Megan grasped his hand

and raising it to her mouth, kissed it. With their hands still entwined, she lowered them onto her sheet-covered lap.

"I don't know if there could have been a man in my life or not. I never took the time to find out. Until tonight—no, until you—I never wanted a relationship."

"Why, Megan?" Pres asked, very much aware of the depths of his feelings for her.

Megan closed her eyes momentarily. "Because I'm afraid of what a relationship means."

"Which is?"

"A stumbling block in the way of my dreams."

"Megan," Pres began, trying to find the right words to tell her that he would never stand in her way. But she stopped him from speaking by placing her hand across his mouth.

"No more words. Please, just hold me."

Dear Reader,

Spellbinders! That's what we're striving for. The editors at Silhouette are determined to capture your imagination and win your heart with every single book we publish. Each month, six Special Editions are chosen with *you* in mind.

Our authors are our inspiration. Writers such as Nora Roberts, Tracy Sinclair, Kathleen Eagle, Carole Halston and Linda Howard—to name but a few—are masters at creating endearing characters and heart-rending love stories. Their characters are everyday people—just like you and me—whose lives have been touched by love, whose dream and desire suddenly comes true!

So find a cozy, quiet place to read, and create your own special moment with a Silhouette Special Edition.

Sincerely,

Rosalind Noonan
Senior Editor
SILHOUETTE BOOKS

MONICA BARRIE
Emerald Love, Sapphire Dreams

Silhouette Special Edition

Published by Silhouette Books New York

America's Publisher of Contemporary Romance

With my deep thanks and appreciation for their help to:
Oceanographer Christopher R. Miller, PhD.
Researcher Leslie O'gwin-Rivers
Silver star scuba-diving instructor Bob Schmidt of the Scuba Training Center, who has already forgiven me for taking certain literary license.

M.B.
Spring Valley, N.Y.

SILHOUETTE BOOKS
300 East 42nd St., New York, N.Y. 10017

ISBN: 0-373-09330-6

First Silhouette Books printing August 1986

America's Publisher of Contemporary Romance

Printed in the U.S.A.

MONICA BARRIE,

a native of New York State, has traveled extensively around the world but has returned to settle in New York. A prolific romance writer, Monica's tightly woven emotional stories are drawn from her inherent understanding of relationships between men and women.

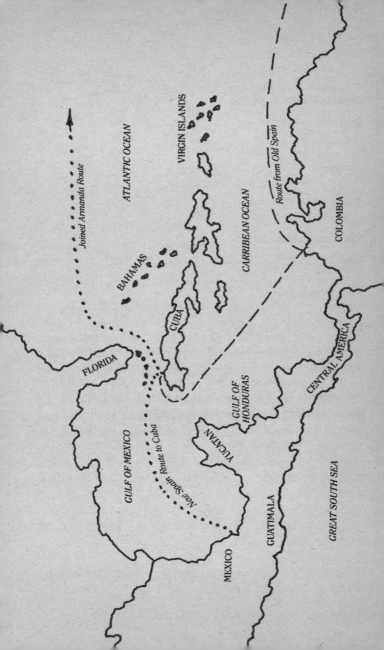

Chapter One

With a quick and practiced glance at the departure board, Megan Teal saw that flight 231 would be boarding in twenty minutes. All around her, excited conversation filled the air.

Noting the departure gate for her flight, Megan shifted her overnight bag to her other shoulder and started forward. Before she could take a second step, she heard her name called out.

Turning, Megan saw Celia Meadows, the Miami flight attendant supervisor, running toward her. When Celia was almost at Megan's side, she slowed down.

"Megan," Celia called again, "help!"

"Don't even ask," Megan warned her friend and ex-supervisor.

"Please...."

Megan shook her head adamantly. "Yesterday was my last flight. As of midnight, I no longer work for Central."

"That's not technically accurate," Celia replied. "You're not officially off our personnel records for another two weeks. That's the way you wanted it, remember?"

Megan remembered. She had accrued two extra weeks of vacation, and chose to use them to end her four-weeks' notice to the airline.

"Only one flight, I promise."

Megan glanced at her watch. "Sorry, I'm going to St. Thomas in twenty minutes."

"I know, flight 231. Anne Reichter came down with the flu. Could you take her place on 231? Please, Megan."

In all good conscience, Megan couldn't refuse. It was the flight she was already booked on and, as a flight attendant, she hadn't paid for the ticket anyway. "No return flight," she stated adamantly.

"Fine."

"Who's the senior attendant?"

"Anne was. Now it's you."

"Okay," Megan said.

"The other attendants are waiting. I have a uniform in my office for you," Celia informed her with a smile.

"Pretty sure of yourself, weren't you?"

"After working with you for five years, shouldn't I be?"

"Old predictable Megan."

"No, dependable Megan," Celia corrected before slipping her arm through Megan's and starting them toward her office.

Pres Wyman settled his tall frame into the comfortable first-class seat in the first row of the smoking section. After buckling his seat belt, he opened his attaché case and took out a cellophane-wrapped box of Nat Sherman cigarettes.

Pres never smoked—it wasn't a smart idea when you made your living beneath the ocean. Well, almost never. He only smoked on airplanes. Pres laughed derisively. He wasn't afraid of diving deep beneath the ocean's surface; yet, whenever he flew, his stomach turned to acid. It wasn't fear in the accepted sense of the word, he just didn't like not being in control of his own destiny. Being a passenger in a plane was equivalent to giving up control to the person who flew it.

Knowing there was nothing he could do about it, he leaned his head back and waited for the plane to take off.

While he waited, his mind wandered back over the past two days and the business meetings he'd had with Bud Schaeffer, of United Salvage and Diving. Bud had asked Pres to come to work for them, as the vice president of salvage operations for the Caribbean.

It was a tempting offer, and one not easily shrugged off. Still, Pres wasn't so sure he would take the job, although he'd admitted to himself that he might have no choice. When Bud had sensed Pres's hesitation, he had ended their meeting by asking Pres to think the offer over and get back to him within a month.

The closing of the cabin doors was just loud enough to draw Pres from his thoughts. The whine of the starting engines made his muscles tense. A few seconds later, the plane backed from the gate and the stewardesses were walking along the aisle on their seat belt inspection tour. He opened his eyes just enough to see them. When he did, his body stiffened as if he'd been struck.

Two stewardesses were almost abreast of his seat. Both were the same height. One had deep chestnut hair, cut short; the other stewardess's hair was dark blond. It wasn't the blonde's hair that was affecting him, it was her face.

So many years, he thought as he forced his muscles to relax. *She hasn't changed, except to become more beautiful,* he said to himself when Megan glanced at him to see if his seat belt was buckled before continuing on her way. Pres thought he caught the slightest telltale flickering of her eyes when she looked at him, but he knew that it would be impossible for her to recognize him now.

Pres smiled. A woman sitting across the aisle smiled back, but he didn't see her. He was still seeing the blond-haired stewardess, and his mind was bringing him back in time, to when he was sixteen and had fallen so foolishly in love with Megan Teal.

The memory wiped away his smile. The long-dormant feelings of humiliation that he'd thought he'd purged from his mind returned. Megan Teal, the beautiful high-school freshman, had been friendly with the tall, clumsy junior whose horn-rimmed glasses, black and oversized, made his blue eyes look more like a frog's than a sixteen-year-old boy's.

His unhappy memories played havoc with his thoughts, and only when he heard Megan's lilting voice on the intercom did he realize that the plane was taxiing.

He sat through the life vest information, and then the oxygen mask instructions, listening to the throaty quality of Megan's voice while watching the brunette attendant demonstrate the safety equipment. When the announcements were over, Pres did his best to banish the unexpected and unpleasant memories that seeing Megan had brought back.

Megan put down the microphone and went to her attendant's seat, which faced the coach section of the plane. Gazing at the rows of passengers, she noted that the coach section was almost full, as the passenger manifest had indicated. In contrast, the first-class section held only eight passengers. Megan was surprised that the flight was as full as it was. This time of year the islands were very hot and uncomfortable.

Just before the plane began its ascent, Martha Grant, an attendant whom Megan had known for several years, sat down beside her.

"I'm surprised you took the flight. I thought you'd be on your way to California."

Megan sighed. "I have to make a slight detour."

"Vacation?"

"Not quite," Megan replied. "But this will be my last flight," she stated just before the high whine of the jet's engines ended their conversation.

But it did not end Megan's own problem—which was the reason she was going to St. Thomas instead of already being in California and setting up her new apartment.

Still, Megan realized that she had no right to complain or feel bad for herself. She fervently hoped that her plans would only be put on hold for a little while.

Megan's biggest problem was that she felt like a fool on a fool's errand. She could deal with the knowledge that there was no possibility of refusing to help out her brother with his farfetched idea of finding a sunken treasure ship, but being forced to accept his idea as truth did not sit at all well with her.

Megan almost laughed out loud, but she didn't. It should have been funny, but it wasn't. Too many things had happened for it to be a joke. *How could everything be so different from what I had planned, and happen in so short a time?*

When Megan had given her notice to the airline six weeks ago, she had intended to return to UCLA and enter the graduate program in anthropology. Megan had worked hard and had saved for five years so that she would be able to study for her master's and doctorate. A week after receiving her acceptance into the program, she'd given her notice to the airline, believing that all her plans had finally worked out the way she had intended.

The wonderful feeling of accomplishment had lasted until Bruce's accident, when his need to enlist her in his cause put a screeching halt to her own plans. Megan wanted to be angry with him, but she couldn't find that anger within herself. Not for the older brother, older by twelve years, who, from the time she was eleven, had raised her and had sacrificed the early years of his career for her.

As an oceanographer, Bruce Teal had planned on doing research, but when their parents had died, he'd taken on the responsibility of raising Megan instead of letting her go to live with their aunt and uncle in Connecticut. Without complaint, Bruce had postponed his research and travel to teach college classes. But in the summers he traveled everywhere, always bringing Megan with him.

Megan shivered. It wasn't the coolness in the cabin that caused her skin to goose bump; rather, it was the thought of something else. Gold, untold amounts of it.

Two years ago, Bruce had discovered several old Caribbean charts. On a lark, he'd had them authenticated. When they were declared genuine, Bruce had told Megan that he was in possession of something extremely valuable. The charts had been drawn up for King Philip III of Spain: they were a composite of the information on all his lost treasure ships from the Americas, with eyewitness accounts and locations of several of the lost ships.

Megan had not been as excited as Bruce. Nor did she believe in pirate stories and lost treasures. "It's your middle-age-crisis pipe dream," she'd told him.

Bruce had smiled tolerantly at his younger sister, but his eyes had told her that he believed in the charts.

"Megan, if I can find just one," he'd told her, "there will be enough gold, jewels and artifacts to bring in all the money I need to start my foundation and to pay for your schooling." His words had served to reinforce her awareness of her brother's dream to one day open an oceanographic foundation dedicated to teaching the general public about the potentials of the world's oceans.

Still, Megan had been a doubter until Bruce located the first sunken galleon. Only the galleon had already been looted. But that hadn't discouraged Bruce. *No,* Megan thought bitterly, *the ocean had, and that's why I'm here.*

Why did it have to happen now? she asked herself. Quickly she cast away the unworthy thought. It wasn't Bruce's fault that he had been hurt. A chill raced along Megan's spine. Bruce's accident could have been worse.

Bruce might have died in his quest to find the second sunken galleon.

Megan chalked up to coincidence the fact that Bruce was diving for the second ship, which supposedly had gone down eight miles off the coast of St. Thomas, at the same time that she had given her notice to the airline.

Megan remembered the horrifying phone call she'd gotten from Sandi Majors, Bruce's fiancée and Megan's ex-roommate. She had just returned from a stateside flight when Sandi called with the news of Bruce's brush with death.

He had been on the ocean floor, looking for the second ship, when his diving apparatus had malfunctioned. In order to save his life, he'd quickly swum the hundred and twenty feet to the surface.

The Coast Guard had rushed Bruce to their decompression chamber because of a severe case of the bends. But, Sandi had assured her, he was alive and would recover his health. Except for his ears, she explained in a trembling voice, which had been badly damaged.

When Bruce and Sandi returned to Miami, Megan learned that he would have to undergo a series of operations to repair his inner ears.

And that was when Bruce had asked Megan to help him.

"Of course. What can I do?" she offered immediately.

"Don't say yes until you know what it is," Bruce warned her.

Megan had already decided that whatever Bruce asked, she would do, especially after all the years that he'd given to her. "What do you want me to do?" she reiterated.

"Find the second galleon for me."

Megan stared at him as if he were a ghost. "I . . . I'm not a diver," she said when her voice had returned.

"But you can dive. I taught you and I taught you well."

"But to look for a treasure ship . . ."

"Megan, I need that ship, and I can't go myself."

"What about Sandi?" she asked in a quick and unthinking reaction. Bruce didn't have to tell her the answer. She already knew. Sandi, although an oceanographer, had severe allergies and could not risk diving below thirty feet. If she had an attack, she could not take the time to decompress before getting to the surface.

After realizing that she was all Bruce had, Megan said the only thing she could. "All right." She didn't tell Bruce about her plans for UCLA, or even that she'd given notice to the airlines; there was no point to it.

"Thank you," he replied. His words and expression chased away Megan's self-pity. "You'll have to take a leave of absence from the airline, then hire an experienced salvage diver. There are two good ones on St. Thomas. You'll dive at the coordinates I give you, and when you find the ship...you'll know what to do." *Will I really?* Megan wondered, opening her eyes at the same time as the double ring of the airplane's tone bell sounded.

Martha Grant sighed and looked at Megan. "Time to go to work."

Rising from the seat, Megan saw that the No Smoking sign was already off, and the smokers were lighting up.

She started toward the first-class cabin to check on Carla Simmons. This was Carla's first solo as a first-class section attendant, and she had been somewhat nervous before takeoff. Just as Megan entered first class, she saw Carla walking toward one of the smokers. Megan had noticed the man when she'd done the seat belt inspection and had gazed at him for several seconds longer than she should have.

There was an aura surrounding the man. It wasn't his handsomeness—although he was very good-looking. Straight deep brown hair capped a well tanned face. His jawline was firm, as were his high-boned cheeks. Earlier, when she'd checked his seat belt, his clear blue eyes had seemed to reach out to her from beneath dark brows.

Even seated, Megan could tell that he was tall and powerfully built. She had the sensation that he was a strong man, not only physically strong, but strong of character as well. Megan categorized him as a powerful executive in a major corporation.

As a flight attendant, Megan had learned to recognize various types of people. It was too bad that he was a smoker, she thought. She knew that because this was her last flight as a stewardess, she could finally end the self-imposed rules she had lived by these past five years—never date a passenger; always be professional. But before that thought could blossom, Megan called up her oldest and most important rule. No involvement, no relationships, period!

While she walked toward Carla and the man, she heard Carla ask him to put out his cigar, and she knew that Carla was making a mistake.

"This is not a cigar," the man patiently explained to Carla as he held up the thin, brown-wrapped cigarette.

"It looks like a cigar, and it smells like one!" Carla retorted. "Please put it out."

"No," Pres Wyman said. The single word was rife with irritation.

Carla stared down at him, her back arched stiffly, her hands firmly planted on her hips. "Sir, smoking cigars is against flight regulations. You'll have to put it out."

Pres's stare was unrelenting. "This is a cigarette and complies with your regulation."

"Sir—"

"I'll handle this, Carla," Megan cut in, using the calmest of voices. "Sorry about the problem. That is a Sherman cigarette you're smoking, isn't it?" she asked Pres.

"Yes, it is," he said, looking into the green depths of her eyes and feeling the effects of a dozen years of emotions erupt in his mind. His teenage crush. Humiliation. A sharp sting of old and misplaced anger. Yet he realized that Megan still had not recognized him. He was far from the same person she had known twelve years ago.

Smiling, Megan turned to Carla. "It is a cigarette, Carla, and it's okay." When she glanced back at the passenger, she said, "I'm sorry for the problem, sir, but it does look like a small cigar. Looks can be deceiving. Carla was just trying to do her job, and to keep all the passengers comfortable."

"Yes, *looks* can be deceiving," Pres said acerbically, his eyes locking with Megan's. "She *looks* intelligent," he added, pointing the cigarette at Carla without looking at her.

Megan's breath hissed out. She stared at the man, and her cheeks flamed scarlet. "And you, sir, look like a gentleman but have the manners of a goat!"

With that, Megan started away, but her anger stopped her retreat. She turned back to chastise the man, but whatever she was about to say flew from her mind when the man riveted her with another glacial stare.

Some primitive force from deep within his eyes struck at her in a way she had never before felt. When she was able to break the stare, she turned and walked determinedly back to the galley, with Carla close on her heels.

"He was wrong!" Carla whispered heatedly. "But you can get in trouble for what you said."

Megan shook her head. A sardonic smile curved on her lips. "No I can't. This is my last flight. But damn it, he was rude!"

"How was I to know it wasn't a cigar?" Carla asked.

"Experience. Don't worry about it, Carla," Megan advised, trying to soothe the younger woman's bruised ego. "Why don't you pull out the serving cart, and I'll work with you in first class."

Carla thanked her and did what Megan said. For the next fifteen minutes she and Megan served drinks to the first-class passengers. When they reached the rude passenger, Megan forced herself to keep her voice level.

"Would you care for a drink?" Megan asked, holding out the complimentary glass of champagne.

Pres looked at her, not at the glass of bubbling wine in her hand. "Coffee. Please," he added.

Megan poured his coffee and offered cream and sugar, which he declined.

"Thank you."

"You're welcome," Megan said. While she served the man behind the rude passenger, she saw him light up another of the brown cigarettes. He didn't inhale the smoke; rather, he drew on the cigarette and blew the smoke out. Strange, she thought to herself.

She kept a covert watch on the man until the last first-class passenger was served. Leaving first class, Megan looked into the coach section and saw that the other flight attendants were behind. She motioned for Carla to keep her eye on first class while she went to help in coach.

Flight 231 landed in St. Thomas not quite four hours after lifting off from Miami International Airport. The passengers, as usual, could not wait for the plane to settle to a stop and the doors to open before they jammed the aisles.

From her position at the forward exit, Megan said, "Thank you for flying Central Airlines, and have a nice vacation," at least seventy times.

When the plane was finally empty, she breathed a sigh of relief that was mixed with sadness at the knowledge that this really was her last flight as a flight attendant.

"Excuse me," came a deep voice from behind her.

Whirling, Megan found herself face-to-face with the first-class passenger who had given Carla such a hard time. Strangely, as she gazed at him, the anger she had felt earlier did not reappear; instead, her stomach filled with butterflies.

"Yes?" she asked.

Pres smiled disarmingly. "I just wanted to say that I was out of line with what I said before."

"That's very considerate of you."

"Miss Teal," Pres said, making a show of looking at her nameplate. "Ah, it is Miss?"

"Yes."

"I'd like to add to my apology with a dinner."

This time Megan's mouth turned as dry as the Sahara. "I'm sorry, but I don't date passengers. And your apology should be addressed to the attendant to whom you were so rude."

Pres Wyman's eyes turned cold. "I see, still the same," Pres said before stepping past her and shaking his head.

Puzzled by his comment, Megan studied his broad back as he walked down the ramp and almost regretted her words of reproval, as well as turning down his invitation to dinner.

But Megan wasn't here for a vacation, or for a love affair. She was here to work, and to help her brother. That wasn't the only reason she had turned down the passenger. Megan sensed, with an intuitiveness that frightened her, that whomever he was, he was trouble. And Megan didn't need any more trouble.

"Enjoy your last flight?" Captain Thorton asked as he came up to Megan.

"Smooth as can be, John," Megan replied. She had flown with John Thorton many times over the past five years and knew him to be a dependable pilot.

"Where are you staying?" he asked.

"My brother's villa. The oceanographic institute he works for maintains it. It's near Frenchman's Reef."

"Enjoy yourself," the captain said as he shook her hand. "We'll miss you."

Megan's eyes misted. "I'll miss all of you too."

An hour later, with her postflight duties completed, customs over and done with, and her two suitcases in hand, Megan went to the airport entrance and hailed a taxi.

After the driver put her suitcases into the trunk, Megan gave him her destination. Settling back as the cab started on its way, Megan opened a window and inhaled the salt air breeze of St. Thomas as it washed across her face.

Glancing at her watch, she saw that it was almost three-thirty. Today was already gone, she realized. Tomorrow, she would visit the first diver, Chad Bradly, and see if he was available for hire. If not, she would see the second man, a P. J. Wyman.

For some reason, the name P. J. Wyman had a familiar ring to it, and Megan guessed that it had probably been the name of a passenger on one of her flights. Because of her years of flying, Megan often heard the same name over and over. Usually they would belong to people she had never before seen.

When the driver left the airport and maneuvered into the mainstream of traffic, Megan did not look at the ramshackle houses lining the airport road, as they did on many Caribbean islands. She had been to St. Thomas enough times for the sight not to affect her as it once had, although she still did not feel comfortable when she passed such squalor set on so beautiful an island. But once they were out of Charlotte Amalie, St. Thomas's capital, the countryside turned lush and tropical.

The crystal clearness of the blue ocean drew her eyes like a magnet, and as she stared at the Caribbean, she began to look forward to diving within its depths.

Soon, she told herself. *And with luck, I'll find the ship quickly and begin school in September.*

Chapter Two

Slowing the motor scooter, Megan carefully turned into the dirt drive of the Bradly Dive Shop. When she stopped and shut off the engine, she looked around. The small building was constructed of white-painted concrete block, with a corrugated roof and the usual funnels for the cisterns to catch the rainfall.

Across the building's front, and gleaming in the mid-morning sun, was the diagonal red and white of the universal diving symbol. Above the open door was a small sign informing those who entered that Chad Bradly was the proprietor.

When she stepped inside the shop and out of the hot sun, she found only the most negligible relief. The shop's interior was almost as hot as outside, and much stuffier.

"Can I be of some assistance?" came a distinctly British voice from behind her. Turning, Megan watched as a lanky man of medium height approached from the rear of the shop. Beneath fine blond hair was a high forehead and pale gray eyes in a too-thin face. While he walked toward her, Megan was conscious of the way his pale eyes looked her over from eyebrows to knees.

"I'm looking for Mr. Bradly."

"You've found him, luv," Bradly said.

Megan stiffened. She disliked being called anything other than her name. Too many male passengers used too many different "cute" names when summoning her—she called them diminutive names. "My name is Megan Teal, and I'm here about hiring you for a salvage job. My brother, Bruce Teal, recommended you." Megan saw Chad Bradly had picked up on her diplomatic rebuke and turned business-like. "Well, Miss Teal, you've come to the right place. I'm sure we can make some sort of arrangement, but I've a rather busy schedule. When are you planning on doing this salvage?"

"Immediately."

"Impossible. As I said, I'm very busy."

Pointedly, Megan looked around the empty shop and the neatly arranged rows of scuba tanks lining the wall. "Seems rather slow at the moment."

"At the moment," Bradly agreed. "However, I'm leaving this afternoon on a two-week diving charter. I'll be back on the twelfth. That's the best I can do for you."

"I really didn't want to wait that long," Megan said.

"Sorry, luv. I can start the thirteenth, but not any sooner."

Again Megan reacted to his use of the diminutive. "Well, if I can't find someone else by then, I'll be back."

"There's no one better," he stated. "That's why I was recommended. By the way, what kind of salvage are you diving for?"

Megan smiled. "Maybe you'll find out, but I doubt it . . . luv," she added in parting. When she stepped into the sunshine, she felt as though a weight had been lifted from her shoulders. She had taken a strong dislike to Chad Bradly and was relieved to discover he was unavailable.

"Well, P. J. Wyman, I hope you're not too busy," she said as she started the motor scooter.

Fifteen minutes later, Megan was at the P. J. Wyman Diving and Salvage Company. The building was larger than Bradly's dive shop, and although it was also constructed of concrete block, it looked more dignified. When she went to the door, she found it locked. Tacked to the door was a succinct note: "On boat out back."

Megan walked around the building and paused when she reached the wooden walkway. Behind the building, in a lagoonlike bay that could have come from a Hollywood motion picture, a twenty-seven-foot cabin cruiser with a flying bridge was moored to a small dock.

Because of the many summers she had accompanied Bruce on his research trips, Megan had learned a good deal about boats. When she saw this particular one, her breath caught. The boat was a good twenty years old. It was a Chris Craft, and it had been immaculately kept up, as a boat of that caliber should be.

Megan sensed the end of her search was near when she saw the boat. A surging of the confidence that had been lacking when she'd spoken to Chad Bradly returned. The cabin cruiser told her that its owner cared about the boat. In turn, that told her that the owner respected the ocean.

By the time she reached the dock, she was praying that P. J. Wyman would be available for her charter. But when she stood at the side of the boat and looked around, she saw no one.

Pres was standing in the bow hatch, stowing a long length of rope. His powerful muscles rippled and strained, not from the work he was doing, but from the tension that had been a part of him since he'd boarded the flight from Miami.

Seeing Megan Teal had brought back old memories, and old wounds, and made him very much aware of the way his life had once been and of the changes that had taken place.

A low simmering anger fed the tension in his body. When he'd waited in his seat until all the passengers had deplaned, he'd done so to apologize to Megan for his rude behavior. He had not been proud of himself for allowing his control to slip. When he'd apologized to her, and asked her to dinner so that he could tell her who he was, she had once again found a way to humiliate him. But this time she had done it without laughing at him.

Shaking his head, Pres tried to stop thinking about the beautiful woman and to concentrate on the day ahead. He had no plans and no diving charters. Instead, he was getting ready to take a couple of days off, to dive in the waters off St. John to clear his mind so that he could make the decision that would affect the rest of his life.

He had settled the last of the rope in place and was starting to straighten up when he heard footsteps coming along the dock. Glancing over the top of the hatch, his already taut muscles knotted. Of all the people in the world, Megan Teal was the last one he expected to see again.

Rather than go out to greet her, he stayed where he was, which was safely out of sight, while he wondered what she was doing at his boat.

Without his wanting it to happen, his emotions began to stir. Her blond hair sparkled in the sun. Her long, tanned legs, barely contained by white shorts, glistened boldly. Her white top, patterned with diagonal blue stripes, did nothing to conceal her full breasts while accenting her narrow waist. But what Pres saw, more than anything else, was the exquisite beauty of Megan Teal's face. A beauty that almost, but not quite, made him leave his hidden position behind the open hatch.

"Mr. Wyman?" Megan called when she found the deck deserted.

"Over here," came a deep voice from the bow. The voice's timbre stirred something familiar in her memory.

"I'd like to speak with you about a salvage charter," Megan called as she started along the dock toward the bow. "Are you available?"

"That all depends... *Megan*," Pres said as he lifted himself onto the bow deck and stared at Megan's shocked expression.

The instant Megan saw P. J. Wyman, her head whirled madly. "You," she whispered.

"Me," Pres agreed. As she stared at him, he jumped from the bow to the dock and walked over to her. "It's been a long time, *Megan*," he said, emphasizing her name once again.

"Long... What's been a long time? Since yesterday? And how did you find out my name?" she asked, finally pushing aside the consternation his appearance had caused within her.

"I've known your name for twelve years. Ever since Des Plains High School. But I guess I didn't make a very big impression, did I? Or maybe it's because I don't wear glasses anymore."

Megan felt as though her mind were being overloaded beneath the twin assaults of seeing him here and hearing his confusing spray of words. "I..." She tried to speak, but nothing came out.

"I was just as surprised yesterday as you are today. Think, Megan! Think about a foolish, gawky junior who fell in love with you when you were a freshman in high school in Illinois. Think about Preston Wyman, whom it took five months to ask you for a date and how it took you three seconds of laughing and giggling before you were able to say no."

Megan's eyes widened. Her breathing stopped momentarily. A multitude of memories rushed through her mind. "You can't be," she whispered. The only Preston Wyman she had ever known had been in her high school. That Preston Wyman had been a clumsy, skinny, too tall boy with oversized glasses.

"Oh my Lord," she whispered.

"Not quite," Pres said tersely.

The shock of finding out who P. J. Wyman was wiped away his last, laconic words. Yet, in the slow-motion movie that was her mind, the moment seemed to last for an eternity while his deep blue eyes held hers in an open gaze. His strong jaw jutted forward defiantly. His generous mouth was but a thin, taut line.

A wash of memories sped through Megan's head in a kaleidoscope of half-formed images, none of which matched the powerful man who stood so close to her.

Once again Megan shook her head. It was an act of denial, while at the same time it was an act of discovery. She had never realized how deep and how blue Pres Wyman's eyes were. *How could I have?* she asked herself, remembering that in school Pres had always worn glasses. And, even though the lenses of the glasses weren't overly thick, the horn-rim frames were too large for his face, which ended up making his eyes appear weak.

Preston Wyman had been tall, even in school, but twelve years ago he had been awkwardly skinny and clumsy. The man standing before her was anything but skinny, and somehow she knew he could never be clumsy.

"I can't believe this is happening," she whispered at last.

"I can," Pres said simply. "Which brings us to the next question: why are you here? You mentioned something about a charter?"

The shock of discovering who P. J. Wyman was eased when Pres's voice took on a businesslike tone. Megan took a slow but deep breath before speaking.

"Well, actually..." she began, but stopped, unable to ask what she had originally come to P. J. Wyman for. Megan thought of the optimism she'd felt when she first saw P. J. Wyman's office building and boat. Now she was no longer certain that Pres Wyman was the man to hire for the salvage operation.

Pres, gazing at her, waited. But when the silence dragged on, his impatience grew. "Are you going to say that you made a mistake and excuse yourself politely, now that you know who I am?"

Megan blushed furiously. The hot rush of her blood rose over her face, making her want, even more than before, to turn and run. But instead of retreating, she held her ground. "Are you always so blunt with your potential clients?"

"Only when I've known them for as long as I've known you."

"No, Preston, you don't know me at all. You never did."

Pres didn't smile or frown; rather, he leaned casually against the dock's railing. His unmistakable attitude said that he had nothing better to do than just gaze at her.

Megan forced herself to take stock of her situation. Her brother was depending on her. It was he who had asked her to hire either Bradly or Wyman. Knowing that she had to at least try to follow his instructions, Megan swallowed her pride. She looked up at the blue sky, and then at the calm water of the bay, before turning back to Pres.

"I'm looking for a diver for a salvage operation. It's a confidential matter—no one must know about it at all."

"As long as it's not illegal."

"It's far from that," Megan assured him, immediately hiding the small trace of irritation that his uncalled-for comment brought out.

After six years of diving, Pres had learned how to judge the reply to that one very important question. He believed, not because of her words but because of her facial expression, that Megan was telling the truth. "What is the salvage job?"

Megan looked away for a moment. When she turned back to him, her stomach twisted ever so slightly. She wasn't sure whether it was because of what must happen next, or because of the way Pres looked against the backdrop of the emerald ocean and blue sky. "I can't tell you."

Pres's annoyance with her answer was evident in his words. "What are you going to do, blindfold me and take me to the dive areas?"

"Don't be sarcastic. I can't tell you about the job until you've accepted it."

"I think you have what is generally considered to be a quandary," Pres informed her in a light, almost mocking voice. "But, because of our past, ah relationship, I'll give you the courtesy of thinking about it."

Megan stiffened at his reply, and her anger rose swiftly. "You have a hell of a lot of nerve! I came here to make you a business proposal, and all you do is make acrid, lofty and sarcastic comments."

"And just what am I supposed to do?" Pres demanded, his temper finally getting the best of him. "Someone out of my past appears on my boat to hire me. But then she says that she can't tell me what the job is until I've accepted it. Really, Megan, melodrama has its place, but that place is not under the ocean, where lives are at stake."

"I'm not being melodramatic," Megan protested. But she was able to understand what Pres was saying, and she could, almost, agree with him.

"What would you call it?"

"Following instructions. Look Pres, all I can say is that I'm authorized to offer you a minimum pay of five thousand dollars for the dive, or ten percent of the salvage, whichever is greater. Of course, all expenses will be paid."

Pres stared at her for several seconds. Her offer, and the words that had preceded it, rumbled in his mind. The monetary offer was the best he'd had in a while, but without knowing what the job entailed, he could not judge if the pay was worth it.

"I was under the impression that you were an airline stewardess. Now you're telling me that you're working for someone else?"

"That's right," she replied without elaborating. For now, who and what she was, was none of Pres's business.

They fell silent again, each studying the other warily, until Megan, waiting for some response to her proposal, shrugged her shoulders. "Very well," Megan said in a rigid voice, "I made the offer. That's all I can do at the moment. But I would like you to give *me* the courtesy of thinking it over."

"Of course I shall," Pres replied in a level voice.

"I . . . I'll give you a call."

"All right," Pres replied.

Megan started back toward the building but stopped after only three steps. Looking over her shoulder at Pres, she experienced another of those unfamiliar twistings within her stomach.

"Pres, I..." Megan paused, took a deep breath and drew herself straighter. "What happened before was between two immature teenagers. What went on twelve years ago should have no bearing on our lives . . . now."

Pres didn't reply. Megan shrugged, thinking to herself that she had tried, and went to her motor scooter. But with each step she took, she was very aware that Pres Wyman's eyes followed her retreat.

As soon as Megan disappeared around the corner of his office, Pres willed his taut muscles to relax. Although he had not shown how much Megan's surprise visit had affected him, he was glad that she was gone.

Pres tried not to think of her, or even of her outrageous and unacceptable offer; instead, he went below deck, wondering if some quirk of fate might bring him a real client.

Pres worked for a full five minutes before he gave up trying to clean the cabin, as well as trying to push Megan Teal from his mind. He went up to the bow, looked down at the clear blue-green water and dived in, hoping that the swim would help ease his twisting thoughts.

Megan lay back on the lounge and gazed out at the setting sun, which had become a simmering orange-yellow jewel hovering just above the western horizon.

The view from the balcony of the villa, which sat on a hill overlooking Frenchman's Reef and the modern hotel that tried to dominate the landscape, and the raw beauty of the Caribbean became the tranquilizer she was so desperately in need of.

Lifting the glass of ice tea, she took a long sip before putting it on the table next to her. Since the moment she'd arrived at Miami International Airport, nothing had gone the way she had expected.

She hadn't really minded having to work, but whatever enjoyment there might have been on her final flight had been taken from her by Pres Wyman. *Oh, how he must have been laughing at me,* she told herself.

She found herself wishing that Chad Bradly had been free for this job. But he hadn't been free, and Megan knew that she could not have taken Bradly's irritating, condescending ways for more than an hour, no matter how much she needed a diver.

"Luv!" she said sarcastically while wondering why P. J. Wyman had to be Pres Wyman from Des Plains, Illinois. "Of all people!"

Megan tried to calm her troubled thoughts by thinking of something pleasant. What would happen at the end of August was pleasant. It was more than pleasant, Megan believed, for it would signal Megan's final success: The beginning of the end in achieving her goal of getting her doctoral degree and entering the world of anthropology.

Since the age of seventeen, Megan had dreamed of the day she would attain her goal. Her ambition was to be either the head of an anthropological team, expanding the limits of modern knowledge in the hopes of discovering something vital to mankind, or the head of the anthropology department of a museum. Megan admitted many times that her ambitions and goals were selfish as well as humanitarian. But above all, they were the dreams she had lived with ever since discovering the intellectually exciting field she wanted to become an important part of.

Megan had worked hard at achieving her professional objectives from the moment she knew what they were. Although she had enjoyed herself in high school and college, she had never let herself get carried too far afield from where she was heading. Megan never allowed herself to lose track of her ultimate goal—even when fate had conspired to hold her back.

Fate had stepped in when she graduated from college and was accepted in the graduate studies program at UCLA. At the same time as she had told her brother about her acceptance, she learned the true extent of her brother's financial position, which was not good enough to support her in graduate school.

And, when Megan realized that her brother had sacrificed the early part of his career for her, it shocked her and made her rethink her future. She came to the decision that she could not keep asking Bruce to support her and give up his own ambitions.

That was when Megan went to work for the airline. Never once in the years that she was a flight attendant had she ever lost track of her objectives. Not even in the face of her brother's unwarranted disapproval of what she was trying to do.

She remembered one time in particular, when she and Bruce had been talking about her life. Bruce had made a joke about her lack of "living a real life." She'd struck out angrily at him, verbally lashing him for his thoughtless words.

Bruce withstood her anger until she was finished, and he calmly responded with, "Megan, you have to have more than just work and the desire to go on with your education. You need friends and dates, and interests to share with others. That's just as important as anything else."

Megan didn't listen to him. "When I've done what I've set out to do, then I'll have the time for other things."

"Don't waste the good years on an obsession, Megan."

"So now I'm obsessed? It's so easy to say that, isn't it? Especially when you've got what you want!"

She knew immediately that she'd hurt Bruce with her thoughtless comments, but she wasn't able to apologize. Rather, she ran from the room.

Much later, Bruce had sought her out. He'd found her in her bedroom, half lying across the aqua chintz bedspread that had been her mother's, and gently stroked her hair. "Meg, it's just that I remember when I was your age, and how hard it was to watch everyone around me having fun while I worked."

Megan, tears forming in her eyes, turned guiltily away. "I'm the one who should be apologizing. I had no right saying what I did. I know how hard it was for you."

Bruce had just smiled at her. "It's forgotten. And Meg, it wasn't *that* hard. And it was worthwhile. All of it. But please, Megan, don't keep yourself separated from life. Please."

Megan pushed away the thoughts of the past and, looking west, saw the sun had shrunk to a narrow arc above the horizon. A few scattered clouds glowed violet and coral from the last rays of the fading day. To the east, darkness crept into the sky.

"Like it's creeping into my mind," she murmured as Pres Wyman's face began to form before her eyes. "No!" she shouted to his image.

But the image would not fade as the sun was doing; rather, it grew stronger. His blue eyes, staring in silent accusation, made Megan shudder. "I couldn't help it! Damn you, Preston Wyman, I was just a child!"

As she spoke to the man who was miles away, her memory of a day she had not thought about in twelve years arose in her mind with a sharpness that surprised her.

Megan, Ruth Gaines, and Kate Hanson walked along the locker-lined hall of Des Plains High School, whispering and giggling at their private jokes. But Megan, while she laughed with her friends, had still not quite gotten used to the coldness of the school in general, not even after five months.

To Megan, Des Plains High School was vastly different from junior high. It was larger, with more kids and more classes. There were strict rules that each grade followed, not school rules, but rules that had grown out of tradition. Freshmen were the lowest on the totem pole, and they were expected to stay together, or restrict themselves to a few friends from the sophomore class.

Most did, except for those girls who succumbed to the lure of the older boys. However, Megan had made one friend who wasn't a freshman; he was a junior. Although her friends constantly teased her about him, Megan liked Preston Wyman.

Preston was different and reminded Megan a little of her older brother. Like Bruce, he was shy and smart and never joked around. Megan only wished he wasn't so clumsy.

Preston had befriended her during her first week of school, when she had been late for a class and he had been the hall monitor. Instead of giving her a tardy slip, he had just told her to hurry up. Later that day, she had seen him in the hall and thanked him for what he'd done.

From that point on, they spoke every day. Preston gave her tips on how to do certain things, and was always around when she needed help.

It didn't bother her that Preston wasn't as good-looking as most of the other boys, for she looked on him only as a friend. But her girlfriends were always making fun of him, and that bothered Megan a lot, and it affected her feelings about her friendship with Preston.

Over the past few weeks, she had become painfully aware that while all her friends were being asked out on dates, she never was, although she knew that she was considered pretty enough to be asked to join the cheerleading squad.

Megan, half listening to another piece of gossip that Kate was giving them, thought about her talk with Ruth the other day. She had confided in Ruth that she was upset because none of the boys liked her. Ruth had told her that it was because of Preston Wyman. Her friend said that the other boys in the freshman and sophomore classes thought that she was… "Ugh," Ruth had said, making a grotesque face, "going with Wyman."

"But I'm not," she'd pleaded. "You know that."

"Get rid of that nerd," Ruth had advised. "He's ruining your life!"

Ruth's words had upset Megan, but they'd also reached their mark. Until high school, Megan had always been a popular girl, and she found it hard to think of herself as an outcast.

When she thought of Preston, she felt sad for him. She knew he couldn't help being too tall for sixteen, and because of that, he was always clumsy. Nor was it his fault that he had to wear glasses, although they could have been better fitted. But the one thing she couldn't understand was why he insisted on dressing the way he did. His clothing plainly marked him as an outcast. He always wore loose pants that were accented by a slide rule hanging from his belt. His white shirt was never without a pen holder in the pocket.

"There he is, *again*," Ruth whispered.

Kate's giggle accompanied Ruth's words, and Megan looked down the hallway and saw Preston walking toward her. Suddenly she was aware of the way, with every step he took, his long and ungainly legs made his entire body look as though he would trip and fall.

His smile, when he saw her, was large and made his horn-rimmed glasses bobble on his nose. For the first time since starting school, Megan was seeing Preston in the same way as her friends.

"He seems serious," Kate whispered.

"Yeah," Ruth agreed. "He's a ner—a man with a mission!"

Once again Ruth and Kate broke up. Megan didn't smile. She was getting tired of hearing her friends pick on Preston, but she could also see the reason why they did.

When Preston reached them, she smiled at him and started to speak, but he stopped her.

"C-c-could I talk to you for a minute?" Preston asked.

Preston's obvious nervousness warned Megan that he had something different in mind than their usual hello. She nodded and stepped closer to him. Ruth and Kate stayed where they were, not two feet behind her, listening intently.

"What?" she asked, looking up at his face and seeing her reflection on his glasses.

"I . . . Could we go somewhere private?" he asked.

Megan knew that she was in trouble. She sensed it deep within her and silently pleaded for Preston to stop. When the early bell rang, she hoped it would help her. "I can't. Class starts in two minutes."

"I . . . Okay. Would you, uh, ah, like to go to the dance with me on Saturday night?"

Megan pictured the way her two friends were staring at her in disbelief. She went pale. They had heard him ask her out. Even though they were her closest friends, she knew they would blab. She knew that if she went to the dance with Preston, she would become the laughingstock of the freshman class. Which meant, as Ruth had told her several times, that once her reputation had been made, it would follow her for the rest of school.

She saw a vision of herself and Preston dancing in the school gymnasium: He towered above her; his big brown shoes were stepping on her toes. He spun her around during a slow dance and fell, dragging her down on top of him!

Megan heard Ruth and Kate laughing behind her, and with the ridiculous vision of her and Preston sprawled on the gym floor still in her mind, she began to giggle. She hadn't planned on doing it, she hadn't wanted to, but she laughed anyway. She stopped giggling when she saw his face. Even at fourteen, she understood the pain reflected on his features.

"Oh Preston, I'm sorry, I'm . . . I'm not laughing at you, it's . . . it's just that we were telling jokes and . . ."

But she knew he could tell that she was lying. Without another word, Preston drew himself straight—straighter than she had ever seen him stand before—and walked away. Never again, in the year and a half that he remained in Des Plains High School, did he talk to her. Not once.

Megan inhaled sharply and brought herself back to the present. "Oh, how stupid I was," she declared. Sadly, Megan realized that when she had laughed at Preston, it had been because of peer pressure, and because she hadn't wanted to be considered different from the other kids in school.

"That is the past!" she half shouted to the tropical dusk, which she knew would be gone as quickly as it had arrived, leaving the island blanketed in darkness.

When the telephone's loud ring broke the silence of the evening, it saved Megan from another flight into the past.

"Hi, kiddo," Bruce said.

"Hi, yourself."

"Did you hire the diver yet?" Bruce asked.

"Chad Bradly was booked up," Megan began hesitantly.

"What about Wyman?"

Megan's tongue froze. When it thawed, she kept her voice on an even pitch. "I spoke to him and made him the offer. He didn't seem excited by it. He wanted to know more, but I wouldn't tell him. Bruce, are you sure you don't want me to tell him what we're looking for?"

"Wyman's a good man," Bruce said. "He's trustworthy, but I can't take any chances."

"He said he wanted to think it over. He'll let me know."

"All right."

"If he doesn't take the job, what should I do?"

"I don't know, Meg. Bradly and Wyman are the two best divers in the Caribbean. And they're the only ones I'd trust to dive with you. But I'll try to check out some other divers," Bruce told her.

"Why don't you just fly here and charter a boat? I'll dive and you can stay topside," Megan suggested.

"I can't fly yet, and besides, I have to get those operations," he reminded her.

"I know," Megan said. "Just wishful thinking on my part."

"Don't worry, Meg, it'll all work out. If you need anything just call."

"I will. Bye," she whispered and hung up.

But Megan wasn't as sure as Bruce was that everything would work out. Especially when it had to do with Pres Wyman.

What happened to him? she wondered. Perhaps because her thoughts had taken her back to high school, reminding her of the way Pres had looked and acted then, she was just now realizing how totally changed he was.

It was more than just a physical transformation, although his physical appearance was as different as night was from day. Megan was certain that he wasn't wearing contact lenses. His eyes had been deep blue and clear, without the telltale glint of plastic.

His awkward and skinny body was no longer skinny; it was as close to perfect as she'd ever seen a man look. Pres's rounded slouch had given way to wide strong shoulders. His chest was broad and tapered to a slim waist. His abdomen was smooth, yet she had seen the way each muscle was individually defined.

Megan stopped herself when she realized the direction her thoughts were taking. Her breathing had become irregular, and there was a slow burning in the lower depths of her stomach. Megan knew she wasn't really comparing the old Pres with the new. What she was doing was thinking of him in a far different light.

"Am I crazy?" she asked herself. "I can't do that... Not now, not yet."

Breaking her train of thought, Megan went into the well-stocked kitchen and made a salad. When she returned to the terrace to eat her dinner, the stars were strewn across the heavens like diamond dust.

Sitting at the table, she speared a jagged piece of lettuce and brought it to her mouth. As she ate, Pres's face again rose to haunt her, and her body reacted to it with all its might.

She put down the fork with trembling fingers and slowly shook her head. *What's happening to me?* she asked herself. Never before had she reacted to a man the way she was now. Never.

"I can't be feeling this," she whispered, trying to tell herself that it was guilt brought on by her memory of what she had done to Pres so long ago.

Closing her eyes, Megan fought against what was stealing into her mind. Her thoughts were fraught with danger and fear—danger for her dream and goal, fear for everything that she was and wanted to become.

Drawing a deep breath, she strengthened her resolve and reaffirmed to herself the promise that she had lived by since leaving college—that she would allow nothing, and no one, to interfere with what she had determined to do with her life.

"And that means you, P. J. Wyman, or whatever it is you're calling yourself!"

Chapter Three

Pres Wyman wasn't calling himself anything; rather, he was sitting on a chair in the rear of the twenty-seven-foot Chris Craft that had once been called the *Lilly Bell*, but was now named the *Cervantes*.

He had chosen the name of the classic Spanish writer because he believed that the late-sixteenth-century author Miguel de Cervantes had been one of those few men who had proved to the world that the impossible was possible, if a person had enough faith in himself. And Don Quixote was only one example of a man's faith.

The gentle bobbing of the *Cervantes* in its calm harbor was in direct counterpoint to Pres's mind, as was his reason for naming his boat the *Cervantes*. Pres's faith was flagging for the first time in years. His dreams were beginning to look as impossible as his efforts to stop thinking about Megan.

He had tried hard throughout the long afternoon and the even longer evening to stop thinking about her. But he could no more stop thinking of Megan than he could tell the president of United Salvage that he would not take the job.

Pres knew that if things did not change soon, he would have no choice but to close down his own business—a business he had started three years ago—and become the head of United Salvage's Caribbean and North American division.

Angrily, Pres stood. He unhooked the mooring lines and, as the *Cervantes* was freed, went to the controls and started the engine. When the throbbing sounds of the twin diesels echoed powerfully, he turned on the forward floodlight and engaged the throttle. The *Cervantes*'s running lights glowed red in the dark night; the floodlight was like a miniature sun, illuminating the night-blackened waters.

When he reached the mouth of the lagoonlike bay, the first of the ocean swells hit the bow. But six years of negotiating the inlet's mouth made his exit seem smooth and easy. And soon he was in the Atlantic and running beneath the stars, determined somehow to clear the fuzziness within his mind and try to rebuild the strength of spirit that he had lost somewhere in the recent past.

"Why did she have to come?" he asked the low-hanging sickle moon that rode just off his port bow.

The moon didn't answer him; instead, it changed into a vision of haunting beauty, complete with blond hair, green eyes and taunting smile.

The moon with Megan's face stayed with him no matter what he did or thought. And while the salt air, blowing across Pres's face at twenty miles per hour, tugged playfully at his hair, it did nothing for his disturbed thoughts.

Two hours after he had left the dock, Pres had still not succeeded in soothing his troubled thoughts. When he emerged from the deeper waters, and the late-night lights of St. Thomas reappeared on the horizon, Pres realized that there was no soothing to be had.

Yet Pres was not ready to go back to the dock, and he cut the throttle. He left the running lights on, and he looked around as the *Cervantes* moved sluggishly with the current. The night was not pitch-black, for the sickle moon and a hundred thousand stars lent their glow to the ocean's rippling surface.

Seeing no ship's lights anywhere, Pres was satisfied that there was nothing close enough to cross his path and decided to let the *Cervantes* drift with the slow-moving current.

Returning to the aft deck, he sat on the padded chair, leaned his head back and stared at the sky. A moment later, he closed his eyes and tried to think clearly but once again thoughts of Megan Teal filled his head.

He didn't allow himself to think back to that one pivotal event in their lives. He had thought about that enough today. He believed that it was no longer important. *In a way,* he told himself, *I owe Megan a thanks for doing what she did.* Pres laughed at his outrageous thought, for he remembered how much he had once hated Megan for what she had done. But there was no merriment in his barking laugh. And, Megan *had* helped him, even though neither of them had known it at the time.

"But I'm not that Pres Wyman anymore," he told himself before he could get sidetracked from what he was trying to do: find a way out of his present, untenable position.

Pres wanted two things: To have a modicum of financial stability, and to be able to keep on diving. United Salvage offered him both. But he was still reluctant to accept their offer and lose his independence.

As these thoughts crossed his mind, the beauty of the night continued to blossom before him. The *Cervantes* was drifting toward St. Thomas, and Pres spotted the blinking beacon that marked the inlet to his dock.

Standing, Pres gazed out at the night ocean for a moment before going to the controls. He thought of Megan and of her salvage job. *Five thousand dollars is nothing to sniff at,* he told himself. Especially if that's a minimum against salvage profits. *But what is she looking for?*

Pres smiled. If there was one thing he liked with a passion equal to diving, it was puzzles. And, he was forced to admit, Megan had done the only thing that could have gotten and then held his interest.

She had handed him a puzzle, a mystery. But along with the puzzle and the salvage operation, Pres realized somberly, would be Megan. Pres wasn't sure if he wanted to be in such close proximity to her.

"What happened, happened a long time ago," Pres said aloud, paraphrasing Megan's earlier words to him. Shrugging, Pres started the *Cervantes*'s engines and tried to make light of the way his crush on fourteen-year-old Megan Teal had hurt him when he was sixteen.

Then he wondered if Megan would actually call him to get an answer, or if he had chased her away. He knew he'd find out soon enough.

Megan listened as the last drops of water dripped into the coffeepot. A moment later the red light went on.

Although she had been up since dawn, she had not dressed and still wore her light nightgown beneath an equally light robe. The sun's rays were slanted in the sky. The early-morning light poured through the kitchen window in an effort to show Megan just how hot it would be in another hour.

But Megan wasn't worried about the heat; she was worried about finding a diver and a boat. Sighing, Megan poured coffee into a cup and started out of the kitchen. She stopped when her eyes fell on the wall calendar.

Gazing at it, she saw that today was August third. She was due in Los Angeles on the twenty-second, one day short of three weeks. Graduate school was scheduled to start September first, exactly four weeks from now.

Megan wanted to be in L.A. by the twenty-second so that she could set up her apartment and do all the things that were necessary when moving to a new place. But if she had to, she would do that after the start of school. The most important thing for her was to be in Los Angeles by August thirtieth, the thirty-first at the latest.

The only conceivable thing that might stop her from reaching L.A. was if she couldn't find the treasure ship. Or if she couldn't get a diver in time.

On the heels of that thought came another. Megan was afraid that if she did not find the sunken ship in time, it would cost her more than just a missed semester.

Megan had scrimped and saved until she had enough money to see her through the first two years of the graduate program. In the third year, she would get an assistant teaching job at UCLA; she had been assured of that.

But she had just enough money to see her through the two years. If she had to postpone one semester, her money would run out a semester early. And, if she went back to work for the airline, she was afraid that she might not have the strength to do it all over again.

"I will find that ship!" she shouted to the calendar. "And I'll find a diver, too!"

Finally Megan stepped out into the morning sun. She stared at the blue Caribbean while she drank her coffee. As the strong hot drink rolled across her tongue, she knew that somehow she would make Pres Wyman take the job.

After finishing the coffee, Megan got dressed. She put on a pale blue leotard and wrapped an off-white cotton island skirt around her hips, securing it with a colorful cloth belt that was part of the skirt's waistband.

She started to put makeup on but stopped herself. Her face was nicely tanned, and for some reason she didn't want to make Pres think she had prettied herself up for him. *This is just business,* she reminded herself, ignoring the irritating little twist her stomach gave to accent her thought.

She slipped on her sandals and left the villa, locking the door behind her. Outside, she drew the Honda motor scooter off its stand. The old scooter started on the first try and, with a noxious billow of smoke from its exhaust and her skirt tucked securely between her thighs, Megan drove down the hill and turned left, heading for the Atlantic side of the island and her inevitable confrontation with Pres Wyman.

The trip took fifteen minutes. Two-thirds of the way there, Megan passed Chad Bradly's dive shop, where she resisted the urge to try Bradly one more time. She knew that even if he had changed his mind, she would not hire him.

When she passed the Pineapple Beach area, she turned off the main road and drove directly to the Wyman Diving and Salvage Company office. Finding the door locked, Megan went around to the dock.

As she neared the dock, and the boat tied to it, she read the name on the aft of the boat for the first time. The boat's name was unusual enough to catch her interest, knowing that most boats were named after women or things but not after long-dead authors.

Crossing the wood-planked dock, she looked into the boat but did not see Pres. Shrugging, she climbed into the boat and started toward the cabin, where she discovered Pres sitting at the table with a coffee cup cradled in his hands.

Megan stayed perfectly still. Pres's head was slightly bowed, as if he were reading a paper, but all he was looking at was the tabletop.

She was more than aware of the imposing figure Pres created, and that he looked very right sitting bare-chested in the galley.

But her moment of silent regard ended when Pres glanced up and saw her. His eyes widened slightly, and Megan knew she had taken him by surprise. Drawing in a deep breath, Megan started toward him. Her hands became little balls at her sides: it was the only sign of her nervousness.

"Have you thought about my offer?" she asked when she entered the well-appointed and very clean galley area of the cabin.

Pres pointed to the seat across from him. "Coffee?" he inquired as Megan sat. When she nodded, Pres stood and went to the stove, where he poured Megan's coffee. "Cream? Sugar?"

"A little cream if it's very strong," Megan said, conscious that her voice was not as steady as she wished, while she did her best not to stare at his imposing back. His only article of clothing was a bathing suit with the telltale red-and-white diving symbol stitched to its side.

While Pres added cream to her coffee, Megan took the opportunity to look around the cabin rather than to stare at his too-broad back, which seemed to have become a magnet for her eyes. The interior of the Chris Craft was in harmonious accord. The galley was stainless steel and mahogany. The seating area held a mahogany table with two benches covered by earth-tone plaid material.

Megan could only make out the barest of details of the sleeping cabin, for the door was partially closed. But what she saw, she liked.

A moment later, Pres sat across from her and slid her cup before her. She picked it up and sniffed at its rich aroma before sipping it. "Thank you," she said, holding the cup in both hands while resting her elbows on the table.

"You're welcome," Pres replied. Although his face was devoid of expression, Megan detected a tightness in his voice.

She started to take another sip, but paused to look at Pres over the cup's rim. His eyes were locked on hers. Her heart skipped a beat. *What's wrong with me?* she asked herself. But she knew. She was feeling guilty.

"I know it's twelve years late in coming," she began, "but I am sorry for what I did to you."

Pres stared at her, but rather than acknowledge her apology, he said, "Tell me about the dive. That *is* why you're here today, isn't it?"

Reluctantly, knowing that any advantage she'd had was gone, Megan nodded her answer.

"What are you looking for?"

Megan shook her head once. "Only if you take the job."

"Have you tried Chad Bradly or Tom Malcome?" Pres asked. "They're good."

"I didn't like Bradly," she said honestly, not mentioning that he had already been booked out. "Only you and he were recommended to me."

Pres digested this latest revelation while holding back the questioning retort that had almost slipped free. *If you didn't like Bradly, why on earth come to see me?*

"Who recommended me to you?" he asked instead, aware of just how stilted and businesslike his tone had become, while he fought to stop himself from falling into the depths of her sea-green eyes.

"My brother," Megan said.

"Who is?" Pres asked, not recalling Megan's having mentioned a brother when he knew her before.

"Bruce Teal."

Her answer took him by surprise. "The oceanographer?"

Megan nodded.

"He's a good man. I worked with him a few years ago when he did some charting in the new section of the underwater park in St. John. I never realized he was your brother. I never made that connection."

A sudden flare of anger whiplashed through Megan, brought on by his last remark and her own defensiveness. "Is that what you mean? Or do you mean that you didn't realize that someone in my family could be nice to you?"

With anger propelling her, Megan slammed her coffee cup down and, ignoring the burning liquid that splashed her fingers, stood.

Before she could slip out of the seat, Pres's hand imprisoned her wrist. Their eyes locked in a silent battle that continued for countless seconds.

As they glared at each other, Megan became aware that she was fighting much more than his hand on her wrist. In fact, she found herself fighting herself, as a sensation of heat unlike any she had ever felt before began radiating upward along her arm from where his fingers circled her wrist.

"Let go of me!" she commanded.

"Sit down!" A heartbeat later, with their eyes still locked together in combat, Pres loosened his hold.

Instantly, Megan jerked her arm free. But she surprised herself by sitting down again instead of leaving. She reached for the coffee, but when her fingers grazed the cup's handle, she stopped. "This won't work, will it?"

"I honestly don't know," Pres admitted. "Why don't you talk to Tom Malcome and see if he's available. He's a good diver."

"I . . ." Megan began before shaking her head in resignation. "You're right, I'll talk with Tom Malcome. Thank you," she added as she stood and started from the galley.

Stepping up onto the deck, Megan took several deep breaths. She could still feel the unwarranted, warm sensation in her arm, which was accented by a low tingling where his fingers had fastened upon her skin. As she rubbed her wrist with her left hand, Megan tried to tell herself that it was just the returning circulation.

Inside the cabin, Pres watched Megan's shapely back disappear as a mighty battle took place within him. He stood. He knew he shouldn't move. He told himself in no uncertain terms that he had to stay where he was until she was gone. But nothing he told himself could stop him from going onto the deck, or stop him from giving in to the emotions that seemed to be growing stronger every time he saw her.

"Megan," he called as he went after her.

Megan froze at the sound of her name. Her body stiffened. Forcing herself to turn around, she gazed at him and waited for him to speak.

"Tell me about the dive," he asked for the third time since yesterday.

A sudden dryness in her throat made Megan's voice come out halfway between a whisper and a coarse cry. "Why?"

"So I can know whether Tom can handle it, or if I should go."

Without her realizing it, Megan's left hand started to reach toward him. She caught herself before he could notice. When she spoke, her voice was tinged with regret. "I can't. I promised Bruce that I wouldn't divulge anything except to the diver I hired."

Instead of being angered at her lack of trust, Pres felt sorry for Megan. She didn't understand what she was asking of him, or of any diver. "Megan," he began, using the low and gentle voice of a teacher talking with a young student, "salvage work is dangerous. No one in their right mind will take an unknown job. Not even for five times your five-thousand-dollar guarantee. A person's life can't be figured in money." Pausing, Pres shifted on his feet. "So, you have another quandary. You'll have to trust me, Megan, trust me that if I decide not to accept your job, I won't tell anyone else about it."

Megan did not hear his words alone; she heard something else besides. She heard truth. In the space of a single breath, the air between them turned electric. She stared at him. Her heart whispered for her to believe him, but her mind reminded her of Bruce's cautioning words.

She wanted to tell him, but she could not go against Bruce's instructions either. That was, she knew, an insurmountable obstacle. Yet the truth of his simple statement made her believe him and ignore her brother's advice. *Trust him,* whispered a little voice within her head.

"You . . . you won't say anything?"

"I've already told you that."

"All right," she whispered. "I'm looking for a Spanish treasure galleon that was lost off St. Thomas four hundred years ago."

A red-hot flash of anger struck through him. Pres fended off the feeling, and he stared at her as if she were something that had just crawled out of the ocean. His eyes narrowed until all that showed were two barely visible horizontal bars of blue.

Shaking his head in disgust, he turned from her and crossed back toward the cabin.

Megan's jaw dropped. Her cheeks turned scarlet, and her hands were balled into tight fists. But this time her hands did not bespeak her nervousness; they spoke of her rage.

"Just a minute!" Megan shouted loudly as anger and humiliation washed through her at his silent dismissal.

Pres whirled, catlike, his eyes still narrowed, his mouth thin-lipped and taut. The muscles covering his abdomen and chest rippled with each strained breath he took. "Wait for what?" he asked, his voice harshly propelling the force of his disgust at what he believed to be her deception. "That was a great story, but it's too bad you couldn't be straight with me. You know, it just might have worked. All you had to do was tell me the truth."

"I did. You asked and that's just what you got: the truth."

Pres's breath whistled out from between the thin double band of his lips to hang in the air above them, preparing Megan for whatever else was to come.

"I don't play games, Megan, not with people, not with lives and not for money. And I damned well won't have someone playing those games with me."

"This isn't a game, Pres," Megan pleaded, taking one step closer to him. "It's real. And I'm doing it for Bruce, not for myself. Bruce knows where the ship is. And I'm going to find it for him, with or without your help."

"Why isn't he here? Why did he send you to hire me?"

"He was hurt."

The tone of her answer made Pres pause. "Hurt? How?"

Megan turned away to stare at the ocean. When she spoke, her voice held no trace of its previous anger. "He was hurt in a diving accident. He...his breathing valve malfunctioned. He was a hundred and twenty feet down, but he made it to the surface."

"Bends?"

"The Coast Guard got to him in time. They brought him to their decompression chamber. He came out of it okay, but his ears were damaged. He can't fly, and he can't dive until he goes through a series of operations."

Pres gazed at Megan's profile, silhouetted by the sun, and felt his insides go cold. His biggest fear—any diver's fear— was of a malfunction during a deep dive. "I'm sorry," he said, and as he gazed at her unmoving profile, something else within him changed. Against his better judgment he said, "All right."

Megan turned to him, her eyebrows knitting together. "All right?"

"I'll take the job," Pres told her.

"Then you do believe me."

"I wouldn't take the job if I didn't."

Megan's sigh was a gentle counterpoint to her earlier emotions and to the surging elation accompanying his last words. Absently, she realized that it didn't matter why he had changed his mind, just that he had. Yet, while that thought swept through her mind, another unbidden thought followed quickly. It was more a feeling than a thought; it was an intuitive sense that Pres had agreed to take the job, not for the money, but for her. It was a thought and a feeling that made her very uneasy.

"By the way," Pres asked as he recrossed the deck to where she stood, "where is the ship, and when do we start looking for it?"

Megan shrugged. "I don't know where the ship is and we start after we go to Key West and talk with Bruce."

"Oh," Pres said in an almost nonchalant afterthought, "there will be one condition."

A warning bell rang loudly within her head, and Megan found herself having to curb her newfound elation. "What condition?"

Pres stared directly into her eyes. No trace of emotion showed on his face. "If, after talking with Bruce, I feel that a treasure salvage is feasible, I want fifteen percent, not ten, plus the expenses for my equipment and boat. However," he said with a half grin, "I'll forgo the five-thousand-dollar guarantee."

"I can't authorize that," Megan retorted swiftly.

Pres's annoying half smile stayed in place. "Call Bruce."

Megan studied Pres's expression, trying to see if she could read beneath the surface, but she could not. And yet she was more than a little relieved that he had put everything into a business perspective. "Why are you willing to take this job when you so evidently hate me?"

Pres's eyes raked across her face. "I don't hate you," he said. "And," he added, his eyes softening, his voice dropping so low that she had to lean forward to hear him, "I need the job and the money. If there is a treasure ship and it's not some wild-eyed fantasy, it will save my business. I have to do that, Megan. As much as you seem to want to find that ship—if it exists—so do I. Does that answer your question?"

Megan's lips were parched. She started to moisten them with her tongue but stopped herself, unwilling to betray any more emotion than Pres was showing. "Yes," she said, "it answers my question. I'll call Bruce."

When she turned from him, a wave of relief washed over her. She had found her diver. Then, almost belatedly, she realized that Pres had so obviously told her that this was to be a business deal, and only that.

Thank heaven, she thought, trying to convince herself that her revelation made her feel better. But she was confused, because all she felt was a funny kind of letdown.

Chapter Four

The flight took off smoothly. When the plane leveled off, Megan shifted in her seat to look down at the emeraldlike jewel that was St. Thomas.

Out of the corner of her eye, she saw Pres was leaning back and had his eyes closed. As far as she was concerned, he was sitting too close to her. She could almost, she believed, feel the heat of his body radiating toward her.

"Stupid," she told herself.

"Why?" Pres asked.

Megan flushed when she realized she'd spoken out loud. "I was . . . I just remembered I left my lipstick at the villa," she said, forgiving herself for the white lie.

"Are you always this tense when you fly?" Pres asked. "I mean, as a stewardess you should be relaxed."

"I am not tense," Megan replied.

"Oh," was Pres's only word.

They stayed silent for almost an hour, and both, at the same time, refused whatever the stewardess offered. But when lunch was served, Megan and Pres ate.

While she ate, she frequently gazed at Pres. When he would catch her, she would fake a smile and return to her food. But when lunch was finished and they were both drinking coffee, she could not hold back her question any longer.

"Pres," she began tentatively, not knowing exactly how to ask the question that had been plaguing her since she first learned who he was.

Pres turned slightly to look at her. The telltale lines that tugged at the corners of her eyes sent him their open message of her inner tension. "Yes?"

"I . . . What happened to you?"

Pres held back his smile at her inevitable question. Everyone he had ever known in Des Plains had at one time or another asked the same thing. "I changed."

"I'm more than aware of that," Megan snapped before clamping her lips together.

This time Pres did smile. "I'll be happy to tell you," he said. "But first, I'd like to know what Bruce's reaction was before he agreed to my fee."

Megan stared out the window at the empty sky. When she answered him, her voice was low and tight. "He seemed quite pleased that you took the job, and it didn't bother him that you wanted more than I offered you."

"I didn't think it would. But it does bother you, doesn't it?"

Megan's head snapped toward him. "Yes, it does. I think you're taking advantage of the situation."

"I'm not," Pres said simply. "I hope you'll understand that later."

"I doubt it."

Pres shrugged. He didn't want Megan to feel that he was milking the situation, but he wasn't prepared to take less for his services, either.

"Are you avoiding my question?" Megan asked, grasping at that to halt the direction their conversation was taking. "It's not just the physical changes I want to know about. I remember you had planned to go to M.I.T.—but I didn't know they taught underwater salvage there."

"They don't. And I didn't go there. And my, ah, physical changes started in the University of Miami."

"Miami?" Megan echoed in surprise, while she tried to tell herself that nothing Pres could say should surprise her.

"Miami, but it's a long story," he warned her.

"It's a long flight," she replied, unable to hold back her growing curiosity. "But didn't you have a scholarship?"

"Uh-huh," Pres said.

"You gave it up?" she asked, shocked at the enormity of his act.

"Yes, but not really. What happened was that in the middle of my senior year of high school, I realized that I was all alone. I had no friends. None."

When Pres spoke, he did so dispassionately, yet Megan was sure she heard the emotional undertones in his voice. She felt her guilt grow stronger but forced it away and waited silently for him to go on.

"I was used to that. It had always been a part of my life at school—most of the kids couldn't handle someone who wasn't made in the same mold as they were. But what I couldn't accept, what became the straw that broke the camel's back, was when Mr. Morris—remember him?" Pres asked quickly.

"The boy's guidance counselor. He was short and stubby," Megan recalled.

"Yup. Well, kind old Mr. Morris was the straw that broke the camel's back. He called me in to his office just after I had gotten notice of the M.I.T. scholarship. He was congratulating me for getting the full scholarship. But then he told me that everyone at Des Plains High School would be eagerly waiting to hear that I had made my mark at M.I.T., and how proud everyone was that I would be representing their school.

"But, Megan," Pres said, his voice not changing one bit as he spoke, "I knew that I wasn't representing Des Plains. I was perfectly aware that on the day I would graduate, I would be forgotten by everyone."

"I don't think that's true," Megan whispered.

"By and large, it is."

"How did Miami fit into the picture?" Megan prompted.

"I decided I wasn't going to do what everyone expected of me. I was going to do something for myself. And that something was to not go to M.I.T. I made a late application to the University of Miami, and two weeks later they accepted me, and matched M.I.T.'s scholarship in electrical engineering."

"I'm sure they did. You weren't a slouch in the brains department."

"No, not in that department," Pres said as he studied her carefully. When she said nothing, Pres leaned back, his head tilted just enough to watch Megan's lovely face and begin his unusual tale.

This time, when he continued telling his story to Megan, he found himself vividly reliving those years that had turned Preston Wyman into a new and different person.

He had arrived at the University of Miami hoping that things would change for him, but they hadn't right away. The change started in the middle of his freshmen year.

He had taken all his required courses, but to hold back his ever-increasing loneliness, he took several elective courses as well. One of the electives was sixteenth-century literature. Pres signed up for this because he'd always enjoyed reading the classics. They had a unique way of transporting him into a fantasy world where he could be stronger than he was.

But this course did not turn out to be what he had expected. The first book he read was *Don Quixote*. He had to write a paper on it, explaining the psychological ramifications of what Cervantes's character had faced.

As he read the novel and tried to understand the underlying motivations as well as the emotions that had guided the writer, he saw one clear theme: that hope was always dominant, and the combination of hope and faith would lend strength to anyone, even to someone who was insane, and make it possible to do the impossible.

The paper he wrote, and the understanding he gleaned from the book, stayed with him, and in the middle of the second semester, when he saw a notice for a scuba-diving club, he remembered Cervantes and Quixote.

Pres had always been fascinated by the sea and had always wanted to learn to dive. Living in Illinois had made that a bit hard. But living in Miami was a different story, and he decided to give diving a try.

He arrived at the proper time and found himself standing in the middle of a group of students, very conscious of the way he looked in comparison to them. He was dismayed because most of the students looked like jocks, and even the average-looking students and co-eds all had good physiques and clear, shining eyes.

Pres was the only one with glasses. Yet something made him stay and listen to the instructor, a graduate student, and the two undergraduate students who were the organizers of the diving club.

When the talk ended, and everyone was asked to sign up if they wanted, Pres hung back. He wanted to join the club, but he didn't think he could make it, not after seeing the others.

When he started to leave, the instructor came over to him. "Change your mind?" he asked.

Pres nodded.

"You ought to give it a chance," the instructor suggested.

Pres looked at the man. He was the same height as Pres but seemed taller. He had a broad chest and powerful muscles. "I don't know if I can do it," Pres admitted. "And I can't see without my glasses."

"That's not a problem. You can get a mask made up with your prescription. They're not too expensive. And as far as being able to do dive or not, nothing's impossible."

The instructor's words struck Pres powerfully, reminding him of Cervantes's impossible dreams. Suddenly, Pres wanted to dive more than anything else.

"Okay," he said, smiling bravely at the instructor.

"Good. Do you work out at all?"

Pres shrugged. "Not very often. I'm usually studying."

"I think you should make some time. It will help."

"Okay," Pres agreed again.

During the first month, the club met in a classroom for instruction to the novice members, and used the pool to familiarize the new members with face masks and fins.

In the second month, the instruction with scuba gear began. It was during the second stage that the instructor, Peter Blanchard, began to spend more time helping Pres.

After the second meeting at the pool, he took Pres aside. "Have you started working out yet?" he asked. Guiltily, Pres shook his head. "Do you really want to dive?"

"Yes," Pres replied forcefully.

"All right, meet me at the gym in the Phys Ed building tomorrow morning at seven."

Pres slept fitfully that night, knowing that the next morning would probably end his hopes for diving. Athletically, Pres had always been a washout. He was certain that he was too clumsy to become a diver.

But when he met Peter in the gym, he was surprised. Not once did Peter get annoyed at Pres's obvious lack of coordination. Instead, he was patient and understanding and worked hard to help Pres.

Pres responded to Peter and pushed himself to his absolute limits. As the months passed, and the semester came to a close, Pres Wyman was feeling differently about himself.

That summer, Pres continued his exercise routine at home, and when he returned to school in the fall, his first objective was to rejoin the diving club and to continue working out at the gym with Peter.

Over the summer, and after reading books on health and nutrition, Pres changed his diet drastically. In Miami, he continued to do the same. Slowly, his physical transformation went on.

By the end of his sophomore year, Pres had turned into another person, one whom *he* even had trouble recognizing. His walk was steadier, he stood straighter, taller, and most of his clothing no longer fit.

Soon he found himself living for the time he would go diving and be able to explore the peaceful world of the ocean. Yet, as the days progressed, Pres became increasingly worried about his eyes.

Everything was blurry, and when he took off his glasses, he wasn't able to focus on anything. He went to an ophthalmologist and explained the situation. After his examination, the doctor took him into his private office and asked a barrage of questions.

When he was finished, the doctor held up Pres's horn-rimmed glasses. "The problem is," he said in a serious voice, a voice that made Pres nervous, "that you seem to have accomplished the impossible, or should I say the improbable."

"I don't understand."

"Let me put it this way. Whatever you've been doing in the past year—your exercise routine, your diet, whatever—you've somehow found a way to correct your vision."

"Correct my vision?"

"Exactly," the doctor said. And then he threw Pres's glasses into the trash can next to his desk. "It appears that your eyes are getting better. You don't need this strong a prescription any longer."

"But everything is out of focus," Pres complained.

"And it will be until we get you contact lenses."

"How is this possible?"

"I don't know your medical history, but I can assure you that it's not a miracle. When I do get your records, I'm sure it will confirm my diagnosis. I believe you had lazy eye muscles as a child and it went unrecognized. You developed a dependency on your glasses instead of following a simple eye-muscle exercise plan. It might not even have been the doctor's fault. He might have made an honest mistake. But for whatever reason, you're showing all the signs of recovering your full sight."

Pres was thunderstruck, but not even that feeling could prepare him for seeing himself without glasses. It was the single biggest change in his life. Yet it was only the beginning of even more drastic changes.

By the middle of his junior year, he was able to throw his contacts away, for his eyesight had become almost perfect. At the same time, he began to date, and he found that girls no longer laughed at him, his body, or his eyes.

By the end of college, Pres had what was considered by many to be a perfect body: he was lean and full muscled without being bulgy.

Three months before graduating, Pres received a dozen job offers, ranging from I.B.M. to General Motors—none of which he accepted. Instead of going from school into his profession, he followed another direction, the road to where his fantasies led.

The week after graduating from school, Pres flew to St. Thomas, where he found a job with a diving salvage company. He worked for them for three years before going out on his own.

After borrowing five thousand dollars from his father to add to the money he had saved, he bought the *Cervantes* and the small building and opened shop.

"And that's the story," Pres said to Megan.

"It's some story, too," Megan replied, holding within herself the deep emotions that his tale had brought out.

"But it doesn't explain what you told me when you said you needed to find the treasure as badly as I did. Why?"

"You really want a lot for your fifteen percent, don't you?" When he saw Megan stiffen at his joke, he reached out quickly and covered her hand. "It was a joke, Megan. Only a joke."

Megan exhaled slowly and withdrew her hand from his. But even when it was free, she could still feel the heat from his hand lingering on her skin. "I'm sorry," she apologized. "I'm just a little edgy."

"I've noticed," he said honestly. When Megan's eyes flashed in warning, he smiled disarmingly. "Back to my tales of woe.

"My first year was a bigger success than I had expected. I paid my father back after the first year, expecting the second year to be even better than the first. But I was wrong. Business for the entire island was off. By the end of the second year, I had to borrow from the bank to keep myself afloat.

"It wasn't mismanagement," he said quickly, "it was the economic situation. The world was in a recession, and I was receding along with it."

"I'm sorry," Megan whispered, sensing just how much of Pres's pride had been bared with his admission.

"It wasn't your fault," he said lightly.

"At least you can't blame that on me."

Pres made himself stop to make sure she had said what she had. When he was sure, he shook his head. "I don't blame you for anything that happened to me."

Megan stared at him and suddenly felt all the tensions that had left return. His eyes roamed over her face. Wherever they passed, heat erupted. Refusing to let her reactions get the better of her, Megan dipped into her reserves of willpower and faced him proudly.

"That's not the way it seemed when I spoke to you the other day." She issued the challenge in a surprisingly steady voice.

"It's the past, Megan. Let's leave it there."

"I won't argue with you about that."

"Good," Pres said.

But the easy, confiding mood had been broken, and the tugging undercurrent of tension returned to fill the air between them, and remained until they reached their final destination of Key West.

Dusk was settling over the southernmost point of the country. Hues ranging from crystal blue to deep crimson banded the sky above Key West. Puffs of clouds, looking like cotton candy, floated toward the coming darkness.

Beneath this magnificent scene, in a hundred-and-fifty year-old Victorian house that had once been owned by a salvage magnate in the mid-eighteen hundreds, Megan introduced Pres to her friend and her brother's fiancée, Sandi Majors.

Sandi was a petite woman the same age as Megan. She had dark brown hair and lively hazel eyes. Sandi had been Megan's roommate in college and, after they'd graduated, had become Bruce's assistant.

Two years ago, Bruce had asked Sandi to marry him and Sandi had agreed. Megan had been very happy for both of them, but she had been disappointed when Bruce and Sandi had not set a wedding date. "We're waiting until the foundation is under way," Sandi had told her.

Megan had argued with Sandi and with Bruce, but she'd had no choice other than to accept their decision—which, they so logically told her, was already made. That was another reason why Megan had to find that lost ship—she wanted to see Sandi and Bruce become a family.

As soon as Sandi and Pres had been introduced, Megan looked around. "Where's Bruce?"

"Bruce had a doctor's appointment in Miami. He was supposed to be back by the time you got here, but he called an hour ago. The doctor wanted him to stay in the hospital overnight so that he could run another battery of tests. He'll be back by noon tomorrow.''

''He's okay?'' Megan asked quickly, worry shadowing her pretty features.

''He's fine. It's just some preoperative tests,'' Sandi said reassuringly before turning her attention to Pres. ''Let's get you settled in and then we can have some dinner.''

Sandi escorted them to the second floor, where Megan left them to go to her room, and Sandi took Pres to a guest room several doors away. The room was large; its floor was highly polished oak. Simple beige curtains that were neither feminine nor masculine framed the two windows that were separated by a full-size bed with a brass headboard.

''The bathroom is over here,'' Sandi said after Pres put his overnight bag on the bed.

Turning, he looked in the direction Sandi was pointing, and he nodded. There was another door next to the bathroom, which he was sure was a closet.

''I'll start dinner,'' Sandi said, ''but there's plenty of time if you want to take a shower.''

''Thank you,'' Pres replied. ''A shower sounds good.''

Smiling again, Sandi left the room and went downstairs. As she prepared dinner, she couldn't help but wonder why Megan had appeared so tense and ill at ease when she and Pres Wyman arrived.

She started to turn on the oven, but as her fingers touched the chrome knob, she paused. She had known Megan for eight years, ever since their freshman year of college. Yet she had never seen Megan ill at ease with anyone before. A random thought occurred to Sandi when she remembered the way she had seen Pres gazing at Megan when they arrived. Her eyes widened; a slow smile spilled across her face. *Could it be?* she asked herself. Then she shook her head, discarding the errant thought as wishful thinking. She knew Megan too well to even think of that possibility.

While Sandi was puzzling over Megan's frame of mind, Megan took a shower and, after drying herself, slipped into a pair of shorts and a halter top that left her shoulders bare.

As she brushed her wet hair, Megan sighed and felt herself relax a little more.

She was tired, almost exhausted, from the vacillating pressures that had been so subtly at play throughout the long journey. Nor, she realized belatedly, had she been prepared for Pres's unusual story, which had evoked a dozen different responses that she had forced herself to hold back from voicing.

And to top it all off, the final leg of the trip had seemed unending. Every time Pres moved in the seat next to hers, she had stiffened involuntarily. Whenever his hand or arm or elbow brushed against her, she'd felt dual sensations of panic and desire. Near the end of the flight, Megan had found herself praying for it to end.

"And it did," she told herself as she put the brush down and left the room she always used when visiting her brother. She went down to the kitchen, where Sandi was still working.

"Hi," Sandi called when she spotted Megan. "You look better now."

"I feel better," she admitted. "It was a long trip. Sandi, Bruce will be okay, won't he?"

Sandi nodded. "If he follows the doctor's orders and does no diving or flying until the operations are over."

"Make sure of that."

"I intend to. What about you? I take it you're still on schedule, now that you have your diver."

Megan looked at Sandi thoughtfully. "So far, so good. Now all we have to do is find the ship. And he's not *my* diver!"

Ignoring her friend's last statement, Sandi said, "I think you should tell Bruce about school. He'll understand."

Megan shook her head adamantly. "I know he'll understand, but that's not the point. I have to do this for Bruce, and for myself. Ever since our parents died, Bruce has done everything for me. Now it's my turn to repay him."

"Megan—"

"The discussion is closed!" Megan stated firmly. "What's for dinner?"

"Roast *Teal* if I had it my way! I swear, you and your brother are the two most stubborn people I ever met. I don't know why I put up with either one of you."

"Because you love us," Megan teased with a smile.

But Sandi didn't smile. "I know I do," she said. Then her features brightened. "Tell me about Pres. He seems...very nice."

"I guess." Megan's response was less than enthusiastic.

Sandi appraised Megan carefully while pretending to be doing something with her hands. She had heard something in Megan's inflection that cautioned her to tread lightly.

"He is a good diver, isn't he?"

Megan shrugged. "Bruce thinks so."

"You don't?"

"I haven't been on a dive with him. But I'm sure he's as good as Bruce thinks."

"He's very good-looking," Sandi said, prodding Megan against her better judgment.

"He didn't used to be."

Sandi knew her face had become an open book, but she couldn't help her expression, or the way she questioned Megan. "He didn't used to be? I don't understand."

"No, he..." Megan paused, wondering if she should say anything to Sandi. But, seeing the look on her friend's face, she knew she owed it to her to explain her statement.

"Pres Wyman and I went to the same high school. He was, ah...one of those, ah—"

"One of those what?"

"Remember all the guys with horn-rimmed glasses and pen holders in their pockets?"

"Sure, and slide rules dangling next to their keys. The geniuses. We called them nerds."

"Exactly. Pres Wyman used to be one of them."

Sandi shook her head in disbelief as a vivid picture of Pres Wyman grew in her mind's eye. His clear, deep-blue eyes accented a generous mouth and strong chin. His tall frame, even which clothed, gave evidence of a powerful, athletic body. "Sure." Sandi drew the single word out sarcastically. "And I'm Cheryl Tiegs."

"He was. He wore large glasses that made his eyes look like a frog's. He slouched, and he was as clumsy as a six-month-old baby. And—"

And suddenly Sandi knew what it was that had puzzled her about Megan's uncharacteristic tenseness with Pres. The sound in her voice and the look in her eyes said everything Megan hadn't. Wisely, Sandi made no comment; rather, she just continued to stare at Megan as if she were crazy.

"And," Megan went on, "I met him when I was fourteen and he was sixteen. He asked me out on a date, and I turned him down."

"So?"

Megan shrugged. "I think he still holds it against me."

Sandi couldn't stop her low laugh from escaping. "Megan, that was a long time ago."

"I know."

"There's more, isn't there?"

"More?" Megan asked, bolstering her defenses against Sandi's insight. "What more could there possibly be?"

Sandi shrugged. "I don't know, just a feeling. The way the two of you looked together. Your nervousness. I've never seen you nervous with anyone before."

"I was worried about Bruce," Megan said, allowing herself the second white lie of the day, and wondering if it was becoming a habit.

"Oh, of course," Sandi replied noncommittally before reaching across the white Formica kitchen table to cover Megan's hand with her own. "I'm your friend, Megan. And I've known you for a long time. What I'm seeing is not what I'm used to seeing. What's made you so frightened?"

"Nothing!" Megan denied emphatically, but inside she could not shake off the lingering sense of doubt about Pres. She could still remember the intensity on his face when he spoke of his need to save his business. Yet, she couldn't bring herself to discuss her suspicions with anyone, so Megan said, "I have no reason to be afraid of anything. It's just that finding the ship is so important. We're talking about a lot of money. And for Bruce's sake, I won't take the chance of Pres finding the ship and not telling us."

"If you feel that way, will you be confident enough about Pres to dive with him?"

Megan nodded. "Even if I didn't, I'd have to."

"That's not the point. Not when your life is at stake."

As Megan pondered Sandi's words, she remembered Pres's sentiments about diving, and about the dangers involved. "I don't think that Pres could be anything other than a good diver."

"Thank you," Pres said as he stepped into the kitchen. He smiled at Megan and then glanced at Sandi. "Smells wonderful."

"I hope it will taste as good as it smells," Sandi said as she stood and went to the oven and looked inside. "Megan, why don't you and Pres go onto the terrace. I've set the table there."

Megan stood, aware that her cheeks were still warm from the blush that had started when she heard Pres's voice. She wondered just how much of the conversation he'd overheard. *Only the last part, please,* she prayed.

The night held an edge of humidity that was a warning of rain to come. Sitting on the wicker love seat on the far side of the darkened terrace, Megan looked up at the sky and thought back to the talk she and Sandi had had earlier.

It was all too apparent to Megan that Sandi had seen through her charade and was aware of the unusual way she had been acting.

The knowledge that Sandi could see through her false front made Megan wonder if Pres could also. This question caused Megan to halt her train of thought and to delve deeper into herself. She had spent the entire time during dinner wondering how much of her talk with Sandi Pres had overheard. But he had seemed calm and unruffled, and she finally decided he had only come downstairs at the very end.

But as much as she had worried about Pres, she had also watched him carefully, unable to keep her eyes from continually gazing at his handsome features.

Stop it! she commanded herself. But she could not draw her mind from its inward travels. Dinner had gone pleasantly enough, and after they'd had coffee and talked for a while longer, Sandi had excused herself, saying that she was tired.

Unthinking, Megan had sat back on the chair as Sandi started to clear the table, and it was Pres who stood to help her. With red cheeks, Megan had joined in.

When the dishes were done, Sandi had bid them goodnight and returned to her apartment, six blocks away. Once again, Megan and Pres had found themselves alone together. After a short but polite time, Megan had pleaded tiredness and gone up to her room.

But she hadn't been able to sleep, and an hour later she had dressed again and come back downstairs. She had gone out to the terrace, thankfully finding that Pres was nowhere around.

The very thoughts that had kept her awake and had forced her to seek the solace of the night air stayed with her. All the questions that were roiling in her head come down to one very simple one. Why was she reacting this way to Pres?

For Megan, the answer wasn't easy. Since high school, she had taken careful pains never to become involved with a man. She had promised herself that, once she earned her degree, she would get into the main swing of the social life she had been denying herself.

Until that time, Megan had determined, it would be best not to date seriously. To fill her empty time, Megan read, played tennis and paddleball, or swam. When she did go on an infrequent date, it was usually to a party where she knew most of the people. She had fun, but she never dated the same man more than once: she knew it wouldn't be safe.

Megan exhaled loudly, confused at where her thoughts were taking her. Pres hadn't asked her for a date. He had made no overture to her at all. She couldn't understand why she was becoming defensive and worried when there was no outward reason.

"Yes, I can," she told herself in a harsh whisper. "There is a reason!" Megan knew that the reason was very simple: Preston Wyman and what she was beginning to feel for him.

Suddenly she could no longer fight what her heart was trying to tell her. And try as she might, she could not deny what was happening to her any more than she could keep pretending that the emotions Pres had unleashed did not exist.

From the moment she had seen Pres Wyman on the plane, she had been attracted to him. When she'd found him again, on his boat, that attraction had grown stronger despite her knowledge of who he was. But she had fought it with all her considerable strength, a strength that was aided by her fear of losing track of her goals.

Another thought made its presence felt. So sobering was it in its sharpness that it helped to ease her harried mind. All her friends had described love as something wonderful. A feeling of warmth ladened with excitement. What she felt was fright laced with desperation. *That can't be love,* she assured herself.

And at last, Megan's taut nerves eased a little, just as the overhead veil of clouds parted to give her a magnificent, brief view of the glowing and star-filled heavens.

But when the clouds again crept over the sparkling jewels of the night, Megan's thoughts returned to her problem— Pres. She reasoned that even if the unfamiliar emotion within her was love, he could never feel the same way about her. His rigid stance toward her these past few days, along with his actions and his words, all pointed to the fact that he still held her childish actions of twelve years ago against her.

After taking the many required undergraduate psychology courses to further her understanding of the basics of human nature—an understanding that was of vast importance in anthropology—she knew that the old incident between her and Pres might possibly have scarred the sixteen-year-old boy for life.

"I am sorry, Pres, I truly am," she whispered. No sooner had the words escaped her lips than a dark shape appeared across the terrace from her. As her breath became lodged in her throat, the shape passed the lighted doorway and revealed itself to be Pres. When he turned and started toward the railing, Megan slowly exhaled, knowing that he hadn't seen her.

Chapter Five

After Sandi left for her apartment, and Megan had gone up to her bedroom, Pres went outside for a walk. He knew himself well enough to understand that if he'd tried to sleep, he would have ended up staring at the ceiling. So he walked the streets of Key West in an effort to tire himself to the point that he would be able to fall asleep the moment his head touched the pillow.

After his aimless walk ended, he returned to the house, accepting the fact that he was still not ready for sleep.

Pres walked around to the back of the house, and stepped onto the terrace, which overlooked the Gulf of Mexico. He paused for a brief moment to look up at the clouds before going to the railing to gaze at the lights of the many boats resting at anchor.

It was a peaceful scene, one that should have calmed him. It did not. His mind was chaotic, his thoughts focused on Megan Teal and his inability to see her as she once was—a cruel and uncaring girl. Instead, Pres saw a beautiful woman who brought out all his passions and desires. She was a woman who had grown from a nymphlike child into an enchantress, and was once again trying to steal his heart.

"Pres," came Megan's voice from behind him. His hands tightened on the railing when he heard her call him, but he thought it was a voice that was only in his mind.

When Megan called his name a second time, he knew that she was behind him, and not in his mind.

Releasing his grip on the railing, Pres spun. Surprise was etched on his features. "I thought you'd be sleeping," he said, moving toward the shadow-shrouded wicker love seat.

Megan, trying to ignore the infernal twisting sensations that rippled through her stomach, stood and clasped her hands together. "I couldn't sleep."

Stopping a foot before her, Pres favored her with a rueful grin. "Neither could I."

Once again, the electricity that always marked their unexpected meetings began to buzz in the air between them. "What's bothering you?" she asked. "Not knowing about the dive?"

Pres took in the way the shadows emphasized her cheekbones. The enticing scent of gardenias floated up from her neck. He liked the way the perfume blended with her own unique scents. "Nothing that simple. Actually, it's you."

Pres's eyes bored into hers. Megan's breath caught; her heart fluttered. When she tried to speak, there were no words, only a myriad of emotions that were cascading haphazardly where the words should have been.

At the same time, she was painfully aware of his physical aura, which seemed to be enveloping her and stealing into her mind and heart. It took her several more seconds of looking into his eyes before she was able to gain a small degree of control over her voice.

Before she could get the first word out from between her lips, Pres moved. His hands seemed to come toward her in slow motion, yet she could not avoid them—her limbs were paralyzed.

In that instant, Megan knew that Pres was going to kiss her. The logical part of her mind screamed its silent warning, but her heart rose up to battle with her logic. Her inner struggle left Megan unable to resist Pres when he drew her toward him. Everything continued to happen in slow motion, and Megan found herself praying that she was dreaming and that this was not reality.

When his mouth found hers, and a million sparks danced across her lips, she knew that this was no ethereal dream. Before she could pull away, a flaming ball erupted deep within her and threatened to take away her sanity. Her lips softened and parted beneath the searing heat of his mouth and tongue before she realized what she was doing.

The explosions of desire within helped her to regain her senses. Fighting valiantly, Megan drew upon her flagging self-control. With a shuddering breath, she broke the deep and passionate kiss.

"No, Pres," she whispered, her voice a husky plea in the overcast night. "This isn't the right time."

Pres stared at her, his chest rising and falling from the effects of the kiss. "Why isn't this the right time?"

She could not meet his open stare; she just shook her head. "It just isn't," she stated.

"I see," Pres replied tersely.

Hearing the tone of his voice, Megan took another backward step. "No you don't" she snapped. Incongruously, as her challenging words faded, and Pres's eyes riveted her fiercely to the spot, Megan became aware of the night sounds of Key West: crickets chirped; a small plane flew overhead; the screech of a car's tires echoed from the road. And through it all Megan struggled to hold back the swelling tide of her anger brought on by Pres's treatment of her.

"Or maybe you do see something. But Pres, it's something you wanted to see happen twelve years ago. Only... we're not in high school anymore. And I won't allow myself to be made to feel guilty for a mistake that happened a long time ago."

Pres stared at her in disbelief. Of all the things she might have said, this was the one thing he had not expected. "Is that what you really think I'm trying to do, make you feel guilty?"

"Aren't you?" she demanded. "Isn't this just a way to salve your bruised ego?"

Pres's features were expressionless except for his eyes, which swept across Megan time and again. When he spoke, his voice was level and as emotionless as his face. "You may have grown up, and you have certainly become more beautiful, but you haven't learned very much about life."

His words, so evenly spoken, stung Megan as no angry rebuke could ever have done. "And you have?"

"Yes," he stated simply. "More than you, it seems."

Infuriated beyond reason by his lofty statement, and hurt more than she wanted to admit, Megan lashed out caustically. "Just what is it that makes you such an expert on people and life?"

"Any number of things," Pres replied. "Or perhaps it's simply that I, at least, can admit to what I feel. And Megan, when we kissed, your reaction told me everything that you won't, or can't, say for yourself."

Megan shook her head in denial and started to walk past him, but when he reached out and put his hand on her shoulder, she stopped as if she'd struck a wall.

"You don't have to run away from me," he said. "And you don't have to worry about me, either. I wouldn't want you to think that my desire for you is based on a...*bruised ego.*"

Megan shrugged Pres's hand from her shoulder and stared defiantly at him. "Then what is it based on?" she challenged.

She realized, too late to help herself, that she had stepped into Pres's cleverly laid trap. But his answer was far from what she'd expected, and it shook her to her very core.

"That's something you have to learn for yourself. Good night," Pres said as he, not Megan, was the first to leave the terrace.

Megan stared at Pres's back until he was gone, fighting desperately to keep up her strength in the face of her newly discovered weakness. The anger that Pres's statements had brought forth still burned within her, and she used that very anger to fight back the burning desires that his kiss had set free within her. Her entire life, the future she had spent years planning and working for, was but a few short weeks away. She would not put all of that in jeopardy for some unknown and unwanted physical need.

Megan remained on the terrace, unable to move, unable to think any further. As a dull fog spread in her mind, tears filled her eyes and spilled onto her cheeks.

A few minutes later, ignoring her tears, Megan went upstairs to her bedroom. After undressing and putting on a white nightgown, she got into bed and turned off the light.

But as she lay in the darkness, seeking her escape, she found herself staring at the ceiling for hours until, just as dawn broke, sleep finally came to ease her tormented mind.

Because she had fallen asleep so late, Megan awoke when the sun was nearing its zenith in the clear blue sky. Glancing at her watch on the bedside table, she saw that it was eleven.

Instead of getting out of bed, she lay safely nestled within the pale-blue sheets until her mind was no longer mired in a swamp.

But when she remembered last night's incident with Pres, a warm flush stole over her body. Megan shifted uncomfortably beneath the sheet.

"No!" she declared before the feeling could grow stronger. Throwing off the top sheet, Megan marched herself into the bathroom and turned on the shower, making sure that the spray of water was cool.

After using the brisk water to help wash away her unwanted desires, she left the shower with a sigh of relief, thankful that her skin was no longer aflame. Sensing that this was but a momentary reprieve, Megan refused to let herself dwell on the previous night, or on the argument that had ended it.

However, one thought remained paramount in her mind: the belief that Pres was trying to repay her for what had happened in high school. After telling herself that Pres hated her, as she so logically wanted to believe, Megan wondered if she was making a mistake about Pres.

Megan had been sure that everything Pres had done or said was because of the way she had treated him in school. But, she reasoned, if such were the case, he wouldn't have accepted the job no matter how badly he needed the money. No, Megan was sure that he would have enjoyed watching her bang her head against a wall trying to find a diver.

Megan closed her eyes. Her breathing became almost nonexistent. Her hands trembled, and she shook her head from side to side.

"I am *not* in love with him!" she whispered. While she dressed, she repeated her statement over and over, until it formed a litany that she could almost believe.

After tucking her T-shirt into the waist of a faded pair of jeans and donning her old worn sandals, Megan brushed her wet hair and left her room. She was as prepared as she could be to face the day, Pres Wyman and whatever new events might occur.

Pres jogged along the winding road, a thin film of perspiration giving a sheen to his bronzed torso. He had awakened early and, as had been his habit since college, done a half-hour exercise workout that he now followed with an hour's jog. The only time he didn't keep to his routine was when he was on a salvage job.

Jogging gave him a chance to think, and he always tried to use this time to puzzle out anything that was bothering him. Pres was bothered today, just as he had been yesterday and the day before—by Megan Teal.

He knew that whatever desires he felt for her had to be held at bay. Pres had surmised that Megan, no matter what she felt for him, was not about to admit it. He believed she wanted to keep their relationship on a strictly business level, and he had made up his mind to do just that.

Turning the corner of the street that ended at Bruce Teal's house, Pres slowed to a walk to let his body cool down. When he got to the house, he went inside and found Sandi in the kitchen making coffee.

She greeted him with a smile and a cheery, "Good morning. I spoke with Bruce a little while ago, and he plans on getting here around ten-thirty, depending on traffic."

"Good," Pres replied. "I'm looking forward to hearing all about the ship."

"Oh," Sandi said with a humorous grin, "you'll hear that and a lot more. I think Bruce has gone a little crazy about these ships. He keeps weaving intricate tales about what life was like on the high seas in the sixteenth century."

"Not a lot of fun, from what I remember of the old books."

"Don't tell that to Bruce. I think he's become a romantic in his old age."

Pres smiled. He heard no derision in her tone, only warmth and love. "The ocean does that to you."

"Coffee will be ready soon. Hungry?" Sandi asked.

"Actually, no. What I'd love to do would be to take a swim."

Sandi cocked her head toward the terrace. "Go ahead. There are rubber sandals by the steps. We don't have sandy beaches here, just rocks, so be careful."

"I will," Pres promised. He swam for a half hour, using every muscle in his body, while enjoying the cool salt water. Returning to the house after the refreshing swim, Pres took a shower and then dressed for the day.

When he came downstairs, he poured himself a cup of coffee, took it outside and sat down at the glass-topped table to wait for Bruce and to think over what Bruce's salvage operation—if it wasn't a wild-goose chase as ninety-nine percent of all treasure hunts were—would mean to him and his future.

It was eleven, not ten-thirty, when Bruce arrived. Standing to greet him, Pres offered Bruce his hand. After saying hello, the two men sat across from each other at the table.

As Pres gazed at him, he saw the familial resemblance between Bruce and Megan. It was in their eyes and their blond hair, through which Bruce was beginning to show some scalp.

"It's been awhile," Bruce said.

"Three years," Pres agreed. "How are you, Bruce? And what the hell happened to you?"

Self-consciously, Bruce fingered the two small flesh-toned plastic devices visible behind his ears. "My demand regulator malfunctioned. The damned thing just fouled somehow. No one's been able to figure it out. It caught me in a bad way. I had just exhaled. I pushed off and raced to the surface... I don't have to tell you what happened afterward."

"No, you don't," Pres said in a low voice.

"I could call you a thief, you know. Fifteen percent!" Bruce said in a tone of false condemnation.

Pres shrugged. "I knew Bradly was booked up. He made that plain enough to me a week before, bragging about the rich client who had booked him for two weeks. But you could have found someone else for the ten percent."

Bruce shook his head. "Not someone with your experience or Bradly's."

"I'm still not sure that there's an old ship in the islands that hasn't been scavenged yet."

"There are several, you can take my word on that."

"That's what I've done so far—or at least your sister's word."

Bruce studied him candidly. "The two of you don't seem to have gotten along too well."

"She told you?"

"She didn't have to. I raised Megan. When I talked with her the other night, her voice told me that she didn't like you, or the idea that I was willing to give you fifteen percent of the find. Why is that?" Bruce asked. His green eyes, the same as Megan's, gazed inquisitively at Pres.

"Megan and I go back a long way," he said offhandedly.

Bruce's eyebrows rose slightly. "College?"

"High school," Megan answered for Pres as she stepped onto the terrace. Both men stood quickly, and Pres watched Megan and Bruce embrace.

"What did the doctor say?" Megan asked as she went to an empty chair, only glancing at Pres from the corner of her eye.

"I'm to have the first operation in a few days."

Megan stiffened, and Bruce reached out and grasped her shoulder. "It's not dangerous, Meg," he assured her. "Now, what is this about high school?"

Before Megan could form an intelligent answer, Pres spoke up. "Megan was a freshman when I was a junior in Des Plains. We just had a little interclass rivalry."

"Oh... I didn't know you were from Illinois," Bruce said as he looked back at Pres.

"It's a small world. But," Pres added, not wanting to stay in the past and have to remember what it represented, "I've been waiting long enough to hear about this mysterious treasure galleon. How 'bout it?"

"Yes," Bruce said with a wide smile, "how about it. Do you want the long version, or the short?"

"I like tall tales," Pres ventured, matching Bruce's smile with one of his own.

But both men ended up looking at Megan, whose breath had hissed out at Pres's flippant response. "It's no joke!"

"No, it isn't," Pres told her. "But it helps if you can keep your sense of humor. You'll learn about that when you're basking under the sun while I'm looking for the ship."

"The hell I will!" Megan declared, realizing for the first time that Pres thought only he would be diving during the search for the ship. "I'll be diving with you."

"Wrong!" Pres stated firmly. "I don't do salvage work with amateurs."

"Who the hell are you calling an amateur?" Megan demanded, her cheeks flaming a brilliant scarlet as she half rose from the chair.

"Hold it," Bruce said, his voice low and authoritative. "Before we go any farther, I want to remind both of you that this is not high school."

"I know what it is," Megan snapped.

"Good," he said, sarcastically drawing out that word and the ones that followed. "I'm glad to hear that, after seeing such a mature display of emotions.

"And as far as Megan being an amateur is concerned," Bruce said, directing his words to Pres, "I trained my sister. She has her certification and has worked with me many times in the past."

Pres just shook his head. "Not on salvage."

"Pres," Bruce said in a patient voice, "this is my operation. You're hired on for a share, but I run it. Is that clear?"

Pres looked from Bruce to Megan. He wanted to say the hell with the job, but he couldn't. It wasn't the money, he realized, but he wasn't ready to accept the alternative— working for United Salvage. And he knew too that without the treasure ship, he'd lose his business. *Don't think of her, think of that!*

Pres exhaled sharply. "I want to check Megan out myself."

"You'll have ample opportunity when you test out the new equipment," Bruce countered. "But for right now, I think it's time I told you the story behind the ships."

Megan, still fuming over their latest argument, folded her arms across her chest and leaned back in the chair. She had heard the story before, but with the dive about to become reality, she made herself pay close attention to Bruce's words. While she listened to the first part of Bruce's story, the part where he'd found the charts, Megan vowed that she would make Preston Wyman eat his words about her being an amateur.

As Pres heard Bruce tell of his discovery and authentication of the charts, he found himself drawn into the intricate web the oceanographer spun. Ten minutes into Bruce's tale, something Bruce said nagged at Pres's mind.

"Until I found the charts, there was no evidence of where these ships were lost. The only notations found in the old records were that they had been lost in the Americas."

"Isn't that unusual?" Pres asked.

"A little, but there was good reason. Spain had lost its dominance of the oceans. Every Spanish ship was a target. King Philip decided that all the routes of the treasure ships would be kept a secret."

"Dumb," Pres commented.

"But necessary. It wasn't a wonderful time for Philip. Drake had destroyed his armada, and Spanish ships were being very cautious. These three in particular were out of Tierra Firma—the Spanish name for South America—and were bound for Spain. Under Philip's orders, they had not taken their regular route, which passed by Cuba and then went along the Florida coast before joining with their armada. Instead, they took a devious route, passing close by the Virgin Islands in their effort to evade the pirates, the British and the French.

"But they'd chosen a bad time, the late summer. Just as they reached St. Thomas, or The Virgins as Columbus had named them, a hurricane struck.

"The ships were caught miles off the coast. Each captain fought the storm in an effort to bring his ship to the islands. Each captain failed. The ships went down, and with them their cargo of gold, silver and jewels, all destined for Philip's court.

"But there were a few survivors. One of them, a ship's officer, drew the charts I found. He accurately placed the first ship. His notation for the second was based on two crew members' observations when their ship went down. There were no survivors from the third. His estimate of where it might have gone down was based on his last sighting of the ship, which was already half submerged."

Pres's excitement mounted, but he tempered it with caution. "What you're telling me is that you're willing to take the word of a man who's been dead for . . . how long? Four hundred years?"

"Give or take a few. And yes, dammit, I am willing to take his word, because it's already proved to be true," Bruce stated.

Puzzled, Pres glanced at Megan. Her eyes were on Bruce, her face devoid of expression. "How did it prove to be true?"

Bruce tapped his hearing aids. "I found the first one. I was looking for the second when my equipment failed."

Pres knew his jaw had dropped, but he didn't care. "You found it?"

Bruce nodded. "There was only one problem. It had been looted."

Pres's eyes narrowed. A muscle ticked on the side of his jaw. "You just told me that no one could have known of these ships. It was completely stripped?"

"Totally. But it wasn't recent. The evidence indicated that the looting was done a long time ago." Bruce paused, knowing he hadn't answered the first part of Pres's question. "And yes, I still believe that no one knows about these ships. Whoever looted it found it by accident. I'm surprised more people hadn't. It's less than two miles off the western tip of St. Thomas, hidden by a coral shelf."

"That's common diving waters," Pres added, picturing the ocean where the ship was. "The ship was intact?"

"To a large degree it was. But there was a lot of rotted wood."

"I'm surprised that there was anything left after four centuries," Pres opined.

"That's the strange thing about the tropical islands. One ship can decompose in a century, another can last hundreds of years longer."

"And you think the other ships are still around?"

"Yes, I do, for two reasons: the second ship went down farther away from the islands, and, it's in a different direction from the first." Bruce paused to fix Pres with a powerful stare. "I know it hasn't been found. I feel it in my heart. And I know approximately where it is."

Once again, the excitement that Pres was trying to hold back reasserted itself. "Finding a sunken ship is like looking for a needle in a haystack," he said, trying to dampen the enthusiasm that was gripping him.

"Not when you've got a magnet and know which part of the haystack the needle was lost in."

"You're an oceanographer. You know what goes on on the ocean floor. Storms shift things, currents play hell with the bottom. After four hundred years, do you really think the ship is still where it went down?"

Bruce laughed. "Not at all. But because I am an oceanographer, I have a pretty good idea where the ship is. I've spent the past two years charting the currents and the plate shifts, as well as tracing every recorded tropical storm. Yes, I think I can pretty well pinpoint the area it's in."

Listening to the absolute confidence in Bruce's voice, Pres began to believe that the oceanographer knew what he was talking about. "All right, let's take a look at the charts."

"Later. First we have lunch, and then we pick up the new equipment. You'll need to test it and familiarize yourself with it tomorrow. We'll have plenty of time for the charts later."

"Okay," Pres said. "What about the contract?"

"Sandi has it inside. You can look it over tonight."

With that, Bruce, Megan and Pres left the terrace, and when Sandi joined them, they went out for lunch.

Sandi glanced up from the neatly typed supply and equipment list that she and Megan were going over. Sitting on the living room couch with Megan, Sandi felt the low edge of excitement dominating the atmosphere of the house. The feeling had turned into something tangible just after they'd returned from picking up the equipment and Bruce and Pres had begun poring over the old charts.

Behind the two women, in the adjacent dining room, the voices of the two men added to the aura of excitement as they compared the original charts to Bruce's present-day survey maps of the ocean floor. Every few minutes, one of the men's voices would rise and a slight argument would ensue.

Sandi, ignoring another sudden upswing in the volume of the men's conversation, glanced at her friend. Not for the first time did she sense that something was bothering Megan, and when they'd finished the list, Sandi suggested they go outside for some fresh air.

"I can't stand listening to them anymore. They're like little boys on Christmas Eve."

"Aren't they?" Megan agreed as she stood.

Outside, they walked down the winding path to the water's edge. There, beneath a partially clouded sky, Megan breathed deeply of the salt air.

"Meg, I know it isn't any of my business," Sandi began, eyeing Megan warily as she uttered the old cliché, "but you've been acting so...uptight all day long. What's wrong?"

Megan laughed uneasily to cover her embarrassment at being so transparent. "If you weren't my friend, I'd tell you to go jump in the ocean."

"But I am," Sandi stated.

"I know."

"Then talk to me. I hate to see you like this. You've always been the one who cheered me up. Let me help you. Please."

Megan shrugged and looked out at the choppy water of the Gulf of Mexico. "It's . . . it's hard to speak about it."

Wisely, Sandi said nothing.

"I'm confused. Really confused. I keep wondering what it is I'm feeling for Pres. I've never been in a situation like this."

Again, Sandi said nothing, and after a few seconds of silence Megan spoke again. "I'm attracted to him. More than any other man I've ever known."

"I had the impression you didn't like him very much."

"It depends on what time of day it is. Last night I hated him!"

Sandi's eyebrows flicked skyward. "That sounds ominous."

"No, just frightening," Megan whispered as she continued to stare out at the ocean. And, without any further prodding on Sandi's part, Megan told her friend what had happened between her and Pres after Sandi had gone home. She did not spare herself or her emotions in the telling, and only when she was done did she look at Sandi.

"And that's the whole seamy story."

"Hardly seamy," Sandi replied. "Megan, sometimes you really show just how old-fashioned you are."

"Why? Because I didn't fall down at his feet and beg him to carry me away to fantasyland?"

"No, because you don't want to recognize your own feelings."

"But you can?" Megan challenged, feeling suddenly as if the whole world were against her. "It's funny. Pres said something similar last night. All right, Sandi, what should I do?"

Sandi shook her head. "I'm not a lonely hearts columnist, and I'm not you. I can't tell you what to do or what not to do. All I can say is that you have to listen to your heart and follow its lead."

"It's not that easy. Especially now. It's the wrong time. School starts in less than a month. And dammit, Sandi, I've worked for a long time to be able to go back to school. I...I don't have room for a relationship, not now."

Sandi took an involuntary step backward and stared at Megan as if she were a stranger. "You don't have room? What kind of a statement is that? Or is your career so all-fired important that you're willing to sacrifice your personal happiness for it?"

"Of course not," Megan said, just a shade too quickly. "It's just that..."

"That you're afraid," Sandi finished for her. "So you use your schooling as an out."

"I thought you said you couldn't give me advice?"

"And I'm not. All I'm trying to do is make you see and hear yourself as I do."

Despite the way she had raised her defenses, Megan did understand what her friend was trying to tell her. She closed her eyes for a second, and when she opened them she took a deep breath. "Perhaps you're right, but I've spent so long chasing my dreams that I don't think I can give up now."

"Why do you have to give up?" Sandi asked, throwing her arms up in exasperation. "I have a relationship. And I have my career."

Megan wished she had an answer for Sandi, but she didn't.

"I'll admit I'm lucky," Sandi added. "Not many women get to have their career and their love at once. But other people manage even if they don't work with the man they're in love with."

"I...I don't know, Sandi. One minute I'm thinking about what life would be like with Pres. The next minute all I want is to get back to school."

"Academia is safe, Megan. It's filled with built-in safe-guards against facing the harsh realities of life," Sandi whispered as she took her friend's arm and guided her back toward the house.

"Which translates into?"

Sandi gazed at a point just over Megan's shoulder. "I don't know for sure. It's something my father told me when I asked him to pay my tuition for graduate school."

"But you got your master's degree at night school."

"Because he wouldn't pay. He said that at the age of twenty-two, it was time that I went into the real world."

"Did you hate him for that?"

"For about three days. Then I went to work for Bruce, remember?"

By eleven o'clock that evening, everything had been settled. The supply lists had been gone over by Pres, and he had been pleased at the thoroughness with which Sandi and Megan had compiled them.

In turn, Bruce had gone over the charts once again for Megan's benefit, pinpointing the location he considered the galleon to be at.

"The new equipment will help. One piece is a newly designed sonar. It's lightweight, and its charge will last for six hours. Another item I got is a metal detector—but it's an experimental model. The designer is a friend of mine, and he assured me that it works perfectly."

"That should make things easier for us," Megan ventured.

Pres shrugged noncommittally. "If they work."

"You'll find out tomorrow," Bruce said, just as Sandi yawned. Glancing at her, he realized that Sandi wasn't tired, but that she was reminding him that they hadn't had any time alone today, and that they wouldn't for the next few days.

"By the way," Bruce said, looking at his sister, "I have to go back to Miami tomorrow."

"Why?" Megan asked.

"The doctor wants me in the hospital by midafternoon. My operation is scheduled for the following morning."

"I'm going with you," Megan stated bluntly.

"No, you aren't," Bruce informed her just as bluntly. As he spoke, his eyes flicked to Sandi. Earlier, Sandi had reluctantly told him about Megan's acceptance to school, after he'd asked Sandi why Megan was pushing so hard to get the salvage operation over with. He had thought it was because she wanted to get back to work so she could continue stockpiling her money for school.

Sandi had told him the reason for Megan's impatience, but had made him promise not to tell. He hoped she would understand if he had to speak of it, because pushing too hard when you were miles at sea was dangerous.

"Bruce—" Megan pleaded.

But Bruce was not about to yield to her sisterly cry. "The operation isn't dangerous. And I don't want you wasting your time—you don't have all that much of it."

"There's plenty of time," Megan told him with more confidence than she felt, misunderstanding his words.

Bruce looked at Sandi again. This time his eyes asked for forgiveness for what he must do. When Sandi gave him a light but discernible nod, Bruce smiled his thanks and turned back to Megan. "Why didn't you tell me about school when I asked you to do this?"

Megan's eyes widened. She glared at Sandi. "You promised." Then she focused on Bruce, all the while aware that Pres was following their three-sided conversation with open interest. "I didn't tell you because it didn't matter. Besides," she added in a voice she hoped did not betray her tenseness, "I think it's time you and Sandi got married. And I know you won't do that until your foundation is under way."

"I could have found another way," Bruce protested.

"It's done! And I'm sure we'll be able to find that old ship before school starts. Isn't that right, Pres?" she asked, favoring him with a dazzling smile she prayed would convey the importance of her message.

Pres's face remained immobile. "With luck," he told the smiling vision sitting next to him.

"All right," Bruce said, "but I want you to leave as soon as you've checked out the new equipment. And you're not coming to the hospital."

"We'll do the testing tomorrow, and leave the following morning," Pres said.

"Okay," Megan agreed. "But I want a phone call as soon as we land in St. Thomas."

"I promise," Sandi said. "And now, if you'll excuse us," she added as she stood and took Bruce's hand. A moment later Pres and Megan were alone in the dining room.

"I guess I'd better get some sleep if we're diving tomorrow. Or should I think of the dive tomorrow as a test for me as well as the equipment?" Megan asked suspiciously. She waited for him to say something, conscious of the sudden tension that leaped between them and all too aware that she had been the one to create it.

"I guess you should get some sleep," Pres replied.

"Have a... good night," she said and started out of the room.

Pres continued to stare at her, until finally, when Megan reached the door, he said, "That would be nice for a change."

Megan's cheeks turned crimson. She whirled to face him. "What is that supposed to mean?"

Wearily, Pres shook his head. "Nothing, Megan, nothing at all. Good night."

"Why do you keep doing this to me?" Megan demanded.

"I'm not doing anything to you, remember? This isn't the right time."

Megan stiffened as if he'd hit her. She searched for some rebuke to his insensitive words, but realized she had nothing to say to him. Without another word, Megan turned and walked away.

Chapter Six

The surface of the Gulf of Mexico was fairly calm, and its effect on the eighteen-foot inboard that Pres and Megan were using was negligible.

The boat was littered with scuba equipment and two odd-looking objects, one squarish and black, the other with a long handle and a wide, flat bottom. Pres had just dropped anchor, and Megan was sitting in the stern, wearing a tank suit and the top half of a wet suit.

Her shoulder-length hair was tied back, and her face was devoid of makeup as she checked the breathing apparatus she would be using.

It was a little past one, and Megan was anxious for the dive to begin. After spending the morning looking over the equipment and getting the two sets of triple-cylinder air tanks filled and checked, Pres had quizzed her on her knowledge of the underwater breathing apparatus.

He had asked her a multitude of questions, designed to trip up anyone without a fair amount of experience. Megan had answered his questions quickly and confidently, but it had infuriated her that when she had finished, all he'd done was to say, "At least you know the theory."

Wisely, Megan had held back her hot retort. After eating a light lunch with Bruce and Sandi and saying goodbye to them when they left for Miami, Megan and Pres had started out into the waters of the Gulf. Pres had, a quarter of a mile later, dropped anchor.

Megan put down the breathing apparatus after she had thoroughly checked it again and gazed toward the bow just as a swell lifted the front of the boat. She watched Pres balancing gracefully against the motion of the boat and saw the way his dark hair was tossed by the breeze. In that moment, with the sun beating down upon his black-clad torso, he looked like a Viking warrior.

Megan banished that errant thought from her mind before it could grow any stronger. *Pres Wyman is no Viking warrior,* she told herself, *more likely, he is the very devil himself.*

"About ready?" Pres asked Megan when he came aft.

"I guess so," she replied.

Pres gazed at her for a few seconds before checking her weight belt to make sure it was set the way he had instructed her, with only five pounds of weight. "Let's go," he said at last as he reached down for her tanks.

When he held them up for her, Megan slipped her arms into the harness and, while he kept the weight off her shoulders and back, she adjusted the straps.

When her own tanks were secured, she picked up Pres's tanks and did the same for him. Neither said thank-you for doing the job that was expected of them.

Sitting on opposite sides of the boat, they put on their fins and masks. Then Pres turned to the equipment they would be testing and tossed both pieces into the Gulf. The sonar device and metal detector were attached to a buoy and would only sink fifty feet—the depth they were diving at.

Without a word to Megan, Pres dropped into the water. Megan took a deep breath and pushed off, knowing that she was about to undergo the hardest test of her life. She was certain that Pres was going to do everything he could to make her appear inadequate.

As the cool water engulfed her, she kicked twice with her feet and popped her head out of the water. After readjusting her face mask and putting in the mouthpiece, Megan dropped down.

The silence, except for the amplified sound of her breathing, was a wonderful balm to her taut nerves. She let herself float for a few moments, eight feet below the surface, before she looked around for Pres.

She found him beneath the boat, waiting for her. She knew he had been watching to see her first reactions. She swam to him and, when she was two feet distant, eloquently shrugged.

Pres motioned for her to follow and went to the line that secured the equipment. When he reached it, he looked back at Megan and gave the signal to dive.

Remembering that this was indeed a test, Megan replied to Pres's orders with the "okay" signal—thumb and forefinger in a circle. She waited for him to start his descent before grasping the line and following him down.

She glanced at her depth gauge the first time she felt pressure on her ears. They were at twenty-five feet. At forty feet, she had acclimated herself to the depth and was enjoying the view.

The water was clear today, almost brilliantly so. Looking up, she saw the surface was like a multifaceted jewel, sparkling with reflected sunlight.

When she dropped the remaining ten feet, she saw that their dive area was at the end of a short coral reef. The hues that glowed upon the reef were a mixture of random colors that no artist could ever hope to duplicate.

To her left, Pres was taking one of the machines off the mooring line. She turned to watch him, and again found herself marveling that, even fifty feet beneath the surface of the sea, Pres was as graceful as at any other time.

Megan knew the first piece of equipment he would use was the sonar. It was a one-foot-square by two-foot-high black box. A handle rose on each side of the box, and centered between the handles was a flat liquid crystal display monitor five inches by seven inches. On the right handle were two controls: an on/off switch, and a monitor magnification button.

When Pres had freed the sonar, he turned to Megan and pointed his finger at her. This was the signal that she was to do the first test.

Again, she gave Pres the "okay" sign and reached for the box. When she took it, its added weight brought her down to the bottom. She looked at the switches and then turned the unit on. A half minute later, the monitor screen glowed green. A dot appeared in the center, and a line began to revolve.

Twisting her head back so she could look at Pres, Megan found that he was gone. She looked up and saw him swimming about five feet above her head. *Of course,* she told herself, *he's going to watch me from above.*

Logically, she knew that where Pres was, was the best way to view things, but illogically, she would have preferred that he be at her side.

Making herself forget him for the moment, Megan pushed off the bottom. She had to use both hands to hold the device so that it would be above the ocean floor.

As she began to work the sonar, she found that nothing was happening, except that the green phosphorescence was maddening. Belatedly, she realized that the device was too close to the ocean floor, and its signal was being bounced back too quickly.

She signaled for Pres to come to her. At a foot's distance, Pres's blue eyes were startling when he stared into her mask. Not wanting to waste time pantomiming what she needed to do, she removed her mouthpiece and leaned forward until her mouth touched his ear.

Using the natural acoustics of the ocean, she shouted, "Too close to the bottom," before quickly slipping her mouthpiece between her teeth and taking a breath.

Able to decipher the muffled shout, Pres nodded and extended his arm, his finger pointing out the direction she should go.

Three minutes later, they were hovering over a chasm on the ocean floor. Megan could not see the bottom, which was too deep for sunlight to filter all the way down. As she started over the lip of the chasm, she realized she was about to make another mistake and stopped herself quickly.

Again, she looked up and motioned to Pres.

When he came next to her, she handed him the sonar and then unclipped her weight belt. With her left hand, she took back the device, and with her right handed him the belt.

Pres nodded and gave her the "okay" sign.

Seeing that Pres's actions were all business, she was determined to act the same way too. Pushing off, she began to swim above the chasm, keeping her depth constant while at the same time peering closely at the sonar screen.

Without having to look up, she knew that Pres was above her, watching her, monitoring her. Because Megan had some experience with shipboard sonar, she knew what to expect. But this unit surprised her, for the first thing that showed was a series of small dots. When she touched the magnification button, the screen flickered and, an instant later, replaced the dots with computer-generated shapes.

What Megan saw was a school of fish. Stopping her forward movement, Megan looked up. She saw that Pres was already coming toward her. When he reached her, he put his face close to the sonar screen for a few seconds before he drew back from the screen to gaze at Megan.

What Megan saw through his face mask surprised her. His eyes were alive with excitement.

Pres signaled her to continue on. And, as he again followed her, he tried to keep himself calm. He had never seen a sonar quite like that one. His excitement stemmed from the fact that, with proper use, the device could find a sunken ship and outline it so that he would be able to tell exactly what kind of a ship it was.

Realizing that he was not paying close attention to Megan, he willed his thoughts to return to only her. He had not been surprised that Megan was a good swimmer; her body was in excellent condition—*too excellent*, he thought as he watched the smooth lines of her thighs and calves, as they powered her above the opening of the small chasm.

Once again, he saw a form take shape on the screen. This time, he did not rush down to look. He recognized the green outline, just as he had recognized the large gray shape twenty feet below them.

Pres's hand went to the handle of his diving knife as the shark turned in a semicircle. But more than the shark, he watched Megan. He saw no telltale stiffening of her limbs, nor did she react by trying to swim away. In fact, she did just the opposite. She slowed, moving just enough to keep herself from dropping into the chasm.

Good, Pres thought, realizing that Megan had been well trained. A moment later, the shark descended and disappeared from sight, as well as from the sonar screen.

Pres checked his chronometer and saw that fifteen minutes had gone by. Kicking twice, he dived down to Megan and tapped her on the shoulder. He signaled her to follow him and led her back to the line and the second piece of equipment.

After untying the metal detector from the line, he signaled Megan to secure the sonar. When that was done, he handed Megan the new piece of equipment, which was a flat-bottomed object with a four-foot handle and a single on/off switch. In the center of the polelike handle was a light. If they were over metal, the light would go on.

Megan took the metal detector from Pres and, remembering Bruce's instruction, turned it on and began to swim. But all too soon she realized that she was too buoyant and she had to stop.

Turning, she signaled Pres for her weight belt. He handed it to her and held the metal detector while she put the belt on. When she started to swim again, Pres rose above her.

Megan checked her air pressure gauge and realized she had been using too much air. *I'm too tense,* she told herself, and made a strong effort to slow down her breathing. She knew that when the dive was over, Pres would check the amount of air she had used. It was one of the ways to judge a diver's experience and competence. If she used too much air, she would fail Pres's test, just as if she'd made a major mistake.

With her breathing better regulated, Megan swam a few inches above the straggly coral reef. Two minutes later, the metal detector's light blinked.

She held herself motionless and looked down to where a small metal object, covered by algae and weed, rested on a piece of coral. Swooping down, Megan freed her knife and touched the object. It flipped over, and she saw that it was a rusted old bolt about three inches long. She looked up at Pres and shrugged.

He signaled her on.

For the next ten minutes, Megan crisscrossed the dive area, luxuriating in the serenity of the ocean. She found two more metal objects, but neither was identifiable because of its age.

As she was floating above a thicker section of the reef, the metal detector's light began to blink rapidly—an indication of a large metal find.

Megan dropped down and looked everywhere. When she was a foot above the reef, she brushed its surface with her gloved hand. Little pieces of debris floated about, obscuring her vision.

Finding nothing, she reversed herself and looked at the metal detector again. It was still blinking madly.

Megan rose higher for a better look. To her left was a small hole in the coral. Swimming closer to the opening, she saw it looked like a miniature cave.

Cautious because she didn't know what might live inside, she began to sweep the metal detector back and forth before the opening. When nothing appeared within the cave's entrance, she relaxed and looked at the detector's light. The blinking red light did not increase its tempo, and she turned to try another direction.

She started away, but the detector snagged on a jagged piece of coral. Turning back, Megan reached down to free the detector.

Above Megan, Pres watched carefully. When she started to make passes above the small cave, a cold chill spread through his body. He had seen too many caves like that in his years of diving, and knew all the possible terrors that lurked within. He started down toward her. The fifteen feet between them seeming like miles. Pres kicked his legs in a powerful effort to speed himself forward. Thankfully, before he reached her, she backed away from the opening and turned around.

His relief was short-lived, for the detector became snagged. And, as Megan tried to free it, her buoyancy allowed her to shift, causing her left side to float toward the cave opening. When her movement stopped again, her left arm was not more than two feet from the cave.

Seeing a slight movement in the mouth of the cave—an iridescent shimmer that told him all he had to know—Pres rushed toward her. In the face of his knowledge, Pres summoned up all his strength in a last-ditch effort to reach Megan. When he was almost there, he saw the rolling length emerge from its hiding place.

Knowing he would have only one chance, he held his arms stretched stiffly before him, his palms out flat. With adrenaline lending him strength, Pres gave one more lunging kick with his finned feet. He struck Megan in the side, sending her spinning in the water at the same instant the moray eel attacked.

As most of the eel's five feet arrowed out of the cave, its needle-toothed mouth was open and searching for the arm that had been moving before it. But Pres had reached Megan first, and instead of getting Megan's arm, the thick-bodied eel struck the metal detector's pole.

Megan, regaining her equilibrium as well as the breath that had been knocked out of her, stared at the deadly battle between metal detector and eel.

An instant later, a shower of sparks raced about the moray's head. The eel arched, stiffened and released the handle of the detector so it could race back to the safety of its cave.

As soon as the eel disappeared, Pres grabbed the detector, yanked hard and freed it from the coral. Turning to Megan, he signaled her to follow him.

By the time they reached the mooring line, Megan's heart was beating normally, but she would never forget the feeling that she'd had when she saw the moray attack the detector. It could have been her arm.

Nine minutes later, they were in the boat. Silently, they both took off their equipment. When her tanks and mask were on the deck, and her gloves off, Megan turned to Pres.

"Thank you," she said, meaning it sincerely. The smile Pres favored her with made her insides turn to jelly.

"You're welcome," he said as he studied her face, looking for a sign of delayed reaction, but surprisingly, he found none.

Megan thought about the metal detector and, without saying anything to Pres, reached over the side and began to pull the line up. When she had the two pieces of equipment dangling from the side of the boat, Pres gave her a hand, and they brought them into the boat.

Megan picked up the twisted handle and looked at it. The blood drained from her face, and her heart was hammering fiercely. The handle, a hollow tube, was ripped open. Ugly gashes marred the surface. The wires inside were torn apart.

"That could have been my arm," she whispered.

"But it wasn't," Pres told her.

Megan looked up at him. Her eyes were wide. "Because you stopped it from getting me."

Pres shook his head. "No, because I did the job I was supposed to. I looked out for my diving partner."

"I—" Megan began, but faltered. She took a deep breath, looked down at the mangled handle, and then back at Pres. "I guess I failed the test," she said, disappointment shading her words and her features for a second, before she turned from him to look back at the metal detector.

Megan was prepared for his words to rake her and believed she deserved whatever he would say. She was ready for him to tell her what a fool she was for even thinking about a deep-water dive. She waited for him to call her an amateur, and to begin a long, self-satisfied diatribe about her inadequacies.

While she waited, Pres reached out and grasped her chin with his fingers. He turned her face toward him and, with no expression, said, "Actually, you did much better than I expected. No, Megan, you didn't fail the test. You just have to learn about some of the hidden dangers."

Megan's breath caught. A maddening heat rippled along her face, radiating from where his fingers lightly touched her jaw. She tried to believe that he was not playing some terrible game with her, tried because she wanted very much to believe him.

"You mean you'll dive with me?" she asked, her words barely loud enough to reach him.

"That's exactly what I mean."

Megan stood on the terrace, enjoying the way the late-night sea breeze rippled the light material of her casual dress. She was wearing the dress she had gone out to dinner in and knew that she should be in bed rather than standing outside.

She and Pres were taking a chartered flight to St. Thomas at nine-thirty the next morning. The day after arriving on the island would find them beginning their first dive.

A little knot of excitement formed in her stomach as she thought about the coming weeks. It was a strange feeling, especially after what the events of the day had brought about. She had been certain, after the incident with the moray, that Pres would refuse to dive with her. He had surprised her by telling her just the opposite.

After they'd returned to the dock, and her spirits were still soaring, they'd gone to a small machine shop and were able to get the metal detector repaired. When they got back to Bruce's house it was five o'clock.

They'd spent another hour packing up the equipment before realizing the time. When they were finished, Pres asked her if she'd like to join him for dinner at one of the local restaurants. Megan had gladly accepted his offer, not because she hadn't wanted to cook—which she hadn't—but because she'd felt a lessening of the tension between them with his acceptance of her as a diving partner.

"Is that really why I went with him?" she asked herself in a whisper as the previous night's talk with Sandi rose to confuse her thoughts again.

Megan looked up at the stars and listened to the crickets. The scent of the ocean tickled her senses and made her aware of how her heart kept vacillating.

Megan knew that to allow herself to become involved with Pres would jeopardize everything she had been working for. Why, she did not know; but that it would, she was positive. *How can I even consider a relationship with someone who thinks so little of me?*

Today's actions, both beneath the ocean's surface and in the boat, made Megan pause in her thoughts. The dangers inherent in a deep ocean dive were innumerable. No one would risk his life diving with someone he could not trust.

If he thinks so little of me, why is he going to dive with me? Megan had no answer to that, except for one. That she was wrong about Pres and his actions toward her.

Before her thoughts could enter yet another convoluted maze that had no exit, she heard footsteps behind her and turned to watch Pres approach her. He wore the same black slacks that encased his powerful thighs. His pale gray designer pullover was open at the throat, allowing small tufts of dark hair to pop out teasingly.

"Hi," Megan said, hoping her voice was not betraying the way her insides were churning.

"Hi," Pres replied as he stopped next to her and looked out at the dark waters.

Gazing at him from the corner of her eye, Megan tried to think of a way of maneuvering the conversation in order to find out what he really thought of her.

"You ought to try and get some sleep," Pres said without looking at her. "It's going to be a long day tomorrow."

As she listened to him, she heard the aloofness that was still in his voice. She shook her head, deciding that somehow she had to break through that and find out what was happening within his mind. "Pres," she called.

Pres looked into her eyes and her determination fizzled as her mind suddenly went blank. "Nothing," she whispered.

When Megan started to turn away, Pres not only realized that she was having trouble with whatever she wanted to say, but could sense the tension that seemed to have been in the air between them all day.

At one point, Pres had wanted to grab her and shake her and make her see him as he was, a man falling in love with a beautiful woman. But he'd remembered her words from the previous night, and knew he had to maintain a modicum of distance between them.

But standing so close to her, feeling her nearness with so much intensity, Pres realized that he didn't want to lose that feeling. "Why are you going back to school?"

Megan glanced at him. "Did you think that my life was just being a stewardess?"

"I didn't know what your life was, or is," Pres replied. "But there's nothing wrong with being a stewardess."

"Unless you want more," Megan said. Turning from Pres, she grasped the terrace railing and looked seaward. She was silent for a moment, and then she slowly began to speak. She told Pres about her dream of becoming an anthropologist, and of the years she had spent trying to achieve her goals. She concluded her narrative by explaining why she was looking for the sunken ship for Bruce. Her story took a half hour, and not once during its telling did she look at him. Only when she had finished did she finally turned back to Pres.

Pres had found himself reacting strongly to Megan's story, for he was able to understand the driving needs that underscored one's desire to attain a goal. He had gone through that himself, on two separate occasions. The first was with his physical transformation; the second was when he had realized that diving would be his career, and his life.

Pres realized this dive meant the same thing to Megan that it did to him: if they were successful they would both be able to reach their lifelong goals. But a note of discord rose to taunt his last thought. "What if it takes more than a few weeks to find the ship?"

"That doesn't matter," Megan said, knowing that it was the truth, despite how much the words hurt her to say.

"But it does," Pres replied.

"There are twelve years between Bruce and myself. While I was in high school, Bruce should have been doing his early research. But instead, he had to teach college in order to raise me. And I'm responsible for holding him back. If he'd been free to pursue his career, he probably would have his foundation already."

"But he doesn't, and I don't think he holds that against you."

"No, Bruce isn't like that," Megan said. "And missing a semester or two is nothing in comparison to what he's done for me."

Pres was surprised by her admissions, and surprised too at the new depths he'd glimpsed within her. Suddenly, the promise he'd made to himself to forget about Megan Teal, except in a businesslike way, fell to the wayside.

"About the other night," Pres began, changing the conversation in the hopes of taking Megan off stride.

But Megan was far from off stride when his words filtered into her ears, and a warning bell went off in her mind. "I don't want to talk about the other night."

"I do. Megan—"

"No!" she shouted much louder than she'd intended. "Please, Pres. I can't think about getting involved with someone right now."

Pres stiffened. "I'm not 'someone!'" he retorted, his voice louder by far than hers had been. "What are you afraid of?"

Megan stared at him, her upper teeth worrying at her lower lip. "You," Megan whispered truthfully. "And me."

Touched by her honest admission, Pres reached toward her. "Megan," he called, his voice deep and husky.

Megan's eyes widened when his arms started toward her. She backstepped but could only go a half step before her legs froze and she lost herself in his eyes. When his hands grasped her shoulders, she trembled beneath his touch.

"I want you, Megan. You, not the girl you used to be, but the woman you are now, today."

Megan's mouth was dry; her breath was trapped in the hollow of her throat. She darted her tongue out to moisten her lips just as the emotions she had been fighting so long broke free. Unable to stop herself, she raised her hand until she felt his cheek in her palm.

She knew he could feel the way she was trembling, just from the light touch of her hand. And, as her heart beat trip-hammer fast, his hands tightened on her shoulders, and he drew her to him.

"Pres," she whispered in the fleeting space of time before his mouth reached hers, and the heat of his lips became a roaring flame.

Chapter Seven

Megan's head spun, but her heart came forth to help steady her and make her understand that what was happening was right. Pres's mouth was like hot cinders upon her lips. And as he held her tightly to him, the heat of his body engulfed her.

Her arms went around his back, not to draw him closer, for she knew that to be impossible, but to hold on to him so that she would not fall. Her breasts, stomach and thighs were pressed against him, and she felt the hardness of his body as if there were no clothing between them.

When the kiss ended, Pres gazed down at her. "I want you, Megan," Pres said in a strong voice, repeating his earlier words.

She met Pres's gaze, unable to speak, and wondered if she would ever be able to find her voice again. Within her, the passions his kiss had ignited continued to grow stronger. And while the logical part of her mind cried for her to awaken from this wild dream, her aching and never-before-admitted needs held her limbs quiescent, refusing to yield to her years of careful logic.

"Megan," Pres whispered, moving his hands upward along her back. His fingers gently and tenderly traced her quivering muscles until he finally cupped her face in his hands.

Megan, her body reacting to his wandering hands and fingers, took a tremulous breath. "Pres, I . . ."

"Be honest with yourself Megan. No games. Not anymore. I won't deny the way I feel about you any longer. I tried," Pres admitted without taking his hands from her face. "I really did."

The strong resolve Megan had used over the years to keep her barriers firm against unwanted emotional entanglements wavered, and another chink in her armor opened, allowing more of her inner turmoil to escape.

"N-no more games," she whispered.

Pres bent and kissed her. It was a gentle kiss. With it, Megan felt not only the reassurance she so desperately craved, but the love that was so much a part of the kiss.

When their lips reluctantly parted, Pres took her hand and started them toward the house. Her frozen muscles moved, obeying him and not herself as she went with him to whatever their destiny might be.

The trip took forever because each step happened in slow motion, or so it seemed to her. And, with every slow step, Megan's stomach grew tighter. Her nerves jangled, and three times she almost stopped.

But they eventually reached the second floor, and the guest room. When they entered, Pres turned on the lights. Megan spun, drawing her hand from his. "Please, turn the lights off."

Seeing the hint of apprehension in her eyes, Pres did what she asked, after which he drew her close and kissed her softly. When the kiss ended, Megan's breathing was again bated, and her heart was racing.

Moving confidently, Pres led her toward the brass bed. There, he enfolded her in his arms, and as he kissed her, he released the reins of his passion.

The kiss deepened and Megan's head spun. She was bombarded by feelings and sensations that stole away reality and replaced it with dreams. His hands were roaming her back, sending sparkling shivers along her skin. From every point that their bodies touched, new flames burst forth.

Megan's legs were weak. The straining interplay of her body and her emotions was becoming unbearable. Slowly, Megan drew her mouth from Pres's, realizing that she must tell him what she'd never spoken aloud to another. But when she tried to look at his face, the darkened room would not let her see his features clearly.

"What?" Pres asked, his voice huskier than before.

Her tongue was held prisoner by momentary panic, a panic brought forth by the fear of what she was about to let happen. But she fought this new fear back. *It's time,* she told herself, *time to become a woman.* And then Pres drew her close.

Those important things she wanted to tell Pres were torn from her mind beneath the maddening assault of his kiss. Somehow, a few minutes later—she never knew exactly how—Megan found herself lying on the large bed with both her clothing and Pres gone.

Suddenly, the sound of the curtains being opened echoed loudly in the quiet room. Turning in the direction of the noise, Megan watched as the pale moonlight entered through the windows.

She gasped, for framed within the subtle illumination stood Pres. As it had happened on the boat, Megan thought he looked like a wandering mythological figure. His broad chest and the sharp V of his waist accented the powerful thighs that were moving steadily toward her.

He's so... beautiful. Her thought made her pause in wonder, because Megan had never before applied that description to a man, especially a naked man. Yet she saw the truth plainly. It was the only description possible for him at that precise moment in time.

The window was open, and although the night was hot and humid, a quiet breeze washed across her. Her nipples hardened. Her skin goose bumped. Megan knew it wasn't the breeze that brought about her reaction; rather, it was the man approaching her.

The sounds of the night and the waves breaking on the rocks outside were all amplified. But when Pres reached the bed, and his large hand caressed her cheek, the only sound she could hear was the rushing of her blood.

She captured Pres's hand in hers and moved it to her mouth. She kissed his open palm, and then looked up at him. "Pres," she whispered. "I..." But again, she could not go on.

Seeing the way the moonlight turned Megan's skin translucent, Pres felt another swelling of desire. But the desire was tempered by the love that had risen so swiftly. And, as he gazed at her and sensed her nervousness, he wanted to reassure her. But no words he could think of would be able to convey what he needed to say. So instead, Pres joined her on the bed and gently showed her by action what he could not put into words.

Their mouths met in a slow and languorous kiss that Pres prolonged until Megan thought her heart would burst. A low longing built within the very depths of her body and grew stronger with each second that passed. And, as her lips parted to admit his questing tongue, her fingers curled on his broad back, holding him firmly to her, before exploring the vastness beneath them.

Once again reality gave way to a dreamlike quality. The night and everything about it became magical. Pres's mouth and hands turned into burning brands that assailed her with such tender mercy that it was as though her body turned to liquid.

When his mouth crossed her breasts, halting only long enough to taste her stiffened peaks, she cried out. A thousand sensations combined to awaken her mind and body and heart, and brought Megan to a new awareness of herself.

His hands and mouth were everywhere, coaxing Megan to strange, new and frightening heights of passion that made her cry out his name.

Just when she found herself praying that he would never stop, his caresses ended. Megan's eyes opened wide. A ray of moonlight spilled over them, framing them as if by a spotlight on a stage. But all Megan saw was Pres. Everything else was darkness.

"I want you," Pres stated. This time he didn't follow his words with a kiss; rather, he waited for Megan and once again held on tightly to the bonds of his self-control.

Megan's body was aflame, in direct opposition to her muscles, which were filled with the most incredible tension. Only when she was finally able to see the blue depths of his eyes did she softly exhale. "I want you too, Pres," she said. "I . . . I need you."

Her words threatened to unleash his mighty passions, but he did not give in to their call; rather, he leaned forward and kissed Megan's now-closed eyes. His lips softly skimmed her skin, traveling along the velvet surface of her cheek, until his mouth finally covered hers again and he could taste the warm sweetness of her lips.

When their mouths were joined, Pres shifted, settling himself between Megan's firm, silken thighs. With the searing heat of their first contact, Megan involuntarily stiffened.

Despite this unexpected reaction, Pres was content to hold her close to him and feel the lushness of her body.

His lips trailed down to her neck. When he kissed the sensitive skin just below her ear, Megan's head began to spin once again. Her hands left his back and wound into the thick mat of his hair. Her fingers played within the dark bounty until she could stand no more and drew his mouth to hers. And, as their tongues danced together, and the fiery sensation of his skin on hers turned more intense, Megan's body moved without her commands.

Megan's muscles yielded to her passion. Her hips arched upward, allowing Pres to gently enter her. The combination of moist heat and pliant flesh encasing him, and his own explosive emotions was a feeling he had never before experienced with such intensity.

But when he moved deeper within her, she stiffened; Pres stopped the instant he felt the barrier within her. His mind reeled with his unexpected discovery of what was about to happen.

Exerting all his self-control, he held his runaway passions fiercely in check, hoping that he hadn't thoughtlessly hurt her.

Megan's limbs were locked: her arms were secured around Pres's back, and the muscles in her thighs trembled uncontrollably. When he'd entered her, the need to engulf him entirely had rushed over her, but the first wondrous pleasure of their joining had brought pain. She had not been able to stop herself from pulling away, nor from fearing what would happen next.

But as Pres lay lightly upon her, the heated tip of his desire within her, she knew that what her heart was crying out was not fear, but its call to trust him. Slowly, her fingers uncurled. She willed herself to relax, and as she followed her own commands, the fires that Pres had unleashed began to blaze again.

Slowly, ever so slowly, she brought her hands upward until she was able to hold his face within them. "Love me, Pres. Make love to me," she whispered.

With her last pleading whisper, Pres completed his entrance and filled her with himself. A searing, sharp, but blessedly fleeting, pain sped through her. She could not stop herself from arching stiffly against him, or from clamping her teeth on her lower lip, but this time she did not draw away; rather, she met him passionately.

Pres kissed and caressed her straining neck until the tension ebbed from her body. Deep within her, he began to move and gently brought Megan willingly with him on a wonderful voyage of learning and loving.

When they reached the very heights of their passionate flight, and their cries mingled as closely as did their bodies, they lay still, holding each other until their breathing softened into wispy sighs and their hearts no longer strained.

Nestled against Pres's side, Megan drew strength from the arms that held her and comfort from the skin that touched her. Her senses cartwheeled, and within her the warmth that had been so strong a part of their lovemaking remained.

Pres's special scent radiated upward from his chest to fill her nostrils. The damp sheen covering his body glowed softly in the moonlight. Her hand, resting lightly on his hip, was never still. His lips, pressing on her hair and scalp, sent thrills pulsing through her.

"Why didn't you tell me?" he asked, his voice muffled within her hair.

Megan closed her eyes. "I don't know. I was afraid. I...I thought it would interfere."

Pres shifted and turned her face to his. "It wouldn't have."

"Then it doesn't matter now, does it?" she asked, her eyes locking with his. *He's so beautiful.*

"It matters," he corrected her gently. "To me, and to you."

Megan smiled. She had no reply, for his statement needed none. Yet the reassurance she felt because he said the words she wanted to hear—though she hadn't even known that she wanted to hear them—only added to the knowledge that she had not made a foolish mistake in letting her heart rule her actions.

Pres smiled back and caressed her shoulder. "You're a woman of many surprises."

"Not really."

"Yes, you are, but I'm not about to get into an argument now," Pres said jokingly.

"Good," Megan teased, "because you'd lose."

"Probably," he admitted, flashing her a grin. "All my defenses are down."

Megan didn't have to say "Me too"; it was written on her features.

Still feeling the afterglow of their lovemaking and the surprisingly unexpected discovery it had produced, Pres found that there was an underlying question that he could not hold back. "Megan, was there no one that you cared for enough to...?"

Megan closed her eyes before his words ended. The question made her uncomfortable, but in her heart she sensed he had not asked it just to make conversation, or to gloat over a conquest. "No, there's never been time," she answered truthfully.

Pres's brows knitted together at her response. And although he didn't want to pursue this subject, her answer left him no choice.

"I would have felt better if you'd said there was never someone you could love. Being compared to time isn't exactly flattering."

Megan sat up and felt her blush rise from her waist to her hairline. She stared down at him and shook her head. "I'm not comparing you... I mean..."

Pres, seeing that he had upset Megan, sat up next to her and put his arm around her shoulders. "It's all right," he told her. "I was only joking."

"No, you weren't only joking."

"Well, somewhat joking," he admitted.

Megan grasped his hand and, raising it to her mouth, kissed it. With their hands still entwined, she lowered them onto her sheet-covered lap.

"I don't know if there could have been a man in my life or not. I never took the time to find out. Until tonight—no, until you—I never wanted a relationship."

"Why, Megan?" Pres asked, very much aware of the depths of his feelings for her.

Megan closed her eyes momentarily. "Because I'm afraid of what a relationship means."

"Which is?"

"A stumbling block in the way of my dreams."

"Megan—" Pres began, trying to find the right words to tell her that he would never stand in her way, but she stopped him from speaking by placing her hand across his mouth.

"No more words. Please, just hold me."

And Pres held her tightly, his strong arms securing her to him. A few minutes later, they slid down into the bed and, while listening to the rhythmic sounds of their hearts, fell asleep in each other's arms.

But the night ended for Megan when the first bands of dawn lightened the sky and demanding cries of gulls searching for their morning meal reached in through the open window.

She woke instantly, remembering not only where she was, but why. Sometime during the night they had let each other go. Megan, lying on her back, gazed at Pres, who was on his side facing her. His hand rested on her stomach, and she realized that the heat from his skin was what had awakened her.

Closing her eyes, Megan tried to go back to sleep but could not. Instead of sleep, the memories of the night paraded through her mind. She turned on her side to face Pres, and his hand slipped to the bed.

His breathing was as deep as his sleep, and she enjoyed the freedom of being able to study him openly. His face was relaxed; the crow's-feet that were always so visible on his handsomely tanned face were gone.

His generous mouth was closed, yet she believed she detected a slight smile on his lips. She hoped it was because of her.

Megan wanted to hold and kiss him, but did not. Instead, she let him sleep and took the opportunity to leave him and have a few minutes to herself before they started off on the next leg of their mad adventure.

Quietly, she leaned over and brushed his lips with hers. Just as quietly she left the bed, retrieved her clothing and went to her room.

After showering and dressing, Megan went downstairs and out onto the terrace. A smile of pleasure transformed her face when she saw that she was in time for the sunrise. When the leading edge of the golden ball peeked above the eastern horizon, she let go a welcoming sigh.

The sun brought forth the new day, and while it rose, Megan thought about the questions Pres had asked after they had made love. Her cheeks flushed with the boldness of her thoughts, but she welcomed the feeling instead of fighting it. Although she had never before given herself to a man, she had no regrets and felt no guilt.

Pres had shown her that waiting for him had been the right thing to do. *What happened between us is good,* she told herself. *It's right.*

But as she silently voiced her feelings, something began to grow within her mind—it was her old fear, the fear she had tried to keep submerged. *What will happen when we find the ship?*

Once again, confusion reigned. The beauty of the morning was diminished, and the love that had glowed last night was somehow not as bright.

No! she cried in silent denial, unable to understand why she was feeling this way after being so happy. *What's wrong with me?*

But Megan already knew what was wrong. She was in love with Pres, and that was the problem.

"How could I have been so weak?" she asked, shaking her head to clear away the mists swirling before her eyes, and hating the ugly truth that rose to taunt her. Because of one night of love, she had endangered everything she had tried so hard to accomplish. And she had even admitted as much to him last night.

What can I do? she asked herself. But there was no answer except to shore up her willpower and go on with her life, with what she had always planned for it to be.

Loving someone shouldn't stop what I want, she tried to tell herself. But with the dissension so rife within her new thoughts, Megan wasn't so sure.

"I won't let this stop me," she promised aloud, as the sun finally inched over the horizon, heralding for all who witnessed its rise that another day had come. The sunrise also reminded Megan that she was another day closer to her deadline.

Pres awakened slowly and stretched his long frame to its fullest. Opening his eyes, he discovered that Megan was gone.

He left his bed quickly and had started for the door then realized that he was naked. He changed direction in midstride and went to the window. The sun was already halfway out of the ocean on its daily pilgrimage to the heavens.

Glancing down, Pres saw Megan was standing on the terrace. His heart swelled with love as he looked at her, and at the way her blond hair sparkled in the morning sun.

"I love you," he whispered. Then he went into the bathroom to shower and shave. When he emerged from his room fifteen minutes later, he went out onto the terrace to join Megan, who was still watching the horizon.

Walking up behind her, Pres slipped his arms about her waist and drew her against him. "Good morning," he whispered, kissing the fragrant skin of her neck. Beneath his lips, her pulse beat strongly.

Megan covered his hands with her palms and moved them in a gentle caress. "Good morning," she replied. The moment she spoke, she realized her voice had betrayed the raging conflict within her.

Pres did not release her when he heard the strain in Megan's voice. Instead, he turned her to him and searched her face. "What's wrong?"

Megan shrugged, unsure of how to answer him. There were a million things wrong, and a million things right.

"Are you regretting last night, now that you've had time to think?"

"No!" Megan answered emphatically. "I'll never regret last night. It's ... I'm just very confused right now."

"Then something is wrong," Pres stated as he gazed at her in his penetrating way.

Megan moistened her lips and stepped back, freeing herself from his light hold. She clasped her hands tightly before her and stared at her fingers. When she looked up at him, her eyes were misty with unshed tears.

"When all of this started," she began, her voice breaking on the last word, "the search for the ship," she quickly clarified, "all it meant was a slight detour from what I had planned. But you," she said, looking directly at him, "you mean more than a slight detour."

A chill raced along Pres's spine, not unlike the one he'd experienced yesterday when Megan had been so close to danger. But nothing of what he felt was reflected on his face. "In what way?" he asked, his voice low and unexpectedly gentle.

"In all ways!" she cried. Pausing to calm her fraying nerves, Megan took a slow breath. "I have my plans set. Everything is arranged. I didn't expect to fall in love. I didn't want to!"

"Is that so terrible?"

"No, it shouldn't be. But I didn't plan on it."

Pres blinked. It was his only outward reaction to her words. "I didn't know love was something to be planned."

"You're not a woman," Megan said.

Caught off guard by her statement, Pres dropped his facade, clearly showing his lack of comprehension.

Megan smiled hesitantly. "As a girl growing up, you make plans for your life: marriage and children and a house with a picket fence are some of those plans. But the older you get, the more those plans change as your priorities change. You think about other things, a career for instance."

"So?" Pres asked.

Megan sighed. "I want my marriage, and my children, and even the house with a picket fence—one day. But I want my career, too. Pres, if I can't reach my goals before going after other things, I'll never attain them."

Pres digested her words, all the while trying not to believe what his mind was telling him. But when she finished, he knew he had not misunderstood her. "What you're saying is that your feelings for me, and mine for you, don't matter right now. All that matters is your career, correct?"

His angry and clipped words struck Megan painfully.

"No," she whispered as she backed away from him.

"It sounds that way to me."

"I'm sorry if it does. I just need you to know that I have to finish what I started out to do." But just one glance at his face told Megan that nothing she could say would help at that moment.

"And you think that having a relationship with me will stop you?" Pres asked, still unwilling to believe that that was exactly what Megan was saying.

"No, Pres," Megan said in a voice that came out in icy contract to Pres's anger. "Or at least I hope not. But almost everyone I know who started out pursuing a career, but then fell in love, never seemed able to have their career."

"Perhaps they never really wanted that career."

"But I do! I want my career!" she stated adamantly.

Pres's eyes became as dull as stone. His lips thinned. "It's a shame you can't let your heart play as important a role in your life as your mind does."

"What are you trying to say?" Megan asked.

"You're the one after the graduate degree. You figure it out," Pres stated pointedly before he started away.

"Pres," Megan called, her heart breaking with the agony of what had happened to them. Pres spun when she spoke his name. When he faced her, his eyes were hard and unforgiving, yet Megan held herself straight and proud.

"I won't... I can't give up school for anyone. I want school, and my career, and I want them badly," she reiterated, working hard to maintain a level tone.

When Pres spoke, his words reached her with the force of a whiplash. "No one asked you to give up anything. Only you never bothered to find that out."

Megan's heart sank when he started away again. Her mind went dark. "Where are you going?" she half shouted.

Pres glanced back over his shoulder. "To get my things."

Megan paled with the knowledge that he was walking out on her. "You're... leaving? But—"

"But nothing," Pres snapped. "*We're* leaving. We have a plane to catch in two hours, or have you changed your mind about going after your brother's treasure ship with me?"

Again, the seesaw battle within threatened to drown her. "I haven't changed my mind. Please, Pres, don't be angry. I just wanted you to understand who I am."

When Pres finally turned all the way around to face her, his body was as rigid as the stare he fixed her with. "Oh, I understand all right. Even more than you do. Last night was just a more grown-up version of what happened in high school, wasn't it? What am I to you," he asked, his voice growing louder, harsher, "the person in your life who you use to gain new experiences?"

Megan's anger, held in thin control until now, burst free with his callous charge. "You don't understand anything other than your own selfish needs. And you certainly don't understand love."

The ghostly smile forming on Pres's lips was a portent of the harsh and vitriolic words to come. "You know, I think you're right. After all, if I understood love, I wouldn't have fallen in love with you after having so much insight into your real character, would I?''

Megan stared at him, her mouth agape. She shook her head in fierce denial. ''You bas—'' But she cut herself off. ''No, I won't sink to your level. You're just getting back at me.''

''My level! I—'' But Pres also cut himself off sharply, as he realized that there was nothing to be gained by continuing the argument. ''If you feel that way, get another diver.''

''There isn't time!''

Pres laughed. ''No, I guess there isn't, not if you don't want to put your career on hold.''

''Would you sacrifice your career and your diving company for me if the situation were reversed?'' Megan challenged, stepping toward him as she spoke. Without giving him a chance to answer for himself, she answered for him. ''Of course not.''

''It's nice to know that someone has all the answers,'' Pres told her, ''even if that someone believes everyone else has the same priorities as she does.''

''Are you trying to deny that what I said is true?''

''What's the point?'' he asked, and then turned and walked away before Megan could reply.

When he reached the doorway, he paused. ''Last night never happened,'' he stated as he glared at her. ''Never.''

But the dull ache centered within her told Megan the truth. Last night had happened. Only now she saw Pres's true nature and knew that she had committed her biggest folly.

And while she tried to tell herself that she had been a fool, the tears that rained upon her cheeks called her a liar.

''What am I going to do?'' she asked the clear blue sky above her. ''What?''

Chapter Eight

The *Cervantes* cut through the Atlantic, its foaming wake
the only disturbance upon the glassy August sea. Pres stood
on the bridge, his hands at the controls, keeping the cruiser
moving smoothly toward the dive area.

The morning sun was roasting the world with uncaring
abandon, but after having lived for six years beneath tropical skies, its intensity did not bother Pres.

Megan was at the bow. Her hands loosely gripped the
railing while she watched the water ahead. Behind her, Pres
studied her almost statuelike stance.

The air tossed her hair randomly about, and he noticed
that during the almost two weeks of their diving, the sun had
streaked her hair to an almost white-blond hue. It was a
color that contrasted strongly with her now deeply tanned
face.

Pres thought her hair was also a color that suited her
perfectly. *No you don't,* Pres told himself, refusing to let his
mind wander to where it should not. Pres understood the

danger in thinking of Megan in any terms other than business, and had worked steadfastly at maintaining his distance.

His outrage had long since eased. What had replaced it was a sense of remorse. Megan had graced him with a gift he had not asked for, but one he had accepted with love. It was a gift that could only be shared once in a lifetime. Instead, what happened the morning after they made love had made that gift seem unimportant.

No matter how many times he told himself that he hated her for what she had done to him, he could not deny that he loved her. *But that means nothing,* he reminded himself.

Pres was not the same person he had been in high school, when a younger Megan Teal had broken his heart. And because he wasn't the same easily hurt boy, he was able to reason out what his feelings were then, and now. In high school, what he'd felt for Megan was the adolescent crush a gawky, unsophisticated and hopeful boy felt for a beautiful and nearly reachable young girl.

What he felt now was passion and love for the woman he had thought Megan to be, but who she obviously was not.

I'm in love with a fantasy, he told himself.

He shook his inharmonious thoughts away and concentrated on his job. Looking first at the compass, and then at the onboard navigational computer, Pres saw that the *Cervantes* was within a half mile of their last dive sight.

It was time to prepare for the day ahead. "Keep a sharp eye," he called to Megan, who was looking for the marking buoys. He knew she heard him, although she gave no sign of acknowledgment.

Her action reminded him that, just as he had kept his distance from her, so had she from him—which he tried to believe was just as well.

Megan heard Pres's warning that they were nearing the dive area and continued to search the ocean's surface, all the while relishing the cool sea air that washed across her skin.

August in the Virgin Islands was hot. The trade winds were weak at this time of year. The air was almost stagnant.

She had found the only relief from the oppressive tropical heat was when she and Pres were on the boat, either going to the dive area or returning; and, of course, when they were beneath the calm, almost mirrorlike ocean.

Megan scanned the ocean's surface, seeking the triple buoys marking their last dive location. Today was the eleventh day of diving, and the twelfth day since they'd left Key West.

Looking over her shoulder for a brief second, Megan glanced at the bridge, where Pres's cutting figure presided. A slight shudder rippled along her skin, but she cut it off before it could grow into something more. She closed her eyes for a second and, when she opened them, made herself look for the buoys. *Thank heaven he acts as though nothing ever happened.* And it was true. From the moment they'd taken the taxi to the airport in Key West, Pres had behaved as if their lovemaking had been but one of Megan's dreams.

He never once mentioned anything about *that* night to her. He only spoke about the business at hand: diving and locating the Spanish galleon. He never touched her, accidentally or intentionally. The only time his hands came in contact with her was when she had her wet suit on and he was helping her with her equipment.

She was grateful for his aloofness, but it tore her apart. Whenever he was near her, she wanted to touch him, to taste the subtleness of his lips, to feel his strong arms holding her securely. But she never let her professional facade slip.

Megan did her best to match Pres's cool, precise and methodical manner in both her attitude and her speech. But the obviously restrained nature in which they worked and talked had taken its toll on Megan.

On the first day in St. Thomas, Megan's nerves had been frayed to the breaking point. Self-recriminations slid easily into her mind. With one thought, she condemned herself for what had happened; with the next, she realized that no matter what the future might bring, her memory of their one night of lovemaking would always be there to whisper of her love for Pres, and her joy at having been able to have that single night, if no others.

After unpacking in her brother's villa—the villa owned by the Florida Oceanographic Institute—Megan had paced in an effort to suppress the thoughts and emotions that were trying to drown her. She knew that she must find a way to contain her anger, to hide her love for Pres and to fight the feeling of shame growing within her mind and heart.

Her shame stemmed from Pres's accusation that she had used him to gain experience. She had wanted to deny his cruel and taunting charges, but she had been unable to. Not because they were true, but because she was certain that he would misconstrue anything she might say to him.

She believed that he would take her explanation as an excuse or a defensive statement and not the truth. She wondered how she could have let her emotions get so out of hand that she had become a pawn to them, instead of controlling them as she had always done.

Megan wanted to blame Sandi for weakening her defenses with her nonadvice and warm understanding, but she could not blame her friend for what she had done to herself.

But, before that long night ended, Megan had found a small grain of strength on which to start rebuilding the foundations of her defenses against Pres, and against the world. She knew that unless she armored herself against her emotional need for Pres, she would be helpless in the coming days.

From the first day of their diving, Megan had drawn upon that lonely grain of strength, and she reacted to Pres without reacting to her emotions. She learned, too, that the days spent with Pres passed quickly as they searched the ocean floor for the old galleon.

But it was the nights that were unbearable. Every one lasted a lifetime, and when the sun rose in the mornings, Megan was already awake.

The nights were hard on Megan. The lush tropical skies and the heavy scents of fruit and flowers assaulted her mind, her heart, and all her senses, bringing out in her the knowledge that she was absolutely alone in the world.

Megan refused to surrender to her loneliness and despair; instead, she continued to strengthen her resolve. When the first week of diving ended, Megan was again secure in the knowledge that she would soon be at school and following her life's path. But Megan thought about her career only when she was alone, for whenever Pres was near, logical thinking was impossible.

"There!" Megan cried, pointing to three red buoys forming a triangle in the middle of nowhere.

The *Cervantes* slowed; the throaty sound of its twin engines died. Megan held on to the railing until the *Cervantes* leveled off, and as the whine of the electric winch lowering the anchor reverberated, Megan went into the cabin and put on her wet suit.

When Pres had finished securing the bridge and lowering the search equipment into the water by means of another winch, Megan came out onto the deck, her black rubber wet suit acting like a sauna on her skin. Five minutes later, Pres had donned his wet suit also.

They went through the slow ritual of checking over their equipment, just as they had before leaving the dock. It was a routine that they practiced daily, and one Pres would not allow to be changed.

When the inspection was completed, Pres helped Megan into her tanks, and she did the same for him. They both looked at their diving watches, adjusting the timer band so that they would know how long they were under and how much time they had left.

They made three or four one-hour dives each day: two dives in the morning, a third and sometimes a fourth in the afternoon, depending on how tired they were. Pres also insisted that they take at least an hour's break in between, to rest and let their bodies recover from the pressures of deep-water diving.

"Let's find it today," Pres said as he slipped his mask onto his head.

Megan, doing the same, paused to look at him. But she said nothing, for there was nothing to say. Pres had uttered the same words every day for the past eleven days, just before their first dive.

Despite the emotional upheaval lying unvoiced between them, they worked well as a team. In perfect unison, they stepped onto the diving platform and jumped into the water. As always happened when she was so far from land, Megan felt the water engulf her and draw her down. She fought the first uneasy qualms of being at the mercy of the ocean's depths: it was a feeling that had been born on the first day they started their quest for the old galleon.

Megan was an experienced diver, but this was the first prolonged period of time she had spent in deep ocean waters. Usually, she dived near land when she was with Bruce. However, the sensation of fear eased almost as soon as it had come. After readjusting her mask, Megan did a graceful underwater somersault and swam to the equipment line, where Pres waited.

During the past eleven days, Megan had learned just how good a diving partner Pres was. *He's more than good,* she corrected herself. Pres never rushed a dive. He always waited for her, and never let her get too far out of his sight. And after her initial queasiness upon entering the deep ocean, she always felt safe with him.

When she reached him, he signaled her down. The descent took ten minutes, because they stopped every twenty feet to let their bodies get acclimated to the ever-increasing pressures of the ocean depths. Once at the bottom, Pres quickly unhooked the metal detector and handed it to Megan.

Knowing that air and time were their most valuable commodities, Megan took the detector, gave him the okay sign and started swimming toward the underwater marker Pres had set up at the end of their last search pattern. With each dive, they alternated using the detector. Pres had used it on the last dive yesterday; the first dive was hers.

They used a crisscross pattern for their searching. Although they were looking for a large galleon, they were also looking for any evidence of the ship's presence, such as coins, metal and even old pieces of wood. Finding any of those things would indicate they were not wasting their time.

So far they had found nothing.

As Megan started the first length of her search, she saw something move on the ocean floor. She froze and turned to face it, knowing that if there was danger, she must be aware of what the danger was.

Her breathing accelerated and as she heard her own amplified and quickened sounds, she exerted self-control. Whatever *it* was, was ten feet from her and five feet below. It was also making the coarse ocean floor shift randomly. An instant later, a large form shot out of the sand.

Startled, Megan almost dropped the metal detector. Her heart thudded loudly before she realized what it was. But Megan's heart returned to normal as she witnessed one of nature's most beautiful displays, a nine-foot manta ray rising straight up.

Its diamond shape, winglike fins and long narrow tail all combined to give this creature of the deep the appearance of a jet-fighter plane. Like a jet in the sky, the manta cut through the ocean depths with graceful ease until it disappeared in the distance.

Shaking herself back to her task, Megan resumed her search pattern. In their location, the ocean bottom stretched infinitely, its surface looking more like a rippled lake after a thunderstorm than it did a rock and sand floor. And much like the ocean above, the floor too had its own horizon: a distinct line of darkness that moved with Megan and kept an equal distance.

Megan searched, secure in the knowledge that Pres was always somewhere near, always watching her and the area around them. And while she looked for the galleon, the combination of the silent world of beauty and the job she was doing made time speed by.

Thirty minutes after she had begun her search pattern, Pres tapped her on the shoulder and pointed to his watch.

Megan nodded, seeing that their time was up, and swam back to the equipment line, where she secured the metal detector. They rose slowly to the surface, taking the full amount of time left in their tanks to properly decompress.

When they were on the *Cervantes*, and had their equipment off, Megan sat on a chair and leaned back.

"Tired?" Pres asked as he attached one set of tanks to the compressor to refill them.

Megan shook her head. "No, I guess I'm just weary."

"It happens. We've been at it for eleven days."

"I can't believe we haven't found one single thing yet. Could Bruce be wrong about the location?"

"I don't know," Pres admitted. "But what I do know is that four hundred years is time enough to have torn the ship to shreds and wiped away any evidence of its once being here."

"Is that what you really think?" Megan asked, afraid that he would say yes.

Pres shrugged noncommittally. "I'm looking for that ship, aren't I? That should be your answer." Pres favored her with a half smile as he added, "All I can say for certain is that I understand the ocean enough to realize that anything is possible. Anything."

Megan accepted his words at face value. Leaning back, she closed her eyes, determined to rest for the alloted time before continuing what she was beginning to believe was her brother's insane dream.

"Why couldn't he have become an accountant?" she murmured.

"Excuse me?" Pres asked.

Startled, Megan opened her eyes and belatedly realized she had spoken aloud. "It's nothing," she said. "I was wondering why Bruce didn't become an accountant instead of an oceanographer. Then he could have found all the treasures in the world without leaving his desk."

Pres gazed at her for a moment. His face was expressionless, but he didn't like what he was hearing. "Giving up already?" he asked.

Megan stiffened. She half rose from the chair and then sank back. She forced a smile to her lips. "You'd like that, wouldn't you? Sorry, Pres. I don't give up easily."

"Good," he said, his face still stonelike, "because I never give up."

Megan stared at him, trying her best to read from his face what the underlying message in his words had been. But she learned nothing in the short space of time before he turned back to the equipment.

The hour passed quickly, and by the time they had entered the water again, Megan gladly welcomed its cool relief from the midday sun.

This time, when they reached the bottom, Pres took the metal detector and Megan swam slightly above him and to his right side. Her job was to watch out for him, and to scan the area while his attention was fixed on the detector and on the floor beneath it.

The second dive was Megan's favorite, for it was feeding time for much of the ocean's denizens. Hundreds of varieties of fish swam in schools, feeding upon the vegetation floating near the bottom. In contrast to the previous dive, the ocean floor was now a world of life, and everywhere Megan looked, rainbow colors and darting forms congregated.

It was a peaceful world that lulled her senses, took her mind off her troubles and gave her respite for short periods. These welcome periods of relief from her tortured thoughts were enough to keep her spirits higher than they would have been.

Back to work, she told herself, realizing that she had lost her concentration, which was very, very dangerous.

Spinning in a circle, Megan looked for Pres and found him twenty feet away. As her eyes followed his graceful form, he stopped his forward motion and swung the metal detector in short sideways arcs. Suddenly he released the device.

No sooner had the metal detector dropped to the ocean bottom than Pres followed it. Small clouds of sand and particles of vegetation spurted upward, disturbed by the metal detector's landing.

Megan swam toward Pres, then hovered above him as he swept the sandy floor with light strokes of his gloved hand. He never touched the sand; rather, the waving motions he made moved the sand from beneath him.

He stopped to reach down, and Megan's heart stopped also. When he grasped something, her breath caught. She wanted to know what it was, but instead of rushing down to him, she made herself breathe slowly and methodically as she was supposed to. She waited for Pres to show her his discovery, but he never once looked in her direction.

The instant Pres saw the rectangular object, his senses had come alive. His body began to tingle, and his breathing accelerated. He made himself relax as he began the slow job of moving the coarse sand from the object without touching anything. When the sand above it was gone, Pres studied the object for several seconds before taking out his diving knife and using its cutting edge to work the encrusted sand away from the four sides. When that had been accomplished, he levered the knife under one edge and pried it up.

Once the lower edge was free, he put his knife into its sheath and carefully lifted the object with his gloved hands.

When he brought it close to his mask, he involuntarily wasted a breath in a startled exhale.

Four hundred years of saltwater erosion had not been enough to disguise what he'd found. It was a leather-encased and belted wooden box about three inches high, six inches across, and eight inches long. The brass corners and belt buckles securing the box were badly discolored, but they still held what remained of the leather covering together.

That it was very old, Pres was certain. All that was left of the leather was a thin weblike covering. When he shined his flash on it, the mahogany wood reflected light back at him.

After a few more seconds, Pres aimed his flashlight at the bottom. He held the light steady while sweeping his hand back and forth to move the sand, but he found nothing else.

When he was sure that there were no other objects beneath him, he secured the flash to his belt and looked up at Megan.

Megan's impatience had been growing, but she held her depth and did not go down to Pres. Pres had set down the rules, and she would not break them. She had to stay alert while his concentration was focused elsewhere. It was important. It could save their lives. Just as Megan looked at her chronometer and saw that their time was up, Pres raised his hand high, formed a fist and shook it in a sign of victory.

Megan replied with an okay sign, and then pointed to her watch, letting him know that their time was up.

Pres unhooked a small package from his belt, opened the underwater buoy and took out his mouthpiece. Inserting the mouthpiece into the end of the bright yellow underwater buoy, he filled it with air, after which he tied the buoy to a piece of rock near the find.

At long last Pres gave Megan the signal to ascend. Throughout the long, seemingly endless journey to the surface, Megan's impatience grew to the bursting point. Each time her eyes went to the box, she was sure that Pres had found something important.

...be tempted!

**See inside for special
4 FREE BOOKS offer**

Silhouette Special Edition®

A FREE
Folding Umbrella
and Mystery Gift
await you, too!

← Clip and mail this postpaid card today! ↗

Mail this card today for

4 FREE BOOKS
(a $10.00 value)
this Folding Umbrella and
a Mystery Gift *ALL FREE!*

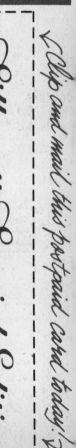

← Clip and mail this postpaid card today! ✌

Silhouette Special Edition ®

Silhouette Books, 120 Brighton Rd., P.O. Box 5084, Clifton, NJ 07015-9956

☐ **YES!** Please send me my four Silhouette Special Edition novels along with my FREE Folding Umbrella and Mystery Gift, as explained in the attached insert. I understand that I am under no obligation to purchase any books.

NAME _____
(please print)

ADDRESS _____

CITY _____ STATE _____ ZIP _____

Terms and prices subject to change.
Your enrollment is subject to acceptance by Silhouette Books.
Silhouette Special Edition is a registered trademark.

CAS086

"What is it?" Megan asked when they stood on the *Cervantes*'s deck.

Pres smiled, unhooked his harness and shrugged off his tanks. Without speaking, he looked pointedly at Megan until she removed her equipment.

"Well?" she asked, barely able to stop herself from stomping her foot on the deck.

"I don't know yet," Pres began as he stared at the box. "But this has all the trappings of a very old seaman's box."

Megan's eyes grew large as she looked at the box. "But it's in such good condition. Are you sure?" she asked when she touched the decaying leather.

Pres didn't answer; instead, he took out his knife and gently peeled the leather away to reveal the smooth wood beneath it. "Mahogany," Pres said. "The leather acted as a protection to the wood. And mahogany is the strongest, the hardest of woods. The sand it was buried in would also protect it. But," he added, "we won't know anything until we open it."

Reaching out, Megan took the box from Pres. She studied the fraying leather straps that held it closed. In between the straps was a brownish-green oblong strip. Pointing to the strip, she asked, "What is this?"

"A plaque of some sort," he ventured when he took the box back. Carefully, Pres used the point of his knife to scrape at the piece of metal. When he did, the leather it was attached to broke apart and the strip fell free.

Bending quickly, Pres picked it up in his left hand and turned it over. The back was the same brownish green as the front. "Brass."

When he rubbed his thumb across the top, he felt some indentations but could see very little beneath the layers of corrosion. "There's an inscription on it."

"Can you read it?" Megan asked impatiently.

Pres shook his head. "Not yet," he stated as he handed her the strip. "In the upper-left cabinet in the galley is my chemical-analysis kit. It has a black vinyl covering. Would you get it please?'' he asked.

When Megan went to the galley, Pres sat in the deck chair and turned his attention to the mahogany box. He wasn't sure how old the box might be. It could be ten years old, or five hundred. Mahogany was used extensively by seagoing men. The corrosion was normal, for brass never corroded the way other metals did. Only a few thin layers of brownish-green coated the metal. Time and water currents could wear at it, but this box had been protected by sand. And whatever was inside the box had registered strongly on the metal detector.

Pres cut the few straggly fibers of leather that held the buckles together. When they separated, he put his knife down and set the box on his lap.

Megan came out just when he had severed the bindings, and she went over to stand behind him. Holding the chemical kit in her left hand, she watched Pres work and prayed that some wonderful twist of fate had given them a clue in their search.

Slowly, more slowly than when he had cleared the sand from the top of the box, he opened it. There was a low ''pop'' when the lid was lifted. The sound was followed by a thin trickle of water spilling out.

Megan held her breath. Pres's strong fingers lifted the top. ''What?'' Megan whispered as she stared at several brown-green pieces of metal.

Pres studied his find, and the excitement he'd tried to hold back began to rise. ''It's a sextant. It's old, Megan, very old.'' As he spoke, his fingers carefully wiped away the mucouslike covering that had once been the oilcloth the instruments were protected with.

After he inspected the pieces without taking them out of their resting places, he asked Megan for the strip of brass and the black kit. Once the kit was opened, Pres removed a vial of clear liquid. Saturating a cotton pad with the mild acid from the vial, he began to wipe the cotton across the brass strip.

Five cotton pads later, he held the now gleaming brass plate up. A smile had long ago formed on his lips, but now he gave full vent to his excitement, a fact that was evident in the tone of his voice. "*Conquistador*—Barcelona," he read. "It must have been the captain's. It could have been washed overboard during the hurricane," Pres added when he placed the brass strip in Megan's hand.

"We're near. Oh, Pres, we must be near the galleon!" Megan cried excitedly.

But Pres did not share her enthusiasm and shook his head slowly. After the initial exhilaration of finding the sextant, reality and the ways of the ocean had followed quickly, reminding him of what he was trying to do. "It's possible, but ocean currents can move small objects for miles in any direction."

Megan refused to listen. "No! I won't accept that! The ship *has* to be near."

"Of course," Pres said, not bothering to hide the sarcasm in his voice, "the ocean wouldn't *dare* interfere with Megan Teal's personal ambitions."

Megan's cheeks flamed. She tightened her fingers into a fist, securing the brass plate within. "You uncaring bastard!"

Pres stared at her, and for the first time since arriving in St. Thomas, he was unable to hold back his true feelings. "That's like the pot calling the kettle black. Who's uncaring in our situation, Megan? Who doesn't want to risk herself in an emotional relationship because she's afraid that love will ruin her life and career?"

"That's not fair," Megan cried in denial.

"No, not from your point of view it isn't," he said, his voice returning to its former coolness. "Shall we go back to work now?" Without waiting for an answer, Pres continued. "Do you want to make us lunch or fill the tanks?"

"The tanks," Megan replied, trying to match the coolness of his voice with hers.

"Of course," he mumbled, as he turned and went down to the galley.

Pres sat on the cushioned chair of the deck, the August sky ablaze with stars. The air barely moved, but he was unaware of the smothering heat and humidity; his mind was occupied with more pressing problems. In his hand was the *Conquistador*'s sextant.

When they had returned to the dock, following two unsuccessful dives, Megan had left for her villa. Pres had spent the next hour cleaning and polishing the sextant until all its pieces shone like new.

After a light dinner, he'd sat down and tried to hold back the growing intuitive sensation that things were about to change.

Gripping the sextant absently, Pres released the cautious hold he had on his thoughts and began to draw upon his intuitive senses. Logically, intellectually, he knew that finding the navigational device meant nothing. It could, as he had told Megan earlier, have been washed overboard long before the ship went down.

But just finding it in the vicinity where Bruce believed the ship had gone down made it hard to believe that the ship wasn't somewhere nearby.

Glancing down, Pres stopped playing with the sextant and looked at it. The brass was warm, holding the heat of his skin within it. As he stared at it, his excitement grew.

He stood and, grasping the device tightly, went into the cabin. Opening the cabinet above the galley table, he withdrew one of the charts Bruce had prepared for him and spread it across the table.

He studied the chart carefully and marked the location of the day's find. He compared that location to the one-square-mile area that Bruce had hopefully pinpointed as the galleon's final resting place.

But Pres knew there was something wrong. He and Megan had crisscrossed that mile, and they had only the sextant to show for eleven days of diving. Closing his eyes, Pres tried to second-guess not only Bruce, but the four centuries of ocean currents.

"Where are you?" he asked as he opened his eyes. "Where!" he shouted, slamming his fist on the table.

Taking a calming breath, he folded the chart and replaced it in the cabinet before returning to his chair on the rear deck.

As he tried to think of a way to locate the galleon, a picture of Megan rose within his mind. He tried to stop it from forming, but this time he was powerless to fend off the emerald-green eyes that stared so unflinchingly at him.

He closed his eyes and released his surging emotions. He pushed aside the denials that had carried him successfully through the past two weeks.

Why did she come back into my life? But he knew that the answer had to do with fate and destiny, and was not something that could be viewed with any sort of logic.

Pres accepted the fact that he loved Megan, and that it was not just leftover emotions of an adolescent that were ruling him. He tried reasoning as logically as he could, but one thing stopped him with its illogicality—Megan's belief that his love for her would interfere with her future.

"What made her that way?" he asked the night. "And what will change her?"

Again, Pres had no answer. He only knew that somehow he must find a way to break through Megan's staunch barriers and show her that she needed more than just a career.

With that thought, the intensity of Megan's image lessened, while the intuitive feeling that he was getting close to the hiding place of the Spanish galleon became stronger.

This time, the picture that rose before him was a vision of what the ship meant to him. Finding it would secure his future. His share of the treasure would make him solvent again, enabling him to stay in St. Thomas and keep his business alive.

Finding the ship would give him one other thing—a reputation. A treasure find the magnitude of the one Bruce claimed this ship contained, would in itself make his reputation as a salvage expert.

But a sobering and jarring thought stopped Pres from enjoying the potential of his find. Because he realized that if and when he found the ship and gained all the rewards of that find, he would lose Megan. With the ship's discovery, Megan's part in the salvage operation would end, freeing her to return to school and the solitary pursuit of her career. *Is it worth it?* he asked himself.

Chapter Nine

On the morning of the seventeenth day, Megan sat bolt upright in bed. Beads of perspiration filmed her face. Her hands and arms hugged her upper torso tightly. Her breathing was harsh and irregular.

"Stop haunting me! Please," she cried futilely to the dream that had awakened her, and to the man responsible for it.

But Megan knew that no amount of pleading would stop these nightly occurrences. Every night since she and Pres had made love, his image had filled her dreams.

Usually, it was the same dream, in which they make love. Afterward, Pres would smile and tell her that she was his. His life was her life. Where he went, she would go; what he did, she would do.

She could not refuse him, in the dream, no matter how hard she tried. Always, at that exact moment, she would wake, trembling and crying.

Megan had reached the point where even thinking about sleep frightened her. *Why did this have to happen?*

Megan railed against the fates that had played with her on the morning after she and Pres had made love. Instead of the understanding she had hoped he would give her, he had shown her that he was unwilling to empathize with what she was going through.

Why can't I have my career, and my love? she wondered, as she left the bed to prepare to face the day. *Why did Bruce have to have that accident?*

Megan quickly drew back that unworthy thought, ashamed at herself for even letting it form.

The telephone rang, breaking the quiet solitude that Bruce and Sandi loved to share when they were working together. Bruce looked up, but when Sandi reached for the phone, he returned to the geodetic survey map he was working on.

"Hello?" Sandi said. When the voice on the other end identified himself, Sandi felt a surge of excitement. It wasn't every day that the United States commissioner of conservation called, even if he had once been the dean of the School of Science at the University of Illinois, and hence Bruce's ex-boss.

Covering the mouthpiece, Sandi told Bruce that Frank Sullivan was on the line.

Bruce's eyebrows flicked up in surprise. The last time he'd spoken to Frank had been two years ago, when he'd applied for a grant to start his foundation. The grant had never materialized because of governmental spending cutbacks.

Puzzled, but glad to speak to his old mentor, Bruce took the phone and said, "Hello, Commissioner."

"Are you still looking for funding, Dr. Teal?"

"Any way I can get it, Dr. Sullivan," he replied, thinking of Megan and Pres searching the Caribbean on his mad mission.

The commissioner laughed at Bruce's tone, and then spoke casually. "Bruce, it seems I've just gotten a windfall.

The House Budget Committee reinstated seven million dollars of the fifteen million they cut back on two years ago. The money is earmarked for conservation funding and grants."

When Frank Sullivan paused, Bruce's hand tightened on the receiver. His mind was at attention; his long-dormant hopes were rising once again.

"However," Commissioner Sullivan added quickly, "any monies coming from my agency must have a minimum of fifty percent in matching funds from the private sector."

Bruce's hopes crashed back into the oblivion they had risen from. "I see," he said in a low voice.

In contrast to his reply, the commissioner chuckled. "The oil companies look like a good bet. They're always looking for tax shelters to offset profits."

"I've tried that route already. How many more times can I listen to someone tell me that their 'funding is already allocated for existing institutes and foundations'?"

"Try again, Bruce," the commissioner advised. "But this time talk to the man on top."

Before he let a caustic retort slip out, Bruce made himself listen to Frank Sullivan's voice more than his words. He heard something, but he wasn't sure what. "Any suggestions? Or would that be out of line?" he asked warily.

"I've never been a political person," Sullivan stated, "but there are certain rules that govern my office."

"I understand," Bruce said truthfully, even as he tried to think of whom he could contact.

"Good. Oh, by the way, I had lunch with Morton Slater, the chairman of Langely Petroleum out of Phoenix. We did a lot of talking about ocean exploration. He's an interesting man. You should meet him sometime."

Bruce, never slow on the uptake, realized immediately what Frank Sullivan was telling him. "Perhaps I should," he agreed. "Is there a time limit on the funding?"

"I'll need the paperwork in sixty days. Thirty would be better. It would get you a larger start-up."

Bruce had to swallow several times before he could speak. When he did, his voice was laden with emotion. "Thank you, Frank. I'll do the best I can."

"I know you will," his old mentor stated confidently before hanging up.

Bruce held on to the phone for a full minute before putting it down. He looked at Sandi, but before he spoke, he bent down and kissed her.

"Ummm," Sandi whispered when their lips parted. "Frank Sullivan should call more often."

"I'll settle for this one time," he said, his voice rising with unrestrained excitement, and he told Sandi what had transpired.

When he was finished, Sandi's eyes were shining as brightly as Bruce's, but she made herself temper her thoughts with reality, for she had lived through all the rejections of the past years.

"Do you think Morton Slater will talk with you?" she asked.

Bruce's smile was devastating. He picked up the phone, saying, "This time, I think I'll be able to get through."

Sandi took the phone from him. "You may be a great scientist, even a genius, but you don't know beans about business. When one calls the *chairman of the board*, one's *secretary* is the person who does it."

"You're not my secretary," Bruce corrected.

"No, but I am your assistant, and I want to be your wife. Making a phone call to further those ends is worth it. Besides, Dr. Teal, first impressions are important. You don't want to appear to be begging for a handout."

Without further ado or argument, Sandi dialed information, obtained the telephone number and made the call.

Ten minutes later, Morton Slater was on the phone. With a huge I-told-you-so smile, Sandi said, "Just one moment, Mr. Slater, Dr. Teal will be right with you."

Bruce wrestled the phone away from Sandi, who was trying to strategically delay him, and introduced himself to

Morton Slater. Exactly two minutes later he hung up. "Lunch next Monday in Phoenix," he informed Sandi.

Sandi's grin faltered. "You can't fly," she reminded him.

"No, but there are trains."

"Yes, there are. And they're very romantic," Sandi whispered, even though she knew she would have to stay here and complete the rush work that the institute needed.

"Oh? I always thought they were bumpy," Bruce said with a straight face.

"Watch it, mister, or I'll trade you in for a marine microbiologist."

"And do what? Raise single-cell children with gills?"

Sandi said nothing; rather, she gave Bruce a shove that landed him back in his chair.

To Megan, the passing day became a mélange of repetitious frustration. And, on the twenty-second day of her odyssey, Megan stared at the blue-green Atlantic from the port side of the *Cervantes*. Anger flamed in her green eyes, giving them a jewellike glow. Her rage was directed at the ocean itself and, as irrational as it was, she could do nothing about it.

Three weeks had passed since she'd boarded the plane on her first trip to St. Thomas. She had less than ten days in which to find the ship.

"Where are you!" she growled. Her frustration at their inability to locate the old wreck gnawed painfully inside her mind.

During the past few days, she and Pres had been at each other like cat and dog. Their nerves were frayed. Their tempers were short.

Not ten minutes ago, they'd had another argument. Pres wanted to move to a different area. Megan had refused, saying that Bruce had chosen this spot, and as long as she was standing in for Bruce, this is where they would dive.

Pres, his face set in stiff lines, had said, "If we keep diving in this spot, we'll end up like two shriveled prunes without a pit between us, much less King Philip's treasure ship."

Megan hadn't been able to stop the laugh that had bubbled out at his incongruous remark. Even Pres's stern features had cracked into a smile, accented by strong and sparkling teeth.

When he'd smiled, Megan had felt her insides go weak, and had taken a half step back to steady herself. In that brief moment, she had once again seen the Pres Wyman that had been her lover, not the Pres Wyman who had become her enemy.

"We're staying here," she had reiterated before walking away from him.

Megan looked at her watch and noted that the hour break was almost over. Glancing at Pres, she saw that he was holding the sonar. They had yet to use the sonar, because they hadn't come across any undersea canyons or chasms, which was what the device was intended for.

But neither the sonar device nor Pres was responsible for her impatient anger. Time was responsible; time was fast replacing Pres Wyman as her enemy.

I hate time. Megan's ridiculous thought echoed hollowly in her mind, growing stronger with each second of precious time that slipped by.

And her time was running out. If they didn't find the ship in ten days, she would miss the start of school, which meant one more wasted year. Another thought, strange and unexpected, made Megan pause. *If we don't find the ship, I won't have to leave.*

Shocked by the way her heart had tricked her, Megan stared at the surface of the water and tried to banish the errant thought. Yet she could not deny what her heart refused to stop telling her. Her love for Pres had not diminished at all during the days they had been searching for the ship. With every argument that hammered another wedge between them, with every heated word and gesture, Megan's heart had remained steadfast in its longing.

"Ready?" Pres asked.

She turned to him with a shadowy smile etched on her lips. "Yes."

"Good," he replied, lifting her tanks for her, "let's go find that ship."

They reentered the water together, descending slowly to the bottom, where Pres took the metal detector and resumed the pattern they had been following all morning.

It was their last dive of the day, and the sun had angled its way nearer the horizon. The light at the ocean's floor was dimmer, causing everything to be seen through a murky haze. Because of that they did not follow their usual routine for the fourth dive of the day.

Instead of Megan's looking for visual signs while Pres searched with the detector, Megan held a powerful underwater spotlight to illuminate the bottom in front of Pres.

The day's last dive was also the scariest dive. Because she could not see into the distance, Megan was forever dwelling on what might be hidden there. Four days ago, a large blue shark had startled her by suddenly appearing at the gloomy perimeter of her light.

She had maintained her courage and self-control, and had flickered the light to warn Pres. Thankfully, the shark had only been curious, not hungry, and had moved on.

Two days after the shark incident, and again during the last dive of the day, they had been surrounded by a school of barracuda. To Megan, and to most experienced divers, the barracuda represented far more danger than any shark— they were known to attack a diver for no reason at all.

Pres had come up to her, flicked off the light and drawn them both down to the ocean floor to try to wait out the deadly school of fish. Just as their air was running low, the barracuda had swum off.

Megan shook the visions of danger from her mind. She was more than cognizant that to keep thinking about those things that might harm her would make her claustrophobic and would threaten her very existence as surely as any danger lurking within the ocean's depths.

Regulating the pace of her breathing, Megan concentrated on her job. Although she could not help occasionally peering into the darkness, any more than she could stop the chills that continually raced across her skin, she also watched Pres and the ocean floor he was searching.

Thankfully, a few minutes later she conquered the fears that tried to erode her confidence and make her flee from the ocean.

She looked at her chronometer and saw that only ten minutes had passed since they'd started the search pattern. *Be there,* she silently begged the old galleon. As the silent prayer went through her mind, she exhaled. She listened to the sound of the released bubbles leaving her mouthpiece and watched them rise upward before the mask. But the sound remained when the bubbles were gone. Belatedly, she realized that she had been hearing the sound for the past five minutes, but her worries about what might lurk in the darkness had prevented her from recognizing the sound for what it was—escaping air.

She almost took another breath—almost. But before she did, she froze. Every nerve in her body became alert. Somehow she knew the sound she was hearing was the sound of danger. She breathed hesitantly. Relief flooded her with the first taste of the bottled air. But just as suddenly as it had come, her relief vanished. Before she could completely fill her lungs the air stopped, cut off by the safety valve.

Panic started to spread, but Megan controlled it. She pulled her mouthpiece out of her mouth to inspect it and the demand regulator. She could detect nothing wrong and pressed the air-release valve. No telltale air bubbles emerged. Growing frantic, she hit the demand regulator with the side of her hand and then put it back in her mouth.

She tried to breathe again. Nothing! Fighting against a diver's worst fears, she took out the mouthpiece and stretched out the air tube. She could find nothing wrong.

Dizziness almost overwhelmed her; on its heels came terror. Megan fought the terror with every ounce of her strength. She still had one hope left. Reaching behind her, Megan grasped the handle of the changeover valve and turned it to free her reserve supply of air. She breathed. The demand regulator stayed closed. There was no air.

The single breath she had taken was all that remained of her oxygen: her lungs had already used most of that breath. Megan's chest was trying to burst open and, as she fought helplessly against the crushing ocean depths, a small, analytical portion of her mind tried to send her down to Pres for help. But she was already too weak to fight back the fear and panic now controlling her every moment.

Megan spun wildly, trying to get to the pressure-reduction valve. As she grasped for the valve, the light fell from her hands and the dizziness became unbearable. In a final effort, she raced for the surface.

The light disappeared and Pres started to look up. Before he could complete the movement, something hard struck his leg. He spun quickly and saw the underwater spotlight.

His muscles tensed. A sense of danger raced rampant in his mind. He looked up at Megan and saw her mouthpiece and demand regulator floating next to her. Her legs were scissoring wildly in an effort to propel her to the surface.

Pres's mind went cold. *No!* he screamed silently, praying that his thought might somehow stop her ascent. Moving purposefully, Pres dropped the metal detector, drew his legs and finned feet beneath him and pushed off the bottom.

Powerful kicks propelled him upward. His arms were stiff at his sides, making his body arrow sleek. When the first burst of speed slowed, he kicked twice more and was within inches of Megan. With one more kick, he reached her foot.

His hand tightened around her ankle like a vise. He yanked down to stop both his and Megan's rise. Megan fought him insanely, and he knew that panic had gained full control of her.

But Pres's strength was the equal of her panic, and he dragged her back down to him. When her face was across from his, and a stream of small bubbles escaped from her mouth, he knew he had won.

Pres pulled her to him. He took his mouthpiece out, and when her face was near his, he grasped her cheeks and squeezed tightly.

Megan jerked back. A thin trail of bubbles came from her barely parted lips. When that happened, Pres forced the mouthpiece between her teeth. She fought him, as he knew she would, but he held strong and pressed the air-release button to force the life-giving substance into her mouth.

Megan's mind had shut down. She knew she was dying and wanted to be left alone. But something was hurting her. She pulled away from it but could not escape. Something was being forced into her mouth. She fought again, but stopped when she tasted cool air. Reflexively, she took a deep gulp.

When the air reached her lungs, the darkness, created mostly by panic and lack of oxygen, began to recede. She opened her eyes and saw Pres's mask-covered face. She exhaled.

Pres motioned for her to breathe again and, when she had, he took the mouthpiece back. For three minutes, Pres kept them on the ocean floor, breathing in turn, until he was sure that Megan was in charge of herself again.

When he determined that Megan was ready, he led them back toward the surface, sharing the air as they carefully ascended and decompressed. Uppermost in Pres's mind wasn't reaching the surface, but holding back the terrible vision that, if he had not stopped her panicked ascent, Megan might have died.

Willing away those chilling thoughts, he concentrated on making the air in a tank designed for one person last the two of them until they reached the surface.

They broke the surface thirty yards from the *Cervantes.* Without a word, Pres started toward the boat, making sure that Megan was always at his side.

Reaching the *Cervantes*, Pres helped Megan onto the diving platform and followed her onto the deck. Only then did the reaction to what had happened set in.

He turned away from her so that she would not see the way his hands shook. Methodically, he unhooked his harness and slid the Aqualung to the deck.

Megan, shivering from her ordeal, tried to remove her tanks but could not. Her hands weren't working. She stared at Pres's back, and when he removed his tanks, she called his name.

Pres whirled. His eyes raked across her face. His mouth was pulled into a narrow and unforgiving line. "What the hell is wrong with you? Are you crazy? Suicidal? Or just plain stupid?"

His words were like a slap, and as if slapped, Megan's head dodged back. Her eyes widened, but no words came out. Tears pooled and fell in the face of his rage.

"You panicked and ran. Damn it all, you know better. I was ten feet under you. All you had to do was get to me, not shoot a hundred and twenty feet to the surface. Or were you trying to see if you would explode?"

"Damn you," Megan grated, unable to stop her tears. Suddenly, she realized that she was no longer trembling and had found her voice. Her muscles, too, were once again hers to command.

With the freedom from her paralysis came a strange out-of-time moment. In that fleeting second, she realized that Pres's stinging words had not been said with cruel intention; rather, their hurtling force had come from his concern for her. *Because I'm his diving partner?*

In the silence that followed, Megan unhooked her harness. "Let me have them," Pres ordered as he reached out and took the tanks from her back.

Before she could turn around, Pres was examining the air hose leading from the pressure-reduction valve at the center of the main apparatus. What he saw turned his blood to ice. Where the tubing was attached was a small crack, but it was just large enough to release a steady and continual stream of air. When the air was gone and water entered the tube, the water had triggered a safety valve in the regulator, which had shut it down to prevent Megan from breathing saltwater instead of air. Not even the ten-minute reserve air supply, which Pres saw she had activated, could possibly have reached the mouthpiece.

He pointed out the crack to Megan. When Megan peered at it, Pres said, "It looks like a manufacturing defect."

"I . . . I thought those things didn't happen."

"If they didn't, I wouldn't be testing our equipment as often as I do," he reminded her. His voice held none of the rage of moments before.

"But the hose is new," Megan said, remembering that Pres had replaced it three days before.

Pres stood. "New or old, it failed. I have to go back down."

"No!" Megan cried involuntarily.

"I left the metal detector and the light," he informed her as he turned and went to where the second set of Aqualungs waited.

While he put the Aqualungs on, he was conscious of Megan staring at him, but he refused to turn and look at her. His anger at what had happened had diminished, but the terrible feeling that he had almost lost her remained. It was that feeling that had made him lash out at her.

Pres picked up the sonar device, stepped onto the diving platform and said in parting, "I guess I get to use this at last." Without any further words, he flipped into the water and disappeared.

Megan stared at the spot where he had gone into water, until the ripples from his entrance, like the outward-flowing rings created by a stone dropped into a lake, disappeared. With a tremulous sigh, she went to a chair and sat heavily.

A moment later, she buried her face in her hands and began to sob. She let her tears run their course, until she was finally able to hold her head up and say, "Thank you, Pres."

Chapter Ten

The sun was a dull orange disk floating above the far horizon when Pres returned to the *Cervantes* and shed his diving gear and wet suit. During the thirty minutes he'd been gone, he had been filled with self-recriminations for his treatment of Megan.

Before he went into the cabin, he approached Megan, who had changed into khaki shorts and a lavender halter top and was standing against the side of the boat, staring into the distance. "I'm sorry, Megan. What I said before was uncalled for."

Megan did not acknowledge his apology when she turned to face him. "Let's stay here tonight so we can start earlier in the morning. We can get an extra dive in," she told him, doing her utmost to forget what had happened less than an hour before. Megan knew that if she didn't return to the ocean depths soon, she might never recover from her terrifying experience.

He had expected some sort of response to his apology, but when she gave none, he did not let his disappointment show. Intuitively, he sensed that she was drawing on her reserves of strength to help herself face what had happened today. Instead of commenting on that, he said, "Yes, time's running out."

"I know," Megan whispered. "It's got to be somewhere around here."

"It is," Pres stated.

"Where?"

Shaking his head, Pres waved his hand toward the sea. "The ocean is like a puzzle. It gives you one clue and hides the next."

"Where does it hide the clues?"

"Usually right under your nose."

"Are we staying here tonight?" Megan asked again.

"If that's what you want," he replied, "but I made lunch. You can make dinner."

With that settled, Pres went into the stateroom and changed, while Megan explored the galley to see what was available.

An hour later, Megan cooked a dinner of omelets and a side dish of herb rice that she had discovered in the pantry cabinet. She also found, in the same cabinet, a bottle of rosé wine.

They ate their meal and spoke in generalities, without making any reference to Megan's earlier near disaster. They each drank two glasses of the excellent wine. After dinner, they brought their coffee out onto the deck.

The sun had dropped behind the horizon moments before they stepped onto the deck. In the minutes following their emergence, they became witness to a unique spectacle: the arrival of the tropical night, which is unlike any other nightfall in the world. Twilight lasts only briefly. For the few short minutes that Pres and Megan watched, the sky was softly lit by a gentle rainbow of pastel colors ranging from pink to gray. While they gazed skyward, the bands seemed to move in a concerted effort to catch the sun. Before Megan or Pres were prepared for it, total darkness had descended.

"It's so beautiful," Megan said breathing the words more than speaking them. "Every time I watch the sunset, it makes me feel ... insignificant in comparison."

Pres looked at her face, lit only by the two running lights on the stern. "You could never be insignificant." Before Megan could recover from his unexpected compliment, Pres rose and turned on the two deck lamps.

Again silence blanketed them. Megan was aware that the heaviness of the night air was nothing in comparison to the thick atmosphere occupying the void between them.

Gazing at Pres, she couldn't help noticing his masculine and handsome form. The plain white T-shirt stretching tightly across his chest reminded Megan of the taut skin beneath. Her breath lodged in her throat; her palms grew damp. Suddenly, she regretted the impulse of asking him to stay in the dive area for the night.

A thought, obscured by everything that had occurred between them since they'd met, came to save her from her worry. Moistening her lips, Megan raised her eyes to his. "Pres, there's something that's been bothering me."

"Only one thing?" he asked warily.

Megan's stomach twisted with his sarcasm. "Please, I don't want to fight with you anymore."

Pres yielded to the plea in her eyes, and to the curtain of sadness reflected back from them. "What's bothering you?" he asked, his voice soothing and gentle.

"We've been together—working together—for three weeks."

"Yes."

"When we met on the plane, it was because you were smoking."

Thinking about the acerbic words that had flown between him and Megan brought a smile to his lips. He nodded, waiting for her to go on.

"I haven't seen you smoke since then."

Pres smiled. His white teeth gleamed against his tanned face, and Megan's heart fluttered. "I don't smoke, except when I fly. It helps to, ah, keep me relaxed."

Megan stared at him, thunderstruck by his admission. "You're afraid to fly?"

Pres shook his head. "Not exactly. I don't like knowing that someone else has some sort of mechanical control over my life. I'm fine driving a car, captaining a boat, or diving in the ocean, but I'm not comfortable handing my life over to some stranger sitting in front of a thousand instruments that he can't possibly keep track of as well as he should."

"Oh," Megan whispered.

"That's all that's bothering you?" Disbelief was etched in his words.

Don't be ridiculous, she wanted to say; instead, she said, "That's all," and looked up at the sky.

Moments before, the sky had been deserted. Now it was alive with a myriad of pinpoint dots. The moon, large and silver, hung a quarter of the way into the sky. Beneath the moon, and like the wide beam of a searchlight, a trail of silver illuminated the now black surface of the ocean, and the *Cervantes* as well.

Megan considered how romantic the setting was: two people sitting in a boat in the middle of the ocean. The moon, winking down benevolently, emphasized her thought. But when an unsuspecting Megan realized where her heart was leading her, she quickly took charge of her meandering thoughts.

"Do you think we'll find it?" Megan asked without looking at Pres.

"We'll find it," Pres replied with more intensity than he had meant to show.

For a brief moment Megan studied his moonlit features, an act that proved too much for her to bear and that forced her to leave her seat and go to the stern.

Pres remained in his seat and leaned over to look at the inky blackness. He could empathize with her action; he was sure she was trying to visualize where the Spanish galleon was hiding.

A montage of thoughts blossomed in Pres's head as he watched Megan lean on the rail. Foremost was the knowledge that he had almost lost Megan today; lost her in a way that would have been permanent.

The idea of never again seeing Megan exploded painfully through him. He realized now that nothing should ever have been allowed to come between them—not her ambitions, not his. The value that he had placed on his own career paled in comparison to what might be gained in a life with Megan.

Rising, Pres moved silently toward her. "Megan," he whispered, reaching out to touch her shoulder.

Megan whirled the instant his fingers touched her bare skin, dislodging them before they could find purchase. The tone he had called her name in sent a warning chill coursing down her backbone.

"No!" she cried, stepping sideways to put distance between them.

"No what?" Pres asked, biting out the words as he tried to control his flash of temper.

Megan stared into the endless blue depths of his eyes. She snapped herself away from the danger lurking within them and said, "I don't know. It . . . it was just a reaction."

"The wrong reaction."

Megan formed a retort, but Pres held his hand out before her, stalling whatever she was about to say. "Before we get into another fight, please let me talk. I have something that needs to be said. When I'm finished you can have your say."

Without waiting for her answer, Pres continued, the deep timbre of his voice holding her in thrall. "I love you, Megan. God knows I've tried not to. But I do."

Megan's head grew light; her breathing became faint. A knot of pressure formed in the pit of her stomach. But she ignored all those things and concentrated on what Pres was saying.

"My only regret is that you believe I want to own you, or to stop you from reaching your goals. And damn it all, I still haven't been able to figure out why you think I would. Nothing we've ever said to each other could have been construed in that way." Pres paused to take a deep breath and relax the tense line of his mouth.

"I would never do that, Megan, that's not the kind of man I am. Everyone has to have a goal in their life, a dream to follow. I found mine, and you should have yours. But I do love you. I have since the first time I saw you in Des Plains."

Megan's head grew even lighter. Her mind spun amid the wild cacophony of confused thoughts his revelation unleashed within her. She tried to speak, but no sound passed the lump that blocked her throat.

Pres, seeing Megan's startled reaction, went on as if he had not stopped. "It's really funny when you think about it. I was sixteen years old when I fell in love with you. But when you...changed—which was the way I had to think of what happened—you made me feel like a fool.

"I told myself you weren't worthy of what I was feeling for you." Pres smiled ruefully. "It took me awhile to convince myself that what I thought of as love was not. I succeeded," he stated emphatically.

"After all, how could an adolescent boy know he had fallen in love? I made myself believe it was a misplaced crush. It worked for twelve years. But," he added with no hint of his previous smile, "when I saw you on the plane, all the old feelings, the anger, the hurt, and the love, came back. I didn't recognize it immediately, but when we were in Key West I did. What I had taken for an immature crush twelve years ago was not. It was exactly what I feel now. Love."

Megan's eyes were like moist mirrors. As she looked at him, the slightly upturned tilt of her head made it impossible for him to read what was in the dark-green orbs. All Pres could see was himself being reflected back.

Turning, he looked out at the ocean and let the easy sway of the *Cervantes* calm him. He moistened his lips but did not look at Megan when he spoke again. "No matter what we've said to each other these past weeks, I believe you love me as much as I love you. And," he added, "I'm finished."

Megan's eyes misted under the force of his confession. Looking at his proud profile, she sensed how dear the cost of speaking those words had been. She realized that Pres was much more than an arrogant man with strong muscles: her proof of that was in the way he had opened his heart and bared his soul.

"I do," she whispered.

Pres continued to look out from the stern with no sign of having heard her. Megan drew in another breath and willed herself to speak louder.

Before she could even form the words, Pres's deep voice filled her ears. "Then why have we been acting the way we have?"

"Because we both want different things," she said quickly.

Pres turned. He gazed at her, drinking his fill of her beautiful features and feeling the stirrings of his desire. "Do we? I don't think so. Or do you really believe that the only commitment you can make is to your career?"

Megan's usual reaction to being questioned about her career started, but she realized just in time that Pres's voice had been totally without sarcasm or anger. His question had been asked openly; his words had the feel of curiosity rather than condemnation.

"It's the only commitment I've ever made," Megan replied truthfully. "But I've never thought about it because I never had reason to."

"Perhaps it's time you did think about it," Pres advised as he swept his eyes across the planes of her cheeks.

A new warmth rose along Megan's skin. It had nothing to do with the tropical heat: the warmth was caused by Pres's nearness, and the way his eyes roamed over her.

"Yes," she said, "it is time to think some more. And Pres," she added, her voice catching on his name, "you are right."

Megan watched in fascination as a single muscle ticked on the side of Pres's chin. "About?" he asked, his eyes fiercely locked upon hers.

"Me," she whispered thickly as she fought to get the next words past the lump that had reappeared in her throat. "I... I do love you very, very much."

When her words faded, Megan had nothing more to say. The silence became maddening; the two-foot distance between them grew into miles. Suddenly, Megan wanted him to kiss her, to draw her to him passionately and smother her lips with his.

But she said nothing of this and tried her utmost to beat back the rising tide of her desires.

Megan's open vulnerability was a visible aura surrounding her. While Pres held on to her last words and let them roll freely in his mind, he resisted the temptation to embrace her and let his need for her go free. The joy he wanted to feel at her admission was not there for with all their words, nothing had been solved. To release his passions now would only start an instant replay of their first lovemaking.

"Megan," he said, his voice dry edged and raspy, "I don't know where to go from here."

"Could you at least hold me?" Her voice sounded as if it came from a million miles away.

An instant later his strong arms secured her to him. Megan's fears fled. She felt safe within the warm harbor created by his arms and body.

Inhaling deeply, she drew in the mix of scents that clung to his body. Faint traces of the salty tang of the ocean mist drying on his shirt intermingled with the other scents, merging harmoniously to produce a new and unique fragrance that tantalized her senses.

Looking up at him, she silently begged him to kiss her. When he obeyed her silent plea, and his mouth descended, she prepared herself for the always frightening explosion it would bring.

Yet no explosion came when their mouths met; rather, Pres's lips were cool and chaste upon hers. This new and unexpected sensation did not frighten her the way their kisses had done before. The very gentleness of the kiss made her draw herself closer to him.

When Pres started to draw back, Megan's hands flew to his hair to stop him from leaving her. She heard a low and tortured groan from his throat. Heat burst forth across his lips.

When his tongue prodded past her lips, she was already opening them, anticipating the way his tongue would slide over the edges of her teeth before exploring her mouth.

Her lungs expanded and her heart pounded mightily, until Pres broke the kiss and firmly set her away from him. "It's late, Megan, and we have to be up early."

Megan shook her head in disbelief. "Why, Pres?"

Pres gave voice to his earlier thought. "We rushed ourselves once and ended up hurting each other. I want to do it right this time."

Sensing that he was protecting them from themselves, and from the powerful desires that toyed with them, Megan did not argue. "All right," she whispered.

Before leaving the deck, she reached up to him and stroked his cheek. The feel of newly grown whiskers teased her palm in a sensuous, thrilling way. "Thank you, Pres, I—" Megan stopped herself. Swallowing hard, she smiled at him. "Good night."

Pres captured her hand and kissed her palm. When he reluctantly let go, he too said good-night.

At the steps leading down to the galley and cabin, Megan paused. She cast a glance at Pres from over her shoulder and was immediately struck by his powerful form. "Which berth should I take?"

"Whichever you want. The sheets are in the overhead cabinet on the left."

Megan smiled her thanks and disappeared below. Pres, nowhere near ready to go to the cabin, leaned against the stern railing and gazed up at the stars.

It was going to be a long night, Pres decided. With his overtaxed desires and needs straining to break free, he could not allow himself go into the cabin until he was sure that Megan was asleep. He knew he could not hold out another time against the longings and passions that Megan had evoked when she came into his arms.

While Pres remained on deck, Megan made the bunk she had chosen, as well as the berth across from her for Pres. After changing out of her clothing and into one of Pres's T-shirts, which she had taken the liberty of borrowing, she slipped beneath the top sheet and closed her eyes.

She was tired and knew that sleep would come soon. She was especially sure of this because the nighttime fears of the recurring dream were not plaguing her tonight. She knew the reason—her admission to Pres of her love for him.

Sleep, she told herself. Turning onto her side, she nestled into the pillow. A heartbeat later her eyes flew open. This was Pres's berth. The mattress carried his scent.

She turned restlessly onto her back and stared at the ceiling. Stars flickered through the portholes. The gentle rocking of the *Cervantes* continued but did not lull her to sleep.

Megan had no idea how long she lay there fighting desires and the troubled thoughts that mingled with them. But her inner clock told her that more than an hour had passed since she'd entered the cabin.

She wanted Pres. She loved Pres. She wanted her career. *Will my career be enough now that I know love?* The uncharacteristic and irrational question nibbled irritatingly at

Megan's mind. When she tried to will it away, it clung tenaciously, bringing yet another upheaval to keep her awake.

She remembered the teasing idea that had come to her before her almost catastrophic last dive—the idea that, if they didn't find the ship by her self-imposed deadline, then all her fears and worries would have been for nothing, for she would miss the opening of school. *And,* she told herself, *I could stay with Pres.*

Not finding the galleon meant not having to make the decision tonight's talk had told her would be necessary. Megan could not ask Pres to give up the life he had created for himself, just as she would not give up her goals for him.

Megan could not understand why life had to be so hard. The only thing she did understand at last was that she loved Pres with all her heart.

While she toyed with that thought, the floorboards creaked and footsteps came toward the cabin. She blanked her mind, closed her eyes and made herself breathe gently and rhythmically.

The footsteps paused in the doorway. Megan's heart began to beat much too fast. She was positive he was looking at her. When a low, husky bark of a laugh echoed out, she almost flinched. But she held fast because she knew that Pres wanted her to be asleep so that they would not have to face their unresolved passions.

When Pres started into the cabin, he stopped at its threshold. The short laugh that escaped his lips was brought out when he saw that, of the three berths available, Megan had chosen the one he always slept in.

Trying not to look at the way the white sheet outlined the not so subtle curves of her body, Pres undressed and slipped between the sheets of the bed Megan had thoughtfully made.

When he was settled in the berth, he made a concerted effort not to look across at Megan. He gave up a few seconds later, turned and let his eyes have their fill.

With the aid of the running lights, which sent a bare hint of illumination into the cabin, and the much stronger rays of the moon, Pres slaked his thirst for her beauty by watching her profile. His lingering gaze soon shifted and traveled over her draped body. Megan's breasts rose and fell beneath the sheet, and his fingers remembered the silken touch of her skin.

His desire swelled uncomfortably, and Pres turned so that his back was to her. *I hate this berth,* he said silently as he sought a comfortable position. Shifting his bulk, he thunked his hand against a beam and a grunt of pain escaped his lips. He turned onto his back.

"Are you okay?" Megan asked, unable to bear the burden of having to lie silent with Pres only inches away.

"Fine," Pres mumbled.

"You don't sound fine."

"Do you always talk in your sleep?"

"I'm not sleeping."

"Yes, you are. Megan, you're sleeping," he said in a strained voice.

"What happened? What was that noise?"

"I broke my wrist," he snapped irritably.

Megan flew from the bed and was next to him in an instant. She grabbed his arm, her fingers exploring his wrist.

"This one?" she asked.

Pres gazed at the concern on her face and slowly shook his head. With Megan's hip pressing close against his side, he was not about to send her away.

Megan released his arm. Leaning across his bare chest, she sought his other arm. When she touched it, her breast, covered only by the thin cotton T-shirt, rubbed across the mat of hair upon his chest.

Sparks ignited. A flush rose on her cheeks. "It's not broken," she said at last.

Pres stared at her, very conscious of the heat that flowed from where her bare hip, exposed from the T-shirt by her sudden movements, touched his side.

"I know," he whispered huskily. "Megan, go back to bed."

"No," she said, her voice sounding much stronger than she felt at the moment. Inside, Megan was trembling. "You said it last time. I'll say it now. I want you, Pres. I love you and I need you."

Pres closed his eyes but could not prevent a groan from rumbling deep in his throat. Half sitting up, Pres reached out, caught Megan in his arms and drew her to him.

Their mouths came together greedily. Their lips hungrily devoured each other. Their tongues, exploring, darting and lingering, were above all communicating.

Megan's breasts were flattened against Pres's chest. The tingling sensation from the contact spread to every part of her body. And, as Pres lay back, Megan went with him. Her mouth was on his, her hands roamed freely along his sides.

The narrow berth soon became her entire world, easily accommodating them both. With trembling hands, Megan removed the T-shirt and pressed her bared breasts to Pres's warm chest. She luxuriated in the sensation of her body on his and accepted greedily the caresses he bestowed upon her.

She would have been content to spend the rest of the night above him, but Pres turned her until he was on top. She found that she enjoyed the weight of his body on hers just as much as she had enjoyed lying on him.

When Pres kissed her, all thoughts disappeared. She felt the growing spear of his desire and instinctively wrapped her legs around his.

Her breathing was sharper. The blood pounded in her body. She could feel his heart beating against her breast. She felt his hardened length seeking entrance.

With a slight shift of her hips, she adjusted herself to him, but she was not prepared for the searing heat that was so much a part of him. When the shock of their contact lessened, Megan welcomed him with all her heart.

"I love you," she whispered when she tore her mouth from his. Her hands sought and found a hold on his back.

They moved together, two people blending into one magical being. The melding of their hearts and bodies became the final surrender to the love they had been fighting.

The burning emotions, the plaintive entreaties and the cries of love they spoke to each other were but a small part of their union of flesh and love. A union that proved to Megan how right their love was, and how necessary.

Sometimes she followed Pres. Other times she led, instinctively and unashamedly moving her body in a rhythm as old as time itself. His body fit snugly with hers. The sensation of skin upon skin, and the sound their bodies created, was accented by the sweet scent of his breath washing across her sweat-dampened neck.

All Megan's senses were heightened. Her body responded to Pres's every move until she reached the point where she believed she could stand no more and, suddenly, everything within her tightened. Her eyes opened. She gazed into the endless blue depths before her. Her legs locked tighter, her arms held faster and her body arched against his. "Pres!" she cried as an incredible wave of pleasure overcame her.

Pres continued to move within her and with Megan flowing with him, was carried beyond the very edge of pleasure and into the realm of ecstasy. With her mind teetering on the rim of the universe, a deep growling moan filled her ears as Pres gave her the final offering of his love.

They collapsed together on the narrow berth and, still joined, waited for their breathing to soften. Little shimmering ripples of pleasure ebbed and flowed within her while she lay contentedly in his arms.

She didn't know how long she lay there, her mind drifting randomly while the soft sway of the *Cervantes* endeavored to seduce her to sleep. It almost succeeded, until Megan realized what was happening.

She didn't want to fall asleep and be robbed of this beautiful time within Pres's arms. She preferred to stay awake, to feel Pres's warm taut skin next to hers and reflect on this most intense of days.

All day, Megan's moods had vacillated between anger, fright and ecstasy. She had almost died today or at the very least could have been severely injured. She had also learned that love was not just a word to be bandied about or feared.

She had no idea about how much the day's events were responsible for tonight's actions. Listening to the calm waves lapping against the *Cervantes*'s hull, Megan searched to find the reason she had given in to her physical desires. What Megan discovered was that she didn't care what the reason was—the satiated feeling of contentment and love was enough for her, for right now.

A low laugh bubbled forth. Suddenly, Megan's mood shifted again. She felt loose, free and extraordinarily happy. It was another first. She couldn't remember when she'd last felt like this. Moving gracefully, a smile curving the delicate bow of her lips, Megan drew away from Pres and sat up.

Pres gazed at her, admiring the way her dark-tipped breasts stood firmly. A light sheen of perspiration made her torso gleam silver in the night. Pres smiled warmly at her as he stroked her arm.

Megan shivered under the light touch but did not draw away. It felt too good. She continued to smile at him and trail her fingertips across the ridges of muscle on his abdomen. Her mood was so light and festive that it made her think of the difference between this night, and when they had made love the first time.

In Key West, everything had been dramatically intense and frightening. Tonight had also been dramatic, intense and wonderful, but far from frightening.

Those thoughts reminded her of what had followed their first lovemaking, and of the embarrassment she had felt at talking about her virginity. There was no such embarrassment tonight. Tonight she was high-spirited.

"Are we going to talk now?"

"About what?" Pres asked.

Megan shrugged. When her shoulders lifted, her breasts bobbed so invitingly that Pres wanted to kiss the tantalizing twin visions. But, sensing a new playfulness in Megan and liking this sudden shift, he managed to hold himself back and follow her lead.

"I don't know," she admitted. "But it's been my experience that after lovemaking, people talk."

"Your experience?" he asked incredulously. "Megan, until a few weeks ago you were a—"

Megan's finger stopped him; her other hand continued to roam across his skin. Wherever her fingertips touched, Pres's skin grew taut.

"Isn't there something to talk about?" she teased.

Pres felt himself stirring and shifted slightly beneath her fingers. "Sleep," he muttered between clenched teeth.

"What about sleep?" she asked, dipping her head down for a quick kiss while her fingers dropped lower on their explorations.

"If you don't stop what you're doing, there won't be any."

"Why?" she asked innocently and without guile. Then her questing fingers found the answer.

"Oh," she whispered. Megan did not take her hand away as a thrill of excitement lanced through her. "Did you *really* want to sleep?"

Instead of answering, Pres reached up and drew her to him. He kissed her deeply before showing her the only possible answer he could give. And, as they joined together, Pres wondered if sleep was even worth bothering with on this very special night.

Chapter Eleven

It was not much before sunrise when Megan slipped from the berth where she and Pres had spent their passionate night and went onto the deck.

She sat silently, her head resting lightly on the cushions. She watched the ocher sky bloom pink and coral, and her mind spun an intricate web of thoughts and worries.

The night had passed as no other in her memory. Her love had leaped forth to temporarily conquer her fears of the future and allow her to enjoy the glorious moments of the present.

Megan wondered if, after their unrestrained lovemaking, anything had really changed. She did not view her question as rhetorical; there was too much at stake to lose herself in linguistic games.

Taking a deep breath, Megan realized that the scent of their night of lovemaking clung to every pore of her skin. A delicious shudder undulated along her length, making her smile with the memories of the night just ended.

She tried to analyze what she was feeling. The first thing that came to mind was love. Danger was her next thought. *From what?* Smiling, Megan knew the answer immediately. The danger was in her mind. The danger was herself, not Pres as she had thought.

Megan shivered despite the ever hot tropical morning. Wrapping her arms around her waist, she pondered possibilities she had never before considered.

The roller-coaster ride that she had lived yesterday had done more than just bring out her fears and let her give herself over to the side of her that craved Pres's love. It had served to show her that not all her hours and days need be filled with the single-minded desperation of going solely after the attainment of a career.

Megan was beginning to see that while reaching toward her longtime goals, there could be time for love, time for joy and time for letting someone within the walls she had erected for self-protection.

Yet even this new knowledge of what could be was tinged with the sadness of what she must decide. When Pres made his impassioned speech, he had told her that he would never willingly interfere with her dreams of her career.

The very fact that there was now another person in her life raised the possibility that he, and their love, might somehow interfere with her dreams. It was an impossible situation that Megan found herself facing, and a situation with which she had no past experiences to guide her.

But experienced or not, Megan knew that somehow she had to find a way to make it all work out.

The instant Pres woke, he knew Megan was gone. He lay still for several minutes, wondering if the night had been but a dream mocking him for his desires.

But the satisfied and pleasant feelings, in his loins as well as his mind, told him that the night had been real. A smile formed on his lips as he thought of last night's Megan, a woman he had never before seen. The smile disappeared as another memory was triggered and showed him another Megan.

The other Megan had also made love with him. And, like today, she had been gone in the morning. When he'd found her, the special moment they had shared had been taken from him. *Will she do it again?*

The power of that thought was enough to propel Pres out of the bed and into his clothing. When he emerged on the deck, it was to a picture that would stay forever in his mind.

Megan, wearing his T-shirt, was sitting in a deck chair. Her head was tossed regally back; her hair hung in waves behind her. Her green eyes were open, gazing skyward. Her arms were wrapped protectively about her waist. Her breasts rose and fell evenly as she breathed.

She's so damn beautiful, he thought passionately.

Pres covered the remaining feet between them, and when he reached her, he bent forward and kissed her forehead. "Good morning."

Megan smiled. Her tongue darted out to moisten her lips. She shifted to look at him. His hair was charmingly disheveled. Last night's portent of a beard to come had turned into an intriguingly dense and stubbly foliage that was trying to obscure his strong chin.

Megan thought he looked unbelievably sexy; her body told her that he was. "A better morning than I ever thought possible," she admitted as her eyes danced merrily across his features.

Pres exhaled slowly, his breath accenting the silence of the sea. "I had my doubts," he admitted.

"Doubts? You?"

"You're a beautiful woman and more naive than I ever believed possible. You're a combination of enchantress and seductress, and you don't even know it. But yes, I had my doubts," he said in an open, honest way. "My experiences with you make doubt almost mandatory."

Before Megan could protest, Pres stopped her with a smile and an upraised hand. "You were gone when I woke, just like the last time. Megan, I don't want a repeat of what happened in Key West. I love you, and together we'll find a way to work things out."

"I want to," Megan said, thinking of how his words echoed her thoughts of moments before.

"We have to," Pres said in a low but emphatic voice. "I'm starved!" he added suddenly, and Megan realized that she was hungry too.

They worked together in the small galley as if they'd been doing it all their lives. And, after eating a large breakfast, Megan checked over the equipment, while Pres put a new air hose on the tanks Megan had used yesterday.

When the repair was completed, Megan looked at Pres. "I've been diving since I was seventeen, and I never had a single mishap. But in the space of three weeks, you've saved my life twice. Pres, I—"

Pres drew Megan to him before she could continue with her misty eyed thank-you, and he kissed her tenderly. "Just remember that if you get into trouble again, come to me. I'll always be there for you."

Megan's first reaction was a warm sensation that flowed mightily through her. Her next reaction was a light, bubbling laugh. When his eyebrows knitted together, she said, "I think I got into trouble the minute you lit that cigarette in the airplane."

"Yeah, I think so," Pres agreed before he stood and motioned Megan to get into her wet suit.

The day, unlike all the others they had spent immersed in the ocean, passed swiftly. The bond they had made during the night remained strong and ever present.

For Megan, those fleeting sensations of fright during those first few seconds she entered the water were gone. Her confidence in diving with Pres, and in loving him, had taken away that fear, along with any fears that her brush with disaster might have implanted in her mind.

When they boarded the *Cervantes* after the last dive of the day, Megan was pleasantly tired and strangely unbothered by their lack of success. Somehow it wasn't as important as it had been on the preceding days.

After their equipment was put away and the anchor raised, the radio blared out the *Cervantes*'s call numbers. Pres answered the marine operator and heard Sandi Majors's voice.

Megan snatched the microphone from him. "Sandi! Where are you?"

"At the villa," her friend stated. "Waiting for you."

"When did you get in?"

"On the four o'clock flight. Are you heading in?"

"We've just weighed anchor. We'll be at Pres's dock in..." She paused to look at Pres questioningly.

"Hour and a half," he said.

"An hour and a half," Megan repeated for Sandi.

"Great, I'll be waiting here. Bye."

"Bye," Megan said. When she replaced the microphone on the radio, she turned to Pres. "This is a surprise," she said happily. A second later, doubt raced through her mind. Blanching, she gripped the edge of Pres's seat.

"Megan," Pres asked when he saw the blood drain from her face, "are you okay?"

Megan nodded, fighting the wave of dizziness. "Could something have happened to Bruce?" The question was not just for Pres, but for herself as well.

Pres reached out and took her hand, even as he steered the boat. "She sounded relaxed. She's probably here for a progress report."

Megan sighed. "Probably." Yet Sandi's presence in St. Thomas was unexpected, and Megan couldn't quite shake the slim thread of uncertainty in her mind.

She worried throughout the hour-and-a-half trip. When they docked, and she started to help Pres with the equipment, he stopped her.

"Go ahead to the villa. I'll catch up later."

"I want to help," she protested.

Pres grabbed her suddenly and pulled her to him. "Then kiss me and get out of my hair!"

Megan did, except that instead of getting out of his hair, she wound her fingers through the dense thicket and held his mouth securely to hers. When she finally released his hair, her legs were shaking.

"I can't believe what you do to me," she whispered in a halting, throaty voice.

"I'm glad to know I'm not the only one who feels that way. Go on now," he commanded. "I'll see you in a little while."

After Megan disappeared around the corner of the dive shop, Pres went back to the *Cervantes* and off-loaded the equipment. He spent an hour cleaning the tanks and the underwater search gear, after which he took a shower and changed into fresh clothing.

As he was about to leave for the villa, the phone rang. Picking it up on the third ring, Pres found himself speaking with Bud Shaeffer, of United Salvage in Miami.

"You're a hard man to get hold of," Shaeffer ventured. "I've been trying since noon yesterday."

"I've been out on a job," Pres replied.

"Well, isn't that a coincidence. It's the very reason I'm calling—the job offer, I mean."

Pres thought rapidly. "Bud, I'm in the third week of a four-week charter. I'm out every day, and I've been busy as hell. Until I finish this job, I won't be able to give you an answer."

"Pres," Shaeffer began, his voice businesslike and well modulated, "I like you. If I didn't I wouldn't have offered you the position. But besides the fact that I do like you and think we'd work well together, you have the talent and experience we need."

"Bud," Pres began, letting Shaeffer's flowery compliments bounce off him easily. But Shaeffer wasn't about to be put off, and he interrupted Pres.

"I can't leave the offer open much longer. We've gotten two new contracts, one in Brazil, the other in the Mediterranean. I want you in Brazil, running that operation. It needs your touch. But if I don't have your answer by noon this Saturday, you'll leave me no choice but to hire someone else.

"Besides," Shaeffer added, "who in his right mind would pass up an opportunity to spend two weeks in Rio de Janeiro?" What Shaeffer did next was to insult Pres's intelligence by adding that he would be giving up a starting salary of seventy-five thousand dollars a year, and the opportunity to became a partner in the salvage company, if he proved himself valuable enough.

"I understand," Pres said.

"I hope so," Shaeffer replied before hanging up.

Pres stared at the phone for several minutes before he rose. Instead of going to his car, he went back to the *Cervantes*. In the cabin, he unfurled Bruce's map and studied it. Looking over his notations of the dive area, he stared at the spot where he'd found the *Conquistador*'s sextant.

"Where are you?" he asked, his voice barely audible as the need to find the ship exploded within him much the way a volcano erupts unexpectedly in the night.

His stomach churned; his mind grew dark. What had once been merely a need to find the ship now became an obsession. Pres's mind locked upon this one objective, in total disregard of all others. It was as irrational as anything that had ever happened to him in his life, but he had no choice.

Too much was at stake. His love for Megan was a force that left him no choice. He must find the ship, and find it before the end of the week.

Turning, Pres looked out the porthole and toward the far horizon. "I will find you!" he shouted.

Twenty minutes after she'd left Pres, and ten minutes after she'd picked up fresh fish at the market, Megan entered the villa. The sun had dropped below the horizon, and the sky was a pastel palette.

After putting the fish on the kitchen counter, she went in search of her friend. She found Sandi on the terrace, drinking a tall glass of ice tea. Sandi's hair was pulled back from her face, and she wore a light cotton print dress.

"Hi," Megan called when she stepped outside.

"Hi yourself," Sandi replied, putting down the ice tea and rising to meet her friend.

They embraced for a moment, and when Sandi sat down on the chaise, Megan joined her. "Bruce isn't with you?"

Sandi shook her head. "He can't fly yet. It may be another year before he can."

"But he's okay?"

"Of course he is. If there was a problem, I would have called."

"When is his next operation?"

"In a month."

"Sandi, he will recover completely, won't he?" she asked, thinking of how badly Bruce would be affected if he couldn't dive again. It was his life.

"The doctors are very optimistic," Sandi said to reassure her.

"He must be bored to death in Key West."

Sandi smiled. Megan thought it was a cat-who-ate-the-canary smile, but she said nothing.

"Actually," Sandi began, "he's not in Key West yet. Or at least he shouldn't be until tomorrow. He's on his way back from Phoenix."

"Phoenix?" Megan responded, the single word rife with puzzlement. "Since when are there oceans in Arizona?"

Sandi laughed. It was a good sound, a happy sound. "Not oceans, oil companies."

Megan said nothing, but her eyes compelled Sandi to continue.

"Megan, I have some wonderful news!" Without waiting, Sandi raced on. She told Megan about the call from Commissioner Sullivan, and about the new funding. She gave a detailed description of the phone call to the chairman of the oil company, to which both women laughed.

"And yesterday, Bruce met with him. Langely Petroleum is going to match the government funding. Not fifty percent, but one hundred percent. Two million dollars! Bruce's foundation is going to become real!"

Seeing the excitement burning on Sandi's face made Megan's heart soar for her friend and for her brother. It was Bruce's dream come true, and Megan almost cried with her happiness.

"And," Sandi said after conquering her excitement, "you can make it to school with a couple of days to spare. If you leave soon."

Megan closed her eyes. Her stomach turned upside down. Her excitement at the good news fled; replacing it was an unexpected sense of sadness.

When she opened her eyes, she saw Sandi's smiling face before her, and it seemed to be spinning in a circle. Quickly, she closed her eyes again.

"Megan?" Sandi called.

Her friends voice sounded as if it were coming through a phone with a bad connection. *Why now?* Megan asked herself bitterly.

"Megan!" Sandi called sharply.

Megan's eyes snapped open. She stared at Sandi.

"What's wrong?"

Megan shook her head. "Nothing... Everything!" she half shouted. Standing, she walked to the edge of the terrace and stared out. In the short space of time that they had talked, twilight had come and gone, reminding her of how all the possibilities that had been born the previous night for her and Pres had suddenly disappeared with Sandi's news.

Taking a sharp breath, Megan turned to Sandi, who was now a backlit and featureless silhouette. "Pres will be here in a little while. I don't want you to tell him about the foundation."

Sandi was nonplussed. Her eyes filled with confusion; her mouth lost its smile. "Why?"

"Because I have a decision to make. An important decision, and I need the next few days to make it in."

Slowly, the look of surprise on Sandi's face gave way to one of comprehension. "It's Pres," she stated, no hint of question in her voice.

Megan nodded curtly.

"I'm sorry, Megan," Sandi said in a low, almost hesitant voice. "I can't do what you're asking."

"Why? It doesn't matter if Pres and I stop now or go on for a few more days. The price will be the same. Sandi, please. I need this time."

"No." Sandi reiterated. "There's more than money at stake. Diving in open water is dangerous. And danger can't be part of some lovers' game."

Megan stiffened, angered and hurt by Sandi's lack of empathy. "This is no game! It's my life, my future. Please, Sandi, you have to try and understand. You have to help me."

Sandi was taken aback by the passion in Megan's words. She had never, in all the years she had known Megan, seen its like. Only when Megan had talked about her career had she come close to sounding like this. But close was all it had been.

Keenly watching Megan's face for her next reaction, Sandi said, "Are you that much in love with Pres?"

Megan wrung her hands together. "God help me, Sandi, yes, I am."

"It's not right, Megan," she began, but Megan turned away. Sandi stood and went to her. She turned her friend to face her, and when Megan was again looking into her eyes, she spoke. "Please listen to me. Deceiving Pres, even if your intentions aren't bad, can only hurt you and Pres."

"It has to be this way, Sandi. I don't want Pres hurt, and I don't want to be hurt myself. But Sandi, it has to be done this way."

"Why, Megan?" Sandi persisted.

Megan started to speak but stopped. She tried to form the words that were right, but they would not come. Her mind was a roiling mass of reasons and answers, but with each one that came forth, another thought chased it back.

It was all too complicated, Megan realized, and she wasn't sure that Sandi would understand. After the previous night's burst of emotions, and the fulfilling words of love she and Pres had spoken to each other, Megan's overwhelming desire to further her education and reach her goals no longer seemed quite as important as it once had.

During the long day of diving, one thought had continually battered at her mind. When she left for school, what would happen to the love that had so brightly appeared? Megan could not help feeling that once she was gone, their love would somehow be diminished by distance and time.

"Sandi," she began after willing some cohesion to her mind, "so much has happened in the past weeks. And now I'm trying to get my priorities straight. Only I can't. I need time. I need the next few days to do that. Please don't say anything to Pres. I promise I'll tell him when the time is right."

Sandi knew she shouldn't agree to this. She was certain that no good could come from deception, but the pain and plea so starkly written on Megan's face overcame her common sense. "All right," she agreed reluctantly.

"Thank you," Megan whispered.

Sandi nodded, then straightened her shoulders. "When is Pres coming?"

"He should be here soon. He thinks that you've come for a progress report," she added pointedly.

"Okay. But how about a little food? Isn't a bride-to-be expected to keep up her strength for the wedding?"

"Certainly!" Megan declared. "You do like snapper?"

"How could an oceanographer not like fish?" Sandi replied with a grin, happy that the heavy tension had lessened.

By the time Megan had cooked the fish and Sandi had prepared the salad, Pres arrived.

"Perfect timing," Megan said when he walked into the house. "Dinner is ready." She glanced at the chart he was carrying and raised her eyebrows in silent question.

Pres said nothing; rather, he put the chart down on a small table and went over to Megan. Drawing her lightly into his arms, he kissed her just as Sandi emerged from the kitchen.

"Hi, Pres," Sandi said, smiling at the blush that colored Megan's tanned face.

"How was your trip?" Pres asked.

"Boring. No air pockets, just Muzak and my reports."

"Speaking of which—" Pres began.

Megan cut him off quickly while casting a warning glance in Sandi's direction. "After dinner. No business until then!" she declared.

Sandi and Pres followed Megan's stern command to the letter, and the meal passed in a pleasant flurry of nonsensical conversation that almost had Megan screaming for it to end.

When the last bite of food was taken and the plates brought into the kitchen, Megan served coffee. Over coffee, the conversation turned to the search for King Philip's ship.

In precise words, Pres told Sandi everything that had happened, and when he reached the point where they'd found the mahogany box and sextant, he handed Sandi the gleaming brass navigational device.

While she studied the ancient navigational instrument, her face a stoic mask, Pres continued his story until reaching their last dive of the day. The only things he omitted were Megan's brush with death and their lovemaking.

When he finished, Sandi gave the sextant back to him. "Where do you go from here?" she asked.

Pres shrugged. "I know that ship is out there somewhere. I feel it in my bones. But it's not where Bruce thinks it is. And Megan," he said, glancing at Megan for an instant, "refuses to leave the search area."

"Bruce is very rarely wrong," Sandi said, watching Pres carefully as she spoke. "He pinpointed the first ship to within a hundred yards."

"Well," Pres said, a rueful smile growing on his generous mouth, "so far he's missed this one by the proverbial mile."

"What do you want to do?" Sandi asked.

Pres's smile turned into a tautly narrow line. Megan's heart fluttered as she stared at him. A sudden heat flowed through her as she remembered the way his mouth had felt on her skin.

"I'd like Bruce to reevaluate his figures to see if there were any mistakes in his original estimate. Perhaps he took too much of a floor shift into account, or maybe he just overlooked one of the storms. While he does that, I want to move to a new search area."

Sandi nodded thoughtfully. "Maybe you should take a day or two off until Bruce can do the work."

Neither Megan nor Sandi were prepared for Pres's violent reply. "No!" he shouted. His open hand slammed onto the table, jarring the coffee cups with its force. Megan watched brown liquid spill onto the white tablecloth and spread in an uneven circle, then she looked at Pres.

The force of his answer held him in thrall for a moment, but when the silence of the room became intense and suffocating, he exhaled. "Sorry," he said, though with no ring of truth in his voice. "Sandi, we don't have an extra day or two to wait around. Megan's time is running out, and so is mine."

Megan's breath caught at his words. She hadn't fully realized just how aware Pres was of the dwindling time.

"I agree with Pres," Megan said to Sandi.

Sandi looked from one to the other. "All right, I'll call Bruce in the morning and ask him to go over his figures again."

"Thank you," Pres said as he reached for the chart behind him. Pushing the coffee cups aside, he opened the chart and began to explain to Sandi where he felt the ship might be. He talked for almost an hour, pointing out the different bottom shifts. When he was finished, Sandi was already half in agreement with his amateur but instinctive way of looking for salvage.

At ten o'clock, Pres said good-night to Sandi and walked to his car with his arm around Megan's waist. At the car door, he turned to her.

"I'll miss you tonight," he whispered.

Megan reached up and stroked his face. A tremor passed through her hand. "I'll miss you too," she replied truthfully.

Pres bent and covered her mouth with his. As his tongue met hers it spoke its silent message of love. When their mouths parted, both were breathing deeper; both felt the heat radiating from their bodies.

A sense of urgency overcame her. "I wish I could be with you tonight," Megan whispered as she buried her head upon his chest.

"In a way, you will be," he told her, kissing her and then sending her back toward the house before he could change his mind and take her with him.

At the door, Megan turned to wave to him. "I love you," she mouthed when the headlights washed across her face. When Pres was gone from sight, she went back into the house, thinking that, once again, so much had changed so quickly. *Why does it have to be this way?*

Chapter Twelve

The night passed fitfully for Pres. Long before sunrise, he had finished loading the equipment onto the *Cervantes* and was sitting on the aft deck, drinking coffee and waiting for Megan.

Pres was very aware of Megan's personal calendar. It was August twenty-fourth and, coincidentally, the twenty-fourth day of Megan's quest. She still had six full days left.

Pres didn't have six days. His schedule had changed with Bud Schaeffer's call. Pres had only three days in which to find the sunken galleon or risk losing any chance for his own future as an independent salvage diver.

Pres was mired within the biggest problem he had ever faced. Finding the galleon in the next six days would give Megan her chance to get to school on time. But if he didn't find the ship in the next three days, he would have to go to work for Bud Shaeffer. Either way, it meant giving up the search for the *Conquistador*.

And what of Megan? he wondered. Suddenly, what he had thought was the most important thing to him was no longer as important. Looking deep within himself, he tried to discern the forces that were now driving him.

He recognized the main force as not being his own ambitions to find the ship; rather, it was a need to prove to Megan that his love for her would not stop her from her personal goal.

Pres finally understood, with a cool clarity that calmed his mind and eased his tension, why it was so important for him to find the ship. He saw, in this moment of crystal introspection, that the only way to prove his love to her, and to reassure her that he did not want to control or own her, was to send her away so that she would come back to him.

To keep her here by default—by not finding the ship in time—would make her turn from him and destroy the love that was so precariously growing between them. His muscles relaxed; the tension of the night drained.

Just as Pres was starting to enjoy the way his mind had settled his disorganized thoughts, a jarring and unwanted insight caught him short.

It was the memory of Megan's impassioned words, when they had argued in Key West, that shattered the harmony he had just found.

Pres wondered if he was kidding himself about Megan. Not kidding himself about what he felt for her, but about what she felt for him.

He couldn't help remembering the other times—the high school days and the passionate night in Key West. He recalled the almost fanatical way Megan was searching for the galleon, in pursuit of her all-encompassing career goals.

Pres halted the direction his mind was taking as he realized the danger of letting stray and discordant thoughts tear at his own self-confidence. Instead, he told himself that the only way he would be able to find out what Megan really wanted—himself, her career, or both—would be to find the ship so that Megan would have no choice but to make her decision.

With Pres's mind somewhat eased by the time Megan arrived, the day started off smoothly enough. By noon they had gotten two dives in and were relaxing and regaining their strength. Megan, sitting across from Pres on the deck, watched him eating a tuna sandwich. All morning, she had been unable to keep her eyes from continually returning to him, or her hands from touching him.

As she took a bite of her sandwich, Pres shifted, and the interplay of muscles that girded his stomach made her own stomach knot. Her abdomen tightened even more when she thought of what might happen in six days or even less. She would have to leave him. The food in her mouth turned into gravel. She had trouble chewing and then forcing the food down. A burning fire built within her. She recognized its flames as those of desire. She wanted Pres. She needed him.

Once the food passed her constricted throat, she took a long drink of diet soda, wiped her mouth and stood. "Pres," she whispered, gazing down at his burnished skin.

Pres looked up. When he saw the tautness of her mouth and recognized the desire in her eyes, he put his sandwich down.

"Make love to me," she pleaded.

Pres stood. Megan started for the cabin. Pres stopped her, his hand encircling her wrist like a steel band. "Not inside," he told her, his voice thick with the passion. "I want to make love to you in the sun."

Megan's cheeks flamed, not with embarrassment, but with a wanton desire that moved her back to him so that he could draw her to him and smother her lips with his.

Beneath the bright disk of the midday sun, with only two towels between her back and the wooden deck, Pres entered Megan with a swiftness that took her breath away. It was a swiftness she matched, in full surrender to Pres and to the love that burst outward from her heart.

The feelings of their noontime lovemaking remained with Megan throughout the last two dives. And while the dives brought them no closer to finding the ship, the emotion that remained after their lovemaking showed Megan just how much more difficult everything was going to be when it came time for her to act upon her future.

Yet during the last dive, something happened to disturb Megan and send a chilling finger of fear to tickle her spine.

Pres was always the one to be careful. He was the senior diver and took his responsibilities seriously. He always monitored their time underwater with the precision of a Swiss watchmaker. On the last of the day's dives, Pres seemed to have lost track of the time.

Megan was above him with the spotlight when she became aware that they had been down for much longer than usual. Looking at her watch, she saw that they were ten minutes past their allotted time. For the first time since starting the search for the galleon, they would have to use reserve air to reach the surface.

She flickered her light in a signal to Pres, but he did not respond. Surprised at his reaction, she swam quickly down to him and tapped him on the shoulder.

Pres spun angrily, shaking her away from him. His actions frightened her; yet they gave her a new determination. She shook her head and pointed to her watch.

Angrily, Pres shook his head in answer. Before she was able to repeat the signal, he looked at his chronometer and back at her. He gave her the okay sign, and they ascended together. Fifty feet from the surface, Megan's air ran out. Calmly, because she had been expecting it, she turned on the reserve air valve and began to breathe again.

Within a minute, Pres had to do the same thing. When they'd stepped onto the *Cervantes*, Megan said nothing while she took off her equipment. After Pres had shed his tanks and taken off the top of his wet suit, she was unable to stop herself from shouting.

"What happened?"

Pres held her gaze for several seconds before speaking. "I lost track of time."

"You never lose track of anything! You're too damned good a diver. Why?" Megan had demanded again.

Pres sighed mightily. He reached out to Megan but stopped himself from touching her. When his hand fell to his side, he finally spoke. "You're right," he told her. "I just didn't want to go up without finding something. Megan, we're close. I know we are!"

"I don't care how close we might be. That ship isn't worth dying for!"

"No, it isn't," Pres replied, but Megan saw something flicker in his eyes. What it was, she wasn't sure. But it bothered her nonetheless.

"Don't ever do that again!" she ordered.

Pres smiled at her. It was a lazy smile that sparkled with the even whiteness of his teeth. "Yes, ma'am," he said soothingly.

"Don't do that!" Megan shouted, anger turning her cheeks crimson. "You scared the hell out of me. You're the one who watches out for me, or did you forget that?"

Pres stared at her, his mouth half open in surprise. Quickly, he closed his lips, wondering if she'd even heard the question she'd asked him.

"I'm sorry, Megan. It won't happen again."

Megan blinked at his sudden change. "Why did it happen at all?"

"Because I wanted more time to look for the ship."

Megan had no reply for his honesty; instead, she crossed the small space separating them and lifted onto the balls of her feet. She kissed him lightly, brushing her lips across his as her fingers grazed the wide expanse of his chest.

"Just don't do it again," she said before turning and disappearing into the cabin.

While she changed, Pres winched the anchor up, started the *Cervantes* and pointed them toward home. At the dock, Megan asked him if he was coming to dinner.

Pres declined, saying that he wanted to go over the charts again.

"You're going to drive yourself crazy," Megan warned him.

"You've already done that," he joked. "But there's someone I want to talk with."

"About the ship?" she asked, alarmed.

Pres stroked her cheek. "My friend knows these waters better than anyone else alive. I won't tell him about the galleon. But Megan," he added, his face set in all-too-serious lines, "don't stop trusting me now."

Megan shook her head. "I . . . no . . . of course not," she said, shocked that he would even think such a thing after everything that had happened between them. When she saw his inquiring eyes studying her, she knew that her innermost thoughts were reflected on her face.

"There was a time you didn't trust me at all," he reminded her.

Megan nodded. "Was," she agreed.

Pres kissed her lightly. "Sandi's waiting for you," he reminded her. "And I'll see you in the morning."

Megan said goodbye after stealing another of those ever-so-light kisses. Ignoring the desire that flared from the feathery fluttering of her lips across his, she turned and went to her scooter.

For some reason, the ride home was endless. Her mind swirled around a hundred different thoughts, never staying still long enough for her to figure out exactly what was troubling her.

Pres's strange behavior on the last dive was one thing that bothered her. His sudden questioning of her trust in him was another. There was also the unusual gleam in his eyes that bespoke so much more of his need to find the ship than he had ever admitted.

When Megan finally reached the villa, she cast aside her troubled ruminations. After parking the scooter, she went into the villa, where she found Sandi talking on the phone.

When Sandi saw her, she covered the mouthpiece. "Bruce," she whispered. "He got home an hour ago."

Megan waited patiently while Sandi explained Pres's request for Bruce to redo his figures. When Sandi paused for a moment, Megan was sure Bruce was asking his fiancée why.

"I'll explain when I get home tomorrow. But do them, Bruce, and quickly, please." After saying this, she told him about Pres's feeling that he had miscalculated somewhere, and that nothing of the sea floor where Pres and Megan had been diving held any real clue about the galleon except for the sextant. And the sextant, Sandi ventured, had most likely been dragged by the current and was far from the *Conquistador*'s watery grave.

After he agreed to do the figures, Sandi handed Megan the phone, and without even saying hello Megan asked, "How's the University of Miami's graduate program in anthropology?"

Used to his sister's sometimes unpredictable ways when something was on her mind, Bruce chuckled. "Better than most people think," he said from the experience of teaching several semesters at the university in order to supplement his income from the oceanographic institute.

"Do you think I can get in?" Megan asked.

"If UCLA took you, Miami wouldn't *dare* refuse. But what happened to UCLA?"

"Would it be so terrible if I went to Miami?"

"Not at all," Bruce said quickly, sensing the warning tone of Megan's voice. "Meg, they'll take you in a second. Want me to check on it?"

"Would you?"

"Sure, but since you're coming back tomorrow with Sandi, wouldn't it be just as easy if I set up an appointment for the day after?"

"No," Megan half shouted. She didn't want to tell Bruce that she hadn't canceled the search yet, or explain the reasons for her actions. "Just check it out for me."

"Okay, kiddo, but why the big mystery?"

"No mystery, Bruce, just some last-minute thoughts. I...I'll see you soon," she added before handing the phone back to Sandi and going into her room to undress and shower.

Ten o'clock found Pres, wearing jeans and a faded blue T-shirt, sitting in a local bar lounge in the heart of Charlotte Amalie.

The long and narrow lounge, known as the Island Star, was dark and crowded. A deep, rocking reggae beat pulsed in the air, propelled outwardly in angry benevolence by the five-piece band at the far end of the room.

The bar itself was crowded three deep with people. The hum of conversation was loud, but not louder than the music. Pres was sitting in a small booth near the entrance, waiting for the man he knew would eventually show up.

Occasionally, someone would leave the bar and come over to the table to say hello. No one stayed, for Pres did not invite company, and the men and women who frequented this place respected a person's privacy and mood.

"'Lo, Pres-ton," came a withered voice filled with all the soft and subtle inflections of an island native. The voice was a perfect match to the man's deep-brown weathered face and lively eyes.

"Hello, Simon," Pres said with a smile. "Drink?" he asked, thinking once again of how his friend looked like a slightly older version of the uncola-man, Panama hat and all.

"I never been one to turn down a spirit, be it from a bottle or from..." Simon rolled his eyes upward in comic relief.

"But I don't think you came here to buy me a drink to soften me up so that you can get me to work cheap for you, Pres-ton," the old islander said with a smile that denied the harshness of his words.

"You know me too well, Simon," Pres said, waving to the waitress to bring Simon a drink. No one had to tell the tall, long-limbed barmaid what Simon drank; everyone knew. Island rum.

"What you be looking to learn now? I thought I taught you everything?"

"If you did," Pres said with a grin that came from deep within, "I'd be rich. I'd be sitting on a yacht drinking champagne instead of beer."

Simon laughed. It was a big, bass laugh that rumbled upward and out, making several people sitting at the bar turn to look at them.

"You still got your good senses, Pres-ton."

As Pres stared at Simon his grin faded. "Sometimes I wonder about that."

Simon said nothing, but his lined face reflected his surprise more eloquently than any words could. The barmaid brought Simon's drink, and after taking a deep pull, he put the glass down.

"You sound like a man with woman troubles. I think maybe you should be talking to Mama Mandie."

Pres shook his head, unable to hold back a short and barking laugh. "No thanks, Simon, I don't need an Obia woman. Witch doctors aren't my cup of tea."

"Then talk to Simon," the old man said kindly.

It was easy to talk to the island native who had befriended him when he'd first arrived on St. Thomas and hired on with a salvage company. Simon had not looked down at him because of his age. All he'd done was to say that his life would be in Pres's hands when they were underwater, and he expected Pres to remember that, and act on it.

He and Simon had dived together for three years. By the end of those years, Pres had become a much better diver because of the things that Simon had taught him. He was also aware of those things Simon had not taught him.

"I can't tell you what I'm looking for," Pres began, "not because I don't trust you, but because I gave my word."

"A man's word is important in these things," Simon said with a sage nod. "I been in that place myself. No one talks treasure."

Pres flinched in surprise. Simon let go another of his huge belly laughs. "It's okay, Pres-ton. When you hear someone say they can't tell what they be looking for, you can be sure it's sunken ships and glorious treasures. I'm only surprised it took you so long to do it. Every diver got to look once, otherwise they wouldn't be no diver. Where are you looking?"

"Northeast of Mandal Bay."

"Near Big Hans Lollick?"

"East," Pres said.

"Old armada route. You looking for big things, Preston," Simon stated.

"Very big, Simon."

"You be careful. I don't like them waters. No good for divers. They change before you know it. Too many deep canyons. Tide suck you down quick!"

"I'm being careful."

"With woman troubles no man can be careful," Simon half joked, but Pres saw Simon's concern etched in the tight wrinkles around the islander's face.

"You taught me how to be careful. I don't forget those things," he reminded Simon, remembering just how quickly he had forgotten his caution earlier that afternoon.

"What be the problem?" Simon asked after taking another deep draft of his rum.

"I found a leather-covered box with the ship's sextant. But I can't find anything else. No other clues."

"Look in straight lines. First look east to west, or west to east. Then north to south or south to north. That box not be washed overboard. If it had, it be carried to one of the islands. No, it be pulled from ship; current maybe drag it along the bottom." Simon paused to give Pres a long, silent look. "How old?"

Pres absently moved his beer glass in circles. "Four hundred years."

Again, Simon laughed. "When I first saw you, Pres-ton, I said to myself, 'That boy, he's crazy coming to the island when he could make his fortune back home.' But I watch you. I see you have a feel for diving. You have the ability. Later I think, 'Simon, maybe you wrong about Pres-ton.' But now I know. Pres-ton, you crazy!"

"Thanks," Pres said.

"But, Pres-ton," Simon added, his voice dropping so no one but Pres would hear him, "only the crazy people find treasure. You keep looking. When you find it, you call old Simon. He help you salvage."

Pres smiled at his friend. "I will, Simon, you already know that."

The big black man nodded sagely. "Pres-ton, there be rumors I heard as a child. Stories that my grandfather tell to me. He said that it be his great-grandfather's grandfather who told him that somewhere off Little Hans Lollick, just past the point where Thatch Cay can't be seen no more, a galleon went down."

Pres stiffened. His hands tightened around the glass; his knuckles turned white.

"By my reckoning, that would be close to the time of the ship you be looking for. And Pres-ton," Simon added, glancing at the way Pres was holding the glass, "if you don't let loose of that glass, you be shark meat for sure."

Pres's fingers reflexively released the glass just before the pressure of his hand would have shattered it into a thousand deadly splinters.

"You're sure, Simon?"

Simon nodded. "I spent a year looking. But I didn't find it. Maybe you have better luck than me, eh?"

"We'll see, Simon. And thank you," Pres added as he stood and put a five-dollar bill on the table. Just when he reached the door, Simon called out and Pres turned.

"You be careful," Simon warned, his voice filled with friendship and concern.

Pres nodded, winked and left the Island Star, its clientele, and its pounding reggae beat behind. He walked through the streets of Charlotte Amalie, trying to digest what he had learned from Simon and to quell the excitement that his friend's words had filled him with, for he still needed Bruce's reevaluation to help in the search.

Pres knew that the spot Simon had spoken of could be anywhere along a ten-mile stretch of ocean. The only thing of which he was certain was that it was not where they had been looking. Pres and Megan had spent the past three weeks directly south of Simon's location.

The sextant was a pointer. Somewhere north of where he'd found it would be the *Conquistador*.

"I have you now," he whispered when he reached his car.

Chapter Thirteen

Megan's mouth turned down in disgust as she looked at herself in the mirror. Dark half moons, riding beneath her eyes, told the story of her night. Her hair, no matter how much she brushed it, would not lie smooth. She was forced to tie it severely back, which only made the circles under her eyes stand out even more.

Long after Sandi had gone to sleep, Megan had stayed awake. The wonderful feelings of love that had helped to relax her had vanished shortly after speaking with Bruce and asking him to check on the University of Miami for her.

Her request to her brother had come with a spontaneity that arose from her desire to be near Pres. Yet it was only after she'd voiced that desire that she realized how far from her chosen path she'd wandered in the past weeks.

The enormity of her request had set the turbulent windmill of her thoughts to spinning, reminding her of what she had always been seeking. The turbulence created by her inner mind forced her to rein in her runaway emotions for

Pres, to stop herself from destroying all the hard work of the past years.

She believed her love for Pres was real too. But somehow this knowledge only added fuel to keep the conflict blazing within her. Her struggles against her emotions had ended up keeping her awake all night long. The deep-rooted fear of losing her identity, as had so many of the girls she had grown up with, had tried to beat her down and make her see the fool she was letting herself become.

The love that had won free from her hard-held restraints told her that she could have much more than just a career. Those warring conflicts, between logic and emotion, made her rethink everything that had happened since she'd met Pres Wyman again after twelve years.

Now, as she prepared to face the day, the thought of Pres, the way his arms had held her and the way his body had felt upon hers was almost too much to bear. "What am I to do?" she asked herself for the umpteenth time.

She was very aware that Pres had never mentioned anything concerning the future. He hadn't asked or spoken to her about what would happen when their time together was up. He'd never asked her to stay, for she had already told him she wouldn't. He'd never said what *he* wanted. It was always what *she* wanted. *Why?*

Her tired-eyed reflection had no answer for her.

Perhaps by not finding the ship she would find her answer, Megan thought, not for the first time. But rationally she knew this was not good enough. She had to make the decision for herself.

Megan admitted that she was not prepared for facing that sort of decision. Her life had been devoted to one objective. She had never given thought to anything else.

Finally, as she applied a little makeup to the shaded area beneath her eyes, she reached the point where she was able to narrow her decision to the most logical choices.

The first choice was to go to the University of Miami, so that she would be near Pres. The next choice was to wait another year before starting school, return to her job and request the Island route so she could have more time with Pres. Her last choice was the simplest: follow her original plan and go to UCLA.

"But which one?" she asked aloud.

"None," she answered, knowing that no decision could be made until she and Pres talked about the future and themselves. What she did know was that she was at long last willing to take a chance and look for more out of life than just the career her tunnel vision had been set upon.

Suddenly, Megan felt better. The tiredness that had been dragging her down eased. The tension drained from her like morning dew trickling from a leaf. A surge of energy and hope came forth.

Going into the kitchen, Megan found Sandi sitting at the table drinking coffee. "You're up early," Megan commented.

Sandi shrugged. "I didn't sleep well. I guess I don't like this place without Bruce here."

Megan poured herself a cup of coffee. When she sat, she gazed at Sandi. "At least you can get married soon."

"I know, it's . . . it's like I've been waiting forever for this time to come."

"The time is here now," Megan told her gently. "And you deserve it. You're a rare person, Sandi Majors. Not many women would have waited for a man the way you have for Bruce."

Sandi straightened her shoulders proudly. "I do deserve it, don't I?" she asked.

"Yes," Megan stated.

"What's going to happen between you and Pres? When are you going to tell him?"

"Soon," Megan promised.

"When I get back to Key West, I'll explain why you stayed, and why I didn't tell Pres about canceling the job. I'll have to be honest with Bruce. I have to tell him about you and Pres. I think Bruce will understand. But about

Pres," Sandi added, her eyes clouding, "I know it will bother him when he learns the search is being called off."

Megan started to nod but stopped. "Because it means I'll be leaving for school?" she asked.

Sandi stared at her without comprehension before realizing what Megan had said. She shook her head. "No, Megan, because it means he won't be able to save his company. You're the one who told me he took the job because he needed to raise enough money to get his company back on its feet."

To Megan's startled reaction, Sandi said, "My how times have changed. When you and Pres first came to Key West, you didn't seem to trust him. You were the one who didn't want him diving without you for fear he'd find the treasure and wouldn't tell you."

As Sandi spoke, her words began to fade from Megan's ears. The enormity of what her friend had just said rocked her to the very core of her being. Megan had all but forgotten that Pres needed to find the ship as quickly and as badly as she and Bruce had.

The earlier days of tension and uncertainty that had strained her and Pres's time together had slowly turned into love, trust and a longing to be with Pres for all time. When her love broke free of its restricting bonds, Megan had forgotten Pres's own quest while she tried to work out her deep-seated problems.

No wonder Pres was pushing so hard. It was the money that Pres was after, she realized, not her love. *He's just using me to get it!* Her silent words brought a bitter taste to her mouth and the sting of tears to her eyes.

Now that she was on the verge of conquering her fears and being able to admit another into the world of her future life, a new tree had fallen to block her path. Megan was not sure she had the strength to wield her emotional ax one more time. "Dear Lord," she whispered.

"What?" Sandi asked.

Megan shook her head and looked at her watch. "I'm going to be late," she said. Rising quickly, she went over to Sandi and kissed her cheek. "Get home safely. I'll call tomorrow."

"You do that," Sandi advised, concerned over Megan's sudden departure and ashen looks.

Megan did not hear her friend's parting words, nor see the look of concern in Sandi's eyes. Sandi's comment about Pres had jogged free the buried memories of those first hard days with Pres. All she saw was Pres's face when he told her why he had demanded the extra percentage for accepting the contract.

She did not see the car she cut off when she shot out of the drive of the villa, nor hear the driver's horn blast as he swerved and barely missed her.

Her mind was besotted with anguish and half-grown fears. Yet Sandi's words had given her pause to think. They had also given Megan reason to doubt the certainty of Pres's love.

She had wondered why Pres was becoming so desperate in his need to find the ship. *Obsessed,* she corrected her thought. He was acting the same way she had during the long years of reaching for her dream.

The last dive of the day, just yesterday, should have told her that something was wrong. The gleam in his eyes when they returned to the *Cervantes,* and he made his excuses for not living up to his responsibilities was the warning she had not seen.

"Have I been a fool?" she asked, letting the wind steal the words from her mouth as she guided the scooter around a turn at a speed much greater than she was aware of.

The trip to Pres's shop turned into a blur of colors, barely seen from the corners of her eyes. But when she arrived and shut the scooter off, she held herself still, knowing that she could not go charging over to Pres and demanding to know if her suspicions were right.

If she was wrong, Pres would never forgive her—again. A false charge, a guilt-laden accusation born of her fears would turn him once and forever against her.

Using the logic that had been fighting against her heart's desire for Pres, Megan decided not to charge bullishly about in a place where only the surefooted ways of a graceful cat would permit her to move in safety.

With a tremulous wrenching of her heart, Megan built her new façade. She would play the game to its hilt. She would learn what passions guided Pres—the treasures of bygone days, or love.

Megan turned the corner of the dive shop. She paused when she saw Pres standing on the *Cervantes*. He saw her and waved. Megan waved back, willing her smile to become full and her arm to rise lightly.

He cupped his hand and shouted, "I left the chart on my desk. Can you get it, please?"

Megan waved her okay and returned to the front door. She walked through the main part of the ship, past the rows of Aqualungs and diving gear, and into Pres's office.

The chart was just where he said it would be, on his desk. She glanced at it quickly before she started to fold it, and she saw several new lines radiating from the first search area they had worked.

Folding the chart, Megan started out. Behind her, the phone rang. She looked at it, debating whether to answer it. The third ring sounded so persistent that she returned to the desk and answered the call with "Wyman Salvage."

"Megan, is that you?" Bruce asked, surprised.

"Good morning, Bruce. Is something wrong?"

"No. I was calling Pres with the figures," her brother said.

"So soon?"

"I started working on the figures after speaking with you. I found one possible point of miscalculation almost immediately. After that I couldn't sleep, so I reworked the whole thing. Everything else checked out. Is Pres there?"

"He's on the boat," Megan said, glancing out the window to where Pres stood on the *Cervantes*'s bow, inspecting a mooring line.

"I wanted to give him the figures."

"I'll take them."

She sensed Bruce's hesitation but stayed silent. "All right," he said at last. "Tell Pres to go seven point two degrees north from the spot he found the sextant. My calculations put the galleon two and a half miles from that point. That's the best I can do. And Megan, tell him it's not a good area. There are a lot of deep canyons and bad currents."

"I'll tell him," she promised after jotting down the new figures.

"Megan, why aren't you coming home with Sandi?"

"Sandi will tell you."

"No, you tell me," Bruce said in the no-nonsense voice he had used with Megan all her adolescent life.

"I want to give it a few more days. Bruce, we can't just walk away from that ship. If we find it, think of the extra money you'll have for the foundation."

"I'd rather know that you were safe," Bruce stated. "Come home with Sandi."

"No!" Megan shouted, clutching the phone tightly. "Dammit, Bruce, I can't!"

"Megan," he said, and his voice carrying over the long miles showed his open concern.

"No, Bruce," Megan said in a milder voice, realizing that she had almost lost control and had spoken out of turn. "Pres is determined to find that ship. He's become obsessed. If we pull out now and he finds it, we'll get nothing. Pres will get it all."

"So that's it," Bruce replied, a knowing tone lacing his words. "It can't happen that way, Megan. Whether you're with him or not when he finds it, the foundation will get its share."

"I don't think so," Megan stated. "And I have no intention of finding out if you're wrong. Goodbye, Bruce."

Megan hung up the phone and walked out of the office. Behind the now closed door, the phone rang again, but this time Megan ignored it and went to the *Cervantes*.

Ten minutes later, the *Cervantes* was on its way out, and Megan, doing her best not to stand close to Pres, told him that Bruce had called with the recalculated figures.

"What are they?" Pres asked, smiling confidently at Megan. He had a feeling that Bruce's new figures would be somewhere near the location he'd worked out last night after talking with Simon.

When Megan gave him the figures, Pres suddenly cut the throttle and let the *Cervantes* drift. Turning to her, he reached out and grabbed her around the waist. Before she was ready for it, he had her against him, his lips hot and demanding on hers.

A flush of heat rushed through her, taking her by surprise as much as the kiss did. She tried to fight back her sudden desire for Pres. Failing in that, Megan helplessly wound her arms around his back. A low, animallike groan reverberated in her throat. She clung to him, pressing her body tightly along his length, returning his kiss with an abandon that shocked her.

Releasing her, Pres gazed down with hooded eyes and said, "If we weren't so close to shore I'd..."

Megan was thankful that he'd stopped himself and given her a moment in which to recover.

Pres looked around to make sure there were no other boats nearby before asking Megan to open the chart.

Megan, still trying to calm the unexpected whirlwind of her passions, was glad for the excuse of action. She opened the chart and held it up for Pres.

"Seven point two degrees north?" he asked.

"That's what he said."

Pres's long, elegant finger moved along the chart, following a path from their original dive location. Megan suddenly pictured his finger skimming along her bare skin, and she almost shuddered in response to her vision. But she willed herself to concentrate on the chart and carefully studied the line his finger made, which corresponded to one of the newer lines on the map. When he stopped, he jabbed his finger against the chart.

"As I said, right under our noses. Or to be exact, a short distance away from where our noses were. It will be there," Pres added as he returned to the controls and left Megan to fold the chart.

Once the *Cervantes* was running smoothly across the face of the Atlantic, and her desires and passions were under her somewhat unsteady control, Megan returned to building her willpower and adding to her determination to learn whether it was she or the treasure that Pres was ultimately after.

The decision she had agonized over throughout the night had been taken from her hands. All Megan had to do now, she realized, was to tell Pres the operation had been canceled and learn his reaction. His response would give her the clue she needed to follow through.

Will it be love or money? she wondered sadly.

Before going to him, Megan studied his broad back. Her heart began to pound horribly. For a fearful moment, Megan was afraid she might faint. But she drew up a lonely shred of courage and took a step toward him. The second step was easier. But the third, which brought her within inches of him, was the hardest step of her entire life.

Moistening her lips, she put her hand on his shoulder to gain Pres's attention. Before she could speak, Pres glanced at her and smiled. The beauty in the smile nearly stopped her heart from beating.

"We'll find it, Megan, and we'll do it before our time is up."

Megan's throat constricted. She doubted if she would be able to speak. She knew somehow she must. "Pres," she began in a hesitant voice, "what if we don't find the ship? Will it be so terrible?"

Pres's expression changed to one of puzzlement before he nodded thoughtfully. "I think it will be terrible. It will hurt your brother, and it will stop you from getting to school. And that, if nothing else, will eventually come between us."

She wanted to ask if that was the only reason, but when she tried to do just that, no words came out; instead, fear broke out in her mind—fear of losing Pres, and fear of being right about his using her to find the treasure. "And your business too," she whispered, "that depends on finding the galleon."

"Yes," Pres responded, "my business too."

With his words, Megan's new life came to an end. A wave of dizziness threatened to fell her. She caught her lower lip between her teeth and bit down until the pain made her gasp. It was the only way she could stop the boat from spinning, shake from her mind the intensity she'd seen in Pres's face and shock herself back into the world of the living.

On the heels of Pres's response came the near certainty of what she dreaded the most. His face, not his words, had told her all she needed to know. Pres was after the treasure. *Fool!* she cried to herself. *Stupid, shameless fool!*

Wordlessly, Megan left Pres to captain the *Cervantes*. She went to the bow, where she sat cross-legged and stared out at the horizon toward which they were heading. There, Megan began to search for a way to rebuild her shattered heart and to strengthen her most prized possession—her mind.

She sat at the bow for an hour, until the *Cervantes* slowed and Megan became aware that they were at the new dive sight.

Refusing to let her emotions betray her, Megan forced herself to work in the same way she had for the past week. The hardest part was when Pres was near her. When his arm touched hers, or when their thighs or hips brushed, little pinpricks of fire danced maddeningly across her skin. She learned, too, that she could not stop her body's traitorous responses to Pres, no matter how she tried.

In the water, however, things were different. The heavy depths separated them and made her feel safe. And the new dive area was so alive with fish and coral reefs that Megan barely thought of Pres and his deception.

Through three dives they wandered along the bottom of a bold new world, this time without the aid of the metal detector, but with the help of the sonar.

Whenever they came upon an undersea canyon or chasm, they would swim over it and watch the magnified screen outline whatever was beneath them.

One time there was a gigantic school of large fish, while another time gave them the outline of a small sunken boat. Megan reveled in the sights the ocean offered.

Large groupers floated along, one almost as big as Pres. A giant sea turtle swam up from one dark chasm, startling Megan for a moment before she realized what it was. But by the end of the third dive, they had still not found the galleon.

When the fourth dive ended, along with their day at sea, Pres's face was etched with lines of disappointment. His almost manic euphoria of the morning was gone. In its place was tiredness.

Again her heart went out to him without her wanting it to. The conflicting emotions heaving within her breast once again conspired to make her weak, but Megan held strong to her earlier promises.

Should I try again? she asked herself, giving in just a little. The love that burned ever so brightly within her told her yes, and she gave in to the needs that she had so recently learned resided within her.

As the *Cervantes* headed back to its dock, Megan joined Pres at the helm. Without realizing what she was doing, she put her hands on his shoulders and massaged his tired muscles. They were tense beneath her fingers. For the first time that day, she realized that Pres had carried the sonar during each of the dives.

"I'll take my turn with the sonar tomorrow," she told him.

Pres smiled. "No argument," he replied. Her fingers felt good on his stiff muscles, and he realized it was the first time all day that Megan had touched him. He had sensed that one of Megan's moods was upon her when she arrived that morning, but he had decided not to mention it unless Megan brought it up. He knew that she was troubled about their relationship and the decisions she would have to make concerning it.

"Tomorrow, Megan. Tomorrow we'll find our ship." Pres didn't say there was any other choice; it had to be tomorrow.

Against the bitter knowledge of what she knew Pres was doing, Megan's aching heart pleaded with her to try one more time to make sure she was right about him.

"If we do find it, do you think our . . . relationship can survive being apart for three years?"

Pres glanced quickly at her. "You asked me that the other day. And it's something I've thought about, a lot. Megan, we have to make it survive."

Despite all her trepidations, Megan leaned her mouth against his back and kissed his salt-laced and savory skin. "If we don't find the ship, it may all be a moot point."

Pres turned, ignoring the controls for a moment. "I'll find it," he stated as he gazed deeply into Megan's eyes.

The intensity controlling Pres's features was like the chilling slap of ice on a burn. It startled and hurt Megan. "Pres," she cried, pleading with him but saying nothing else.

Mistaking her cry for something else, Pres shook his head adamantly. "No more talk, Megan. We'll find that ship. Bruce will have his foundation, and you'll make it to California on time!"

Now! her mind screamed. *Tell him about Bruce now!* Megan swallowed forcefully. "Pres—"

"No more what-ifs!" Pres shouted angrily. "Have some faith in me! Stop talking about what might or might not happen." So saying, Pres turned back to the *Cervantes*'s controls and made the trip back in silence.

At the dock, and with his irritation now well under control, Pres went over to where Megan was wiping down one of the Aqualungs.

Bending, he brushed her shoulder with his fingers. "Megan, I didn't mean to shout at you. It was a long day, and my nerves are on edge."

"I know," Megan said. When she stood, his fingers fell from her shoulders. "We're both tired. Very tired, and I'm sure you're right. We will find the ship soon." Megan yawned after she finished speaking.

"Why don't you stay here tonight?" Pres suggested.

Megan shook her head quickly, and then recovered from her abrupt reaction. "I want to soak in a hot tub for about three hours." Megan's words were both truth and lie. She wanted a bath, but the real reason she needed to leave was so that she would be away from Pres's overwhelming sphere of influence.

"Forgive me?" she asked with a smile she hoped would hold up to his scrutiny.

"Always," Pres replied, stepping close to her and drawing her into his arms. The slight resistance he felt at their contact disappeared almost immediately.

And, as it had happened that morning, when he kissed her she responded totally. Her desire for him flared dangerously. When they parted, he gave her a look that asked her to stay tonight. Megan shook her head and said, "I need that bath."

"Be careful driving home," Pres cautioned.

"I will," Megan promised as she left the boat and went to her scooter, conscious of the way Pres's gaze followed her.

Only on the scooter, with the hot tropical air less intense at thirty miles an hour, did Megan breathe a sigh of relief.

She was still astounded by her body's willing response to Pres. The first kiss that morning had startled her; the kiss tonight had shaken her deeply. She was puzzled by the strong and unwarranted physical reaction she had whenever he was near, especially when she knew that he was only using her to further his own purposes.

Yet Megan accepted what was happening to her as a lesson to be learned. One's body was not necessarily one's friend. *Not for much longer,* she vowed.

Five minutes after she got to the villa, Megan turned on the faucet and impatiently waited for the tub to fill. In the past, when Megan had a serious problem, she had found a way that seemed to help her solve it.

She would fill a bathtub with hot water and bathing oil, make a light sandwich and eat dinner in the tub. The combination of filling her stomach and having her muscles soothed by the warm water had always helped her before. She hoped it would now.

When the tub was filled, and a cheese sandwich and glass of ice tea resided on a small stool, Megan slipped into the bath, leaned her head back and closed her eyes.

An instant later, her eyes were open. "Go away!" she ordered Pres's image.

Surprisingly, his handsome face departed.

Megan reached for the sandwich, lifted it to her mouth and promptly discovered she wasn't hungry.

"So much for plan A," she whispered.

"Now," she continued, talking to herself out loud so she wouldn't feel lonely, particularly when she knew that the comfort of Pres's arms could have been hers for the entire night. "I will be strong," Megan declared.

The four words turned into four separate sobs. She squeezed her eyes shut to stop her tears from escaping. She didn't want to cry anymore.

"Why couldn't you have loved me the way I love you?" Megan asked the face that was now imprinted on the inside of her eyelids. Unable to stop it from happening, Megan found her tears flowed freely, falling to mingle with the fresh water that filled the bathtub.

Chapter Fourteen

For the second day in a row, Megan stared at her tired, shadowy-eyed reflection. Today the dark circles were even more pronounced than yesterday. But unlike the other morning, Megan had no hesitation about applying a base of makeup to cover the evidence of her troubles. She used a makeup advertised to be impervious to water, but she doubted that it would stand up to a day of diving, even though it had always held up well on long flights when she was a stewardess.

That thought made her pause. It seemed like years, not weeks, since she'd been a flight attendant, working a regular route in pursuit of her goal. She felt different now, as if that had been in another lifetime.

Shaking her head, Megan brushed her hair and made herself ready to face the day. She hoped that the day would be better than the long night that had just passed.

After leaving the tub last night, with her thoughts still as unsettled as they had been all day, Megan had tried to sleep.

She had tried and failed. So Megan had spent the night awake, staring at the ceiling. There were times, she knew, that she had drifted off, but she doubted that she'd slept more than an hour at most. The circles beneath her eyes were ample testimony to that fact.

Megan left the bedroom and started out of the villa, but when she passed the telephone, she remembered her promise to call Sandi. Picking up the phone, she dialed the overseas operator and gave the woman Bruce's number.

A few rings later, Bruce's sleepy voice filled her ears. "Morning," Megan said.

"Megan," Bruce said, his voice sharper, more alert. "Are you okay?"

"Of course," Megan blatantly lied, "why wouldn't I be?"

"I don't know," Bruce said with uncharacteristic sharpness. "But I've had a feeling since I spoke with you yesterday that something was wrong."

"Is Sandi there?" Megan asked quickly, not wanting to get into an argument with her brother.

"No. Her flight got into Miami late. She missed the last plane to Key West. I told her to stay in Miami and wait for me. I have an institute lecture to give tomorrow afternoon, so I'll meet her there in the morning," he explained patiently.

With his words, Megan realized that Sandi had not yet had a chance to tell him why Megan was staying on in St. Thomas.

"I want you to come home," Bruce said, repeating the words he had spoken in their last conversation.

"Not yet," Megan said, her voice carrying the sound of steel. "Not till the last day is over."

"Meg, you're being ridiculous about this."

"I'm being myself, and doing what I have to. You taught me that," she stated, making her voice sound calmer than she felt.

"I want this dive ended."

Megan closed her eyes and took a deep breath. "Bruce, I don't want to argue with you. I know what I'm doing. Please, don't fight me. I have to stay here. Bruce, its only for three more days."

Perhaps it was the desperation in her voice, or perhaps the silent prayer for Bruce to understand her needs and stop arguing with her that finally made him give in. Whatever it was, she was thankful for his next words.

"I don't understand why you're doing this, Megan, and I don't for a moment believe that Pres is trying to steal from us. But whatever it is, Sandi seems to think that you know what you're doing. But Meg, I want to be kept posted."

"You will be," Megan promised, breathing a sigh of relief.

"By the way," Bruce added off-handedly, "I spoke with the dean of admissions. The University of Miami will be more than happy to accept you into its graduate program. And you'll have a week more to decide. Miami starts a week later than UCLA."

Two days ago she would have been overjoyed at the prospect of being able to stay closer to Pres. Her heart would have leaped heavenward, and she would have told Pres all about her decision. Today she accepted the impossibility of it. Yet hearing the hopefulness in her brother's voice at the prospect of her staying in Florida, Megan found she couldn't tell him that she was going back to her original plan—yet.

"Just give me a couple of days' notice so I can get your records transferred."

"Okay," Megan said in a low voice. "I have to go now," she added before saying goodbye and leaving the villa.

As Megan drove the scooter toward Pres's, she was more than just a little aware that this was day twenty-seven. And, as she had told Bruce, in three more days it would be over, no matter what.

The horizon was filling with clouds, some light, others dark and threatening. The surface of the Caribbean was choppy. Not bad, but nowhere near as calm as the preceding weeks.

Looking at the sky above the horizon, Megan likened it to her own tormented mind before pushing the thoughts away and turning back to the business at hand.

They had made four dives already, but instead of leaving as they usually did, Pres insisted on a fifth dive. Megan had argued with him, but Pres had remained steadfast. He had pointed to the cloud-gathered horizon, reminding her of the weather reports they'd been receiving all day: a tropical storm was building somewhere in the nearby Atlantic.

She'd continued to argue with him, but he refused to listen; rather, he'd said, "Stay here if you want. I'm going down again."

Megan would not let him go alone and had agreed to the dive. Which was why she found herself in her tanks again, looking at the sky.

"Let's go," Pres summarily ordered.

While Megan adjusted her mask and joined him on the dive platform, she wondered why she had not seen this obsessive side of Pres before the other day.

But it no longer mattered, she tried to tell herself as they entered the darkening waters. At seventy feet, the visibility was barely thirty feet. At the bottom, the visibility was down to twenty feet or so. When Pres unhooked the sonar from the equipment line, Megan took it from him, signaling Pres that it was her turn.

Pres acquiesced, and handed her the one-foot-by-two-foot black box. He unhooked a floodlight and rose above her. They started out slowly in the direction of the spot where they had ended their last search.

As Megan swam, she was aware of the unusual amount of activity on the ocean's floor. Schools of fish no longer swam randomly; they all seemed to be going in a specific direction.

Five feet beneath her, a manta ray sped by. A shiver raced along her spine, for she too sensed the danger of the building storm.

When Megan reached the undersea canyon where they had last searched, she turned on the sonar and increased the screen's magnification. Methodically, she swam in a zigzag pattern along the precipice of the canyon's steep walls. She could not see far into the inky depths and, looking at the sonar screen, she realized that the bottom of the canyon was so deep that it did not register on the small unit, which was designed to read depths of up to a hundred feet from whatever location it was at.

Megan's concentration soon became total. Her eyes rarely left the view screen, except to check on her depth and make sure she had not drifted down into the mouth of the canyon.

Megan continued her zigzag path for twenty minutes until, belatedly, she looked ahead and found that the visibility was growing less. Suddenly, she realized that there was no light guiding her. Glancing quickly about, she saw that Pres was gone. A momentary fear grew, but it faded when she spotted Pres's floodlight moving along a parallel path, twenty-five feet away. *Why is he doing this?* But Megan knew the answer even better now than before. His obsession was making him do things he would never have done before. His greed was overcoming his natural caution and allowing him to take desperate chances. *It could have been so beautiful,* Megan thought. *We could have had a wonderful life together, with love and children and years to enjoy it all.*

Megan's eyes blurred. She immediately stopped her train of thought, knowing that to cry a hundred and twenty feet beneath the ocean's surface was a worse danger than what her heart had let her into.

Forcefully, Megan ordered her tears to stop and, when they had, she focused her attention on the sonar screen. With her eyes riveted to the screen, her muscles jumped spasmodically, and she almost dropped the unit.

Something was registering on it. A partial shape, but Megan knew it was not a living thing, and that it was large.

Looking down, she tried to pierce the murky depths but saw nothing. She cautiously swam a little farther to her left and dropped another six feet. The shape on the screen increased in size.

There was definition to it now. Megan's heart raced. Her breathing increased, dangerously using up quantities of air. But she couldn't help it. She knew what she was looking at. The sonar's screen was showing the image of the stern of an old ship—the distinctively shaped stern of a galleon.

Megan looked down and stopped breathing. Her eyes widened to the size of saucers at the sight that greeted her. Fifteen feet below her was the stern of an old ship. For a moment, Megan thought it was too small to be the galleon. But then she remembered that the old galleons, although large for their time, were nowhere close to the size of today's ocean going vessels.

When the pressure of the ocean reminded her to breathe again, Megan kicking her legs twice and propelled herself farther over the canyon's mouth. This time when she looked down she gasped aloud. The muffled sound of her voice in the water helped her to maintain her senses as the *Conquistador* came into full view.

What was left of the galleon's bow was lodged between two coral shelves that formed a horizontal chasm in the canyon's upper wall. It looked as if some underwater god had used the old ship as a dart and the canyon's wall as the dart board.

One coral shelf, made up of multifarious layers of colorful sea life, was above the galleon, cutting a third of the ship off from view. The shelf beneath it, which was also rampant with pastel shades, precariously held the galleon from slipping into the uncharted depths of the canyon.

Excitement blossomed in her mind. Her muscles stiffened, and then relaxed. Her breathing, again out of control, took her several precious seconds to slow down.

I found it! she cried to herself. Megan closed her eyes and counted slowly to five before opening them again. She needed to make sure this was not some hallucination brought on by her need to find the ship.

When she opened her eyes, the galleon was still there. *Pres!* Turning, she looked for Pres's searchlight. When she saw it, the overwhelming, giddy feeling of discovery fled. Then the first joy of finding the ship was replaced by the knowledge that her and Pres's moment of truth was upon them.

The future was here, and there was nothing left but to learn the whole truth, even though Megan already knew what that truth must be.

The searchlight turned toward her, and Megan signaled Pres with a wave of her excruciatingly heavy arm. She had to wave three times before he acknowledged her signal and started toward her.

As the searchlight grew bright, Megan's hopes dimmed in proportion. When Pres was next to her, she pointed her finger unerringly down at the stern of the Spanish galleon.

Pres looked down. His muscles froze. He looked back at Megan, and then at the ship as if he, too, could not believe it was there after so long a search. Finally, Pres wrenched his muscles into a coordinated effort and, after signaling Megan to come with him, descended to the ship's stern.

They dropped to within yards of the galleon and stared at the barnacle-encrusted wood. Strangely, the ship appeared to be in good condition after almost four centuries. But, Pres reasoned, if it's been in this one spot for so long, it's been protected by the canyon itself.

Dropping lower, aware of Megan at his side, Pres was reminded by his sense of timing that their air was running low. He went down until he could see the hull of the old ship. The disintegrated state of the planking on the bottom of the hull, and the way the sea life of the coral shelf had migrated onto the hull, gave him evidence that the ship had indeed been there for a long time.

Because it was jointly protected by the shelf and the first ten feet of the underwater canyon, the currents within the ocean had not broken the galleon apart as they would have had it been on the unprotected ocean floor. Yet while the galleon was wedged into the shelf, Pres wondered how long it could remain there. A powerful surge in current, dipping into the canyon, would move the galleon. How much of a surge of current that would have to be, Pres couldn't tell.

Looking at his watch, Pres saw that they had to surface. He signaled Megan and unhooked a buoy from his belt. He swam to the stern of the galleon, feeling a sense of history grow strongly within him as he gazed at the haunting image that had carried men over the sea four hundred years ago.

He anchored the buoy to the coral shelf and joined Megan for their slow ascent to the surface.

Fifteen minutes later, and three minutes into their reserve air supply, they broke the surface. The sky was growing dark above them, but the ocean was no rougher than it had been when they'd started the dive.

Once on the boat, and with their equipment shed, Pres crossed the four feet between himself and Megan and encircled her waist with his hands. Lifting her off the deck, he spun her in a wild circle. A grin was plastered on his mouth; his eyes were fevered bright with excitement.

"You found it!" he shouted. Lowering her, he pulled her to him and kissed her deeply.

Megan stiffened, unprepared for his kiss or the way the heated spheres of his lips battered her without mercy. Traiorously, her body responded. Her lips softened and parted, allowing his tongue entry. The rasping of his tongue across the edges of her teeth sent a corresponding shiver along her skin.

His hands eased their pressure on her back and began to move in tight circles. His fingers, through the layer of the wet suit, sent sparks skittering wildly. When his hand dipped to cup the curving firmness of her rear, another explosion was released within her.

Megan, unable to restrain herself, returned his embrace. Her nails dug into the rubber of his wet suit in an effort to stop her head from spinning and her heart from pounding furiously. Megan found herself teetering on the very verge of insanity. Just before it would have become impossible to stop herself from falling into the abyss of her emotional need for Pres, Megan wrenched herself back to reality. It was one thought that saved her: she reminded her protesting heart of the deception of the man who held her so tightly in his embrace.

Pres's body was exploding with passion when he broke their kiss and drew his mouth away. His hand, still caressing the lush curves of her body, slowed. "You found it," he repeated, his voice low and thickened by desire.

Megan backed away from him, unable to stop staring into the frenzied depths of his blue eyes, which suddenly seemed as clouded and unreadable as the ocean from which they had just emerged.

"Did I?" Megan asked her tone solemn and unenthusiastic no matter how hard she tried to keep up the pretense of excitement.

Pres's brows knitted together at her lack of excitement. He shook his head, thinking that, after all the time spent searching for the ship, the enormity of their find had not yet fully registered upon Megan's mind.

"I told you it would be right under our noses."

"Yes, you did," she admitted, forcing a halfhearted smile to her lips. "And now what?"

Looking at the sky, Pres said, "We come back tomorrow and start salvaging. If," he added, "the forecasters are right and the storm is still two days away."

When he spoke, he'd let none of his urgency show through. But he realized that he had done what he'd set out to do, find the ship before their deadline.

Pres almost laughed out loud. He hadn't once, since spotting the galleon, thought about his company or Bud Shaeffer's offer. His only concern was that he'd found the ship for Megan. Pres did not speak of that; rather, he said, "For now, let's set another marker buoy down and start for home."

Megan nodded as a wave of tiredness swept through her. It had been a long day, and she had hardly slept at all during the two previous nights. But she did not allow her exhaustion to show through and helped Pres with the buoy. Ten minutes after releasing the marker, they were on their way back to St. Thomas.

The ride was made in almost total silence. Pres was wrapped up in his own thoughts, and when he tried to speak to Megan, he found that she'd fallen asleep in the deck chair and was unaware of how much rougher the ocean had become.

It was only a few moments before they docked that Megan awoke. But she could not move her tired body while Pres unloaded the equipment. His energy seemed unflagging, and Megan wished she could feel like that.

When everything was done, Pres went over to Megan and shook her free of her lethargy. "You need to get some solid sleep. Do you want me to drive you home?"

Megan shook her head, yawned and stood. Dredging up a smile for his benefit, she said, "No, I'll be fine."

Pres looked at her doubtfully but decided against arguing with her. "Come on, I'll walk you to the scooter."

"You go on ahead. I have to get my things." And saying this, she rose and kissed him lightly. "I'll see you in the morning."

Pres held her face in his hands. His eyes raced across her features. Beneath his roaming gaze, Megan's stomach constricted.

She wanted him to hold her forever; she wanted to scream at him and slap him and hate him for what he was doing to her and to them with his deceptions. She did none of those things. She simply waited for him to release her.

"Good night," he whispered as his hands dropped from her skin.

Megan stood on the deck and watched him until he was gone. When he turned the corner of the building, Megan went into the cabin and gathered her clothing. A wave of dizziness caught her. She sat heavily on the closest berth and closed her eyes until the wave of vertigo passed.

When she tried to stand, her legs would not support her. Realizing that she would not be able to drive back to villa, Megan lay back down in the berth. Before her head had fully settled onto the mattress, Megan was asleep.

The *Cervantes* rocked on the increasingly high swells that were reaching the dock, and on one high sway, the cabin door closed and the latch clicked shut.

With the euphoria of finding the *Conquistador* continuing to supply Pres with energy, Pres spent the hour after saying good-night to Megan cleaning and refilling the air tanks.

When that task was done, Pres made himself an omelet and, as he sat at his deck eating the fluffy mixture of egg and cheese and sipping hot coffee, he began to plan for tomorrow—the first day of salvage.

His first priority would be to run heavy lines from the ship and anchor them into the coral ledges so that no sudden shift of current could rip the galleon from its resting place.

Pres thought about adding a secondary measure of defense against losing the galleon by installing air ballast bags in the ship's hull. By so doing, the extra buoyancy would keep it from dropping too far into the unrecorded depths of the canyon.

But the air ballast bags would only work if the wood of the hull was not completely rotted, which, even considering how good the galleon looked, Pres thought was doubtful.

When he finished eating, Pres drew a diagram of the ship and the coral ledges just the way they were when he'd seen them. Carefully, he marked the spots where securing lines would be placed.

As he sketched out his plans, the phone rang. He answered with a succinct, "Wyman."

"Pres," came Bruce Teal's voice. "I've been trying to reach you since four. Is Megan with you?"

"She's at the villa. Bruce," Pres said, then drew in a preparatory breath and smiled to the phone as if he were speaking to Bruce in person. "We—" But Bruce interrupted Pres before he could tell Bruce about their success.

"Aren't you at least going to congratulate me?" the oceanographer asked.

"For?" Pres began, puzzled by this turn of events and thinking that, if anyone should be congratulated, it was he and Megan.

"For the funding I received to start the foundation!" he stated proudly.

"Funding?" Pres echoed, his voice laden with the remainder of his unvoiced question.

"She . . . she didn't tell you?"

Amid a thousand warning bells blaring in his head, Pres leaned back in his chair. "Tell me what?" he asked in a calm voice that denied the sudden tension swarming through him.

Pres heard Bruce's loud sigh. "I think I knew she hadn't. Not after our last talks. I had hoped she would, but after this morning—"

"Perhaps," Pres said, cutting into Bruce's meandering words, "you'd better tell me what the hell is going on."

"Yes, I guess I'd better." For ten straight minutes Bruce spoke without a pause, telling Pres about the funding and about his orders to cancel the salvage operation.

When he finished his tale, and after a moment of silence, he asked Pres for a favor.

"If I can," Pres replied, fighting the sudden anger that had filled him at Bruce's words.

"Send Megan back."

Pres thought about the galleon, picturing it as clearly as when he had first seen it. "I don't know if that's possible," he admitted.

"Talk to her. Tell her that, even if you find the ship without her, our contract still holds."

"Of course it still holds. Why wouldn't it?" Pres asked, startled by Bruce's words. With Bruce's next words, the anger that had caught him deepened into a fury that turned his every thought to ice.

"I know the two of you have been at odds, and... Oh, hell, Pres, don't take this the wrong way, but Megan's got this crazy idea that if she leaves before you find the ship, you'll claim the salvage for yourself."

"She's wrong," Pres said in a low, tight voice.

"I know that, and so do you. But Megan doesn't know our ways."

"It has nothing to do with *our ways*. It's the law. All right, Bruce," Pres added, "I'll make sure she goes back to Florida tomorrow."

"Thank you, Pres," Bruce said, relieved.

"No, thank *you*," Pres replied stiffly.

He was about to hang up, when Bruce said, "And Pres, that new tropical disturbance seems to be building into a full-fledged hurricane."

"I'll watch out for it," Pres told him.

"The storm may go right across the area you're diving in."

Bruce's caution brought out one of Pres's fears about the storm and its effect on the galleon. "If the storm does come this way, how will it affect the ocean floor?"

"At deeper depths there's usually no problem," Bruce said.

"Which are?"

"Thirty-five meters or so. After that it's negligible unless the storm reaches full hurricane status—winds of a hundred and twenty miles an hour or more—and then anything goes."

"The area where I'm diving is about a hundred and twenty to a hundred and forty feet."

"Forty or so meters," Bruce said, converting the measurement aloud. "The bottom should be fairly safe, but..."

Here it comes, Pres thought.

"...the area you're diving in is a volcanic region. It's dormant for the most part. The canyons and chasms are part of an underwater mountain range. To be honest, no one really knows what happens down there."

Not liking the way Bruce's words were affecting him, Pres prodded the oceanographer for more. Bruce complied freely.

"Most underwater ranges have treacherous currents of their own. When there's a storm, we get a mixing of warmer and colder waters, which can raise all sorts of havoc.

"If this storm kicks up enough of a fuss, and the winds get really high, it can get down to that forty-meter mark or farther. If that happens, and the warmer upper waters mix with the deeper water, it's anyone's guess as to the result.

"Personally," Bruce continued, "I've found that when there's a temperature conflux, it gets pretty violent."

"What's 'pretty violent'?" Pres asked in a subdued voice.

"I've seen deep-water whirlpools that can make a Kansas tornado seem like a mild summer breeze."

"But that shouldn't happen, correct?" Pres ventured.

"It shouldn't, but Pres, the area you're diving in isn't the best. Some of those chasms are too deep to have been charted yet. The currents are rough and cold. I wouldn't set down any firm rules."

"I see," Pres said after a few seconds of silence. "Thanks, Bruce."

"Sure. And Pres, if I were you, I'd stay out of that area for three or four days after the storm passes. Let the sea settle before you go back in."

Long after he'd hung up the phone, Pres continued to stare at the far wall. His anger at what Megan had done to him rose and fell, much in the same way as a storm tide does. And, with Bruce's cautioning words about the storm weighing heavily upon him, he could sit still no longer.

He stood swiftly. The back of his calves caught the chair seat and sent it crashing onto the floor.

"Damn!" The single word exploded like a cannon. Pres shook his head fiercely, the way a male lion does when an enemy approaches. He started to pace the confines of his office, his feet moving him in short, angry and ungraceful steps.

She had done it to him again, Pres realized. And he'd let her. She had taken his love and twisted it to suit her own needs. "Damn her!" he shouted. "And damn me for being such a fool!"

Megan had not stayed because of love. No, she had stayed because she didn't trust him not to steal the salvage. Suddenly, her sea-green eyes were floating before him, and he saw the mocking sparkle that had always been hidden within them. The sparkle was what he had once thought was love.

Berating himself for being a lovesick fool, Pres went to his weather radio and flicked it on. A burst of static filled the air, followed by a monotone voice informing its listeners that the tropical disturbance was indeed reaching hurricane proportions. Estimates of the hurricane's strength were given, followed by the news that once the hurricane began to move, if the storm chose a westward path it could reach the islands late tomorrow.

Pres listened intently while a terrible image grew in his mind, fed by Bruce's earlier words. He saw the *Conquistador*, pulled randomly about by the lower ocean currents, being drawn steadily down into the far reaches of the canyon's depths.

Pres was aware of the possibility that if the hurricane passed over the galleon's resting place, the furies of the storm could unleash powerful bottom tides. If that happened, the point of confluence between the ocean's bottom and the canyon's mouth could become the most dangerous place on the face of the earth.

The colder water in the canyon's deeper reaches would act like a vacuum cleaner on the water above it. The canyon would suck the warmer water downward, creating a tornadolike effect that would drag down anything within the vicinity. And that included the *Conquistador*.

Pres closed his eyes and tried to quell the feelings that his mind brought up. The galleon was his salvation. It would allow him to keep his company and live the life he had always wanted.

But four centuries of ocean waters had left Pres's future dangling on a ledge. If the storm grew as powerful as predicted, the *Conquistador* might not survive the wild currents where the canyon met the ocean floor.

"I can't let that happen," Pres stated. Going to the phone, he called the Coast Guard base and asked for Lieutenant Peter Malcome.

When the native islander was on the phone, Pres asked, "What about the storm, Pete?"

"It's a big one, Pres. Just stay out of the water for a while."

"It may not be that easy. Do you have an exact fix on it?"

"Sure do. We just got a radio report back from the plane. Pres, Ariel—that's the storm's name—is huge. Its center is two hundred and ten nautical miles due east. It's becoming a monster, Pres."

"Speed?"

"None. Ariel hasn't decided on what direction she wants to go in. But we've estimated that if she does head for us, it would hit us around midafternoon tomorrow. We're not taking any chances with this one. We've just issued full hurricane alert," the lieutenant stated.

"Thanks, Pete."

"Pres," Pete Malcome called.

"Yes?"

"Don't do anything stupid. I know you're having a hard time right now, but don't push your luck."

"Me?" Pres asked innocently. "You know me better than that."

"I hope I do," the lieutenant said in farewell.

The moment Pres hung up the phone, he started moving. He loaded four sets of Aqualungs onto the boat, along with six-hundred-foot lengths of rope. He added five heavy-duty stationary underwater floodlights and made sure he had a lot of coffee on board.

Never once did he pause to look into the sleeping cabin, for he was too rushed. Not even on his last trip from the dive shop to the *Cervantes* did he notice Megan's motor scooter still leaning against the shop's wall. All Pres saw was the underwater canyon, and the way the old galleon rested precariously within the clutches of the two coral shelves.

As he unhooked the mooring lines, the angry clouds whirling in the sky parted. A full moon, hanging boldly in the heavens to mock the earth's weather, sent down a silver sheen to guide the *Cervantes* into the deeper ocean waters.

With the throttle at the halfway mark, Pres angled away from the dock and toward the dive sight. But while he steered the boat almost by instinct, he could not stop cursing at himself for becoming an emotional fool and having fallen under Megan Teal's spell once again.

"Never again," he promised the storm clouds that once again hid the moon.

Chapter Fifteen

At exactly midnight, with the spotlight above the bridge of the *Cervantes* illuminating the buoy Pres had left to mark the spot of the sunken galleon, he lowered the anchor.

Once the anchor had found purchase, Pres paused. Sometime during the trip out, the ocean's surface had grown calm. Pres looked up at a cloud-filled sky that obscured the stars but strangely let the moon shine through. The air was still, but not quite stagnant. Pres sniffed, drawing in the scent of salt and humidity.

He remembered all the stories of the ocean before a major storm. What Pres was seeing was the proverbial calm before the storm. For all the ocean's seemingly gentle surface, Pres felt a sensation of fear at what would happen to the sea during the coming afternoon.

Sensing the growing danger of staying out in the ocean for too long, Pres moved quickly. He put on his wet suit and attached all the extra equipment he'd brought to the drop line. Along with the extra equipment, he hooked on three more sets of air tanks. Pres planned on working the galleon for as long as he could. Two sets of tanks were for work; he would use the third to return back to the *Cervantes*.

When he was satisfied that he had not forgotten anything, he lowered the searchlights, tanks, ropes and stakes into the water.

When the equipment was down, he tested his Aqualung, slipped it on and cinched it tight. The last thing he put on was a double-thick pair of insulated gloves.

He lowered the diving platform, turned on his hand-held spotlight and entered the water. Darkness engulfed him immediately. The only light came from the torch in his hand. He looked about until the light flashed over the equipment line, which he followed to the ocean floor.

Pres was more than aware of the dangers inherent in night diving, and in diving alone. But it was a risk he chose to take, and Pres would not let his mind dwell on any thoughts other than success.

At the bottom, he disconnected one floodlight, set it on the floor and turned it on. Brightness flooded the area. Working with the light's aid, Pres unhooked the ropes and stakes and brought them to the ledge above the *Conquistador*.

He made five trips in all, and it was a half hour from the time he reached the ocean floor until he had two floodlights attached to the coral shelf above the *Conquistador*.

Knowing that he had only fifteen minutes of air left in the first set of tanks, Pres took his first inspection tour of the galleon.

The comparative silence of the ocean, combined with the exploration of a ship from the far-distant past, took Pres away from the world of troubles and brought him into a world of peace.

With his diving knife in one hand and his underwater torch in the other, Pres swam along the hull of the *Conquistador* looking for signs of a hull breach, but he found none. In fact, Pres realized that the rotting wood looked much as it might have when the galleon was sailing the route between South America and Spain. The only sign of its ill fortune was that all its masts had been sheared off.

He was careful not to bang into anything, or to prod too forcefully, for he knew that the apparent good condition of the ship was misleading. After four hundred years, the wood and corroding iron might be nothing more than a rotted shell.

Carefully, he swam close to the port hull and gently applied his knife tip to the wood. The blade met a momentary resistance before completely penetrating the wood.

Small bits of decaying timber broke loose. Pres withdrew the knife quickly. He had been right. There was no substance to the hull. It was merely a paperlike shell. The only reason the galleon still retained its shape was because it had been protected from the harsher undersea currents by having become lodged on the coral shelf.

After his inspection tour, Pres rose onto the deck and went into one of the open hatches in the galleon's center.

The darkness within the lower deck was total, but Pres's light illuminated the walls clearly so that he would not inadvertently bump into them. After looking through one empty cabin, he swam along the passageway until he could descend farther. He emerged next in the galley and stopped short.

In the galley, floating among the deteriorating fixtures, most of which were barely recognizable as having been cast from metal, was a fairly large octopus.

Pres backed slowly and carefully out of the room. He did not fear the tentacled denizen of the deep; what he feared was the ink jet that would block his vision and impair his ability to navigate within the confines of the ship.

Just as he reached the sanctuary of the passageway, his air ran out. Quickly, Pres turned on the reserve air and left the galleon. He went over to the second set of tanks and switched over to them.

He was aware that he had only an hour and a half of air left now: the second set's full hour and the first half hour of the third Aqualung set. The remaining air in the third set would have to get him back to the surface.

Pres disregarded his plan of using securing lines to hold the *Conquistador* fast. There was no place to hook the lines to. The hull of the ship was too rotted.

Five minutes after reaching that decision, Pres was ready to look for the treasure cabin of the *Conquistador*. Scooping up a salvage bag, he tied it to his waist and headed toward the stern hatch.

In his mind was a diagram of a Spanish galleon, and of the way it was set up below deck. Usually, there were four levels above the ballast stones that lined the ship's bottom.

The gold and jewels were stored in a small room connected to the captain's cabin on the aft of the ship, on the second deck. On the deck below that, in another storeroom, would be the less valuable metals such as silver.

Pres had recognized this galleon as being of the *Almirante* class. It would have carried little cargo except for treasure—its seagoing duties were more to protect ships in its armada.

That was Pres's last thought before slipping through the hatch and working his way aft along the second deck.

Megan was dreaming. She was being tossed about on a blanket held by six burly men. They were laughing as she flew up into the air, stopped and then fell back into the blanket again. She pleaded with them to stop, but they wouldn't. Finally, as she was again hurtling skyward, she screamed loudly. "No!"

Her voice penetrated the layers of her dream, and Megan's eyes snapped open. An instant later, she was again tossed about, only it wasn't into the air; rather, she was slammed against the wall of the cabin.

Recovering, Megan realized that she was still on the *Cervantes*, and that the bay had gotten much rougher than when she'd fallen asleep. *The storm is coming.* She glanced at her watch and saw it was almost two o'clock.

Sitting up and grasping the edge of the bunk to steady herself, Megan took several deep breaths. The boat continued to buck, and it took considerable effort for Megan to gain her feet without being knocked down again.

She inched her way to the cabin door and stepped into the galley. Again, using whatever handholds were available, she maneuvered her way to the deck. When she reached it, she gasped.

The dock was gone. So was Pres's dive and salvage shop. Megan froze. Her knuckles turned white as she gripped the sides of the doorway with a death hold.

"My God," she whispered when the realization of where she wasn't struck home. And, as one high wave lifted the *Cervantes* into the air, and then crashed it mightily back down, Megan knew where she was—out at sea, in the midst of a storm.

"Pres," she screamed. There was no answer.

Frantically, she tried to find him, but he was nowhere to be found. She worked her way to the side of the boat. When she saw that the diving platform had been lowered, her gasp echoed out once again, this time against a suddenly powerful blast of wind.

Her hair was pulled back harshly, and she felt as if the wind was trying to rip it from her head. Her mind spun dizzily with her efforts to grasp what she was seeing.

In that moment, the heavens chose to unleash a torrent of rain that struck down at her like steel pellets. But the pain of the hard water was nothing in comparison to the knowledge she had just gained.

Pres was diving at night, and in the middle of a hurricane. *Pres is going to die!*

"No!" she shouted defiantly at the forces attacking her. Moving quickly, refusing to let the boat stop her by smashing her against its wooden sides, Megan retreated into the cabin and put on her wet suit.

When she reemerged on the unsteady deck, Megan turned on the weather radio and heard the warning of the storm's unexpectedly early strike.

Without letting herself think too much, Megan picked up the single remaining set of tanks and fought with them until they were on. The *Cervantes* kept tossing about like a matchstick in a draining sink.

The wind howled in Megan's ears. Fear rose bitterly in her mouth. She swallowed hard, forcing the fear back down. Intuitively, Megan sensed that Pres was trying to salvage whatever he could from the galleon. He had already told her that the ship might be dragged down into the undersea canyon at any time.

She didn't think he knew about the storm. *He wouldn't be down there if he did,* she reasoned. A black terror of the stormy ocean welled up in Megan's mind, but she knew she had to warn Pres of his danger. Nothing else mattered anymore—not the galleon, not even her own life—as the true depth of her love burst out and told her that she must save him, even if their love was an impossible dream.

Megan adjusted her mask securely. She concentrated on working her way to the diving platform and, once there, snapped the short safety line that hung around her waist to the equipment line.

No sooner had she done that than another powerful gust of wind caught the *Cervantes*. With the wind, a giant wave lifted it up. Megan's finned feet slipped out from beneath her and sent her reeling backward. She fell, ramming her head against the unyielding wood of the *Cervantes*'s deck.

Darkness rushed over her, but not before the *Cervantes* spun in the water and sent Megan rolling back toward the diving platform. Water rushed over her, and as the darkness pulled her last thoughts from her mind, the ocean drew her into its churning embrace.

Down Megan went. The mouthpiece was clutched tightly between unfeeling teeth as the weights around her belt took all buoyancy from her, allowing the sea to drag her to its very bottom.

Her descent was stopped only when her safety line could not pass the first three heavily laden sacks. But Megan knew nothing of where she floated unconscious, five feet above the ocean's floor.

Pres was lost in the wonder of what he was doing. For a solid hour he'd been liberating heavy gold coins, bars and statuettes from the treasure room that had, indeed, been a part of the captain's cabin.

He was thankful that the interior walls of the galleon had not been as badly ravaged by sea life as had the hull. Still, the work had been slow, but he'd applied himself fully and had filled three salvage bags with gold. By his inexperienced estimate, he had found perhaps a half million dollars in bars, coins and small religious statues.

Twenty minutes earlier, he had exchanged his used-up second set of tanks for the fresh third set and was aware that he had only one more trip left after this one.

Needing to make the most of his time, Pres searched through the decaying ruins of the captain's cabin, in the hopes of finding the jewels that were always so important a part of Spanish treasure ships.

After five wasted minutes, he gave up and returned to the treasure room, where he filled the fourth salvage bag with as much of the golden material as he could fit in it.

He started out, conscious that he was cutting his time close. When he swam through the doorway, into the captain's cabin, he was stopped short and his arm jerked back. Spinning, he saw that the salvage bag had become hooked on an ornament on the wall. He pulled hard, and the bag started to rip.

He reached up to lift the bag off of an intricately carved large brass coat hook. While his gloved fingers fought to get the mesh material free, the ship shuddered all around him and he grabbed on to the hook to steady himself.

Pres stayed like that for a full thirty seconds. When the ship did not move again, he returned to his task. But he saw that the hook had sliced into his glove and held it fast.

Damn! he thought, giving his arm a powerful tug. The glove ripped free, and with the force of the action, the hook tilted down. Before he could reach up to free the salvage bag, the hook, and a two-foot-square section of cabin wall, fell forward, its hinges giving in to the corrosion of the centuries.

Pres's eyes widened when they fastened onto what was now before him. In the watery compartment was a shelf filled with jewels. Giant emeralds winked in the light of his torch. Rubies the size of walnuts glowed blood-red in their showcase of green water. And sapphires, almost as blue-black as the night, were the size of large California grapes.

The value of the gold in the salvage bag was minute compared to what was before Pres's eyes. Slowly, almost fearful that the jewels might vanish before he could reach them, Pres extended his hand.

Not a second after his hand had entered the hidden vault did another tearing, shuddering spasm pass through the ship. This time, the galleon tilted backward.

He held himself immobile and floated out into the center of the cabin, waiting for the ship to stop its tortured groaning. He prayed fervently that it would not slip farther into the canyon.

Every muscle in his body was prepared for flight, yet analytically, Pres knew his chances to win free if the galleon went down were nil. The current created by the ship would suck him along with it.

All of his highly tuned instincts told him the ship was going to go down. He could feel its doom surrounding him in the darkness like an aura of death. He recognized the tortured groans of the galleon's old hull as its final death knell. Pres knew this would be his last chance to get anything else out of the ship.

When the ship quieted for the second time, Pres lunged for the jewel cabinet. He grabbed a handful of jewels, not wasting time to select the best gems, and hoped that whatever he had grabbed would be good.

Moving swiftly, he opened the small mesh pouch at his waist and started to empty the jewels in his hand into it. No sooner had he begun than the ship groaned agonizingly again. This time Pres was thrown about by the backwash of water set in motion by the shifting currents.

As he spun, he pulled the string on the small bag tight and propelled himself toward the passageway. The galleon trembled, shifted and knocked Pres against the side of the door. The old rotted wood caved in beneath his weight, and Pres found himself wedged into the wall. Quickly, Pres pulled himself free and barely scraped through the opening, unaware that the salvage bag at his waist had been ripped open by a jagged piece of wood that had narrowly missed slicing into the side of his wet suit.

As Pres wound his way free of the doomed galleon, he left behind him a trail of jewels that marked the last passage any human being would ever make through the treasure ship.

Propelling himself out of what could have been his watery grave, Pres swam up the chasm wall to the ocean floor before turning and looking at the old galleon. He paused to study the ship and for the first time became aware of the change in the water. The bottom currents were stronger and tried to pull Pres back into the canyon. As he fought against the underwater tide's pull, the large octopus he had come face-to-face with earlier shot past him, powered by undulating waves of its eight mighty tentacles.

A hammerhead shark zipped past a school of fish without pausing to draw them into his cavernous mouth. Pres immediately understood the significance of what he was seeing. A thousand fingers of fear chilled him to his bones.

The hurricane was near. And it was a big storm. That had to be the reason for the underwater panic. Turning, Pres started toward the equipment line, but he froze, his body stiffening with tension and alarm.

Illuminated by the underwater searchlight at the base of the line was another diver. With his hand curled about the handle of his diving knife, Pres warily approached the form while fighting the rising force of the deep-water current. When he was ten yards from the diver, he noticed the diver was floating aimlessly. *Who?* he wondered.

Suddenly, *who* it was didn't matter. Pres realized that this unexpected diver was in trouble. The too-steady rhythm of air bubbles was his signal. No one exerting any effort could breathe such perfect and shallow breaths, not at a hundred and twenty feet of depth.

When he drew closer, he realized that the dark halo surrounding the diver's head was hair. *Megan's hair? She can't be here!* He went to her and peered into her face mask. It was Megan, and her eyes were closed.

Pres shook her but got no response.

He pulled off a glove and sent his fingers to her neck to look for her pulse. He found it and felt its slow and irregular pattern.

What happened? he asked himself pointlessly. Looking around, he saw that her safety line was hooked to the equipment line. He reached toward it to make sure it wasn't snagged. As his fingers touched the connection that had kept her secure against the dragging tide, a fist of water exploded against his chest and sent him tumbling backward.

The indomitable force of the ocean's mighty current caught Pres helplessly within it. He spun head over heels, being tossed about like a child's toy. But finally Pres summoned up the strength to battle back. Lunging desperately, he pushed himself free of the underwater tide's clutches and rose above it. When he steadied himself, he was far from Megan.

But he could still see the searchlight and fought his way back to it. Gone were all thoughts of the galleon. His only objective was the helpless woman moored to the equipment line.

It no longer mattered that she had deceived him and lied to him. Pres knew that life without Megan somewhere on the earth, even if not with him, held no joy for him. His love for her gave him the strength to reach her and to fight the swirling underwater tides that accompanied the storm ravaging the ocean's surface—and Pres was sure that the hurricane was indeed above him.

When he reached Megan's side, he grasped her to him, ignoring the pain where he scraped his hand on her tanks. Within seconds, another roiling wave of ocean current struck them and tried to tear them apart. Pres refused to yield to the ocean's might and kept Megan against him until the water again settled down.

After switching to his final air tank and aware of his extended time beneath the surface, Pres started them upward. He stole a glance at Megan's air gauge and was relieved to see that she still had at least forty minutes of air left. But there could be even more time because her breathing rate was extremely slow. He knew that only a miracle had kept her jaws locked around the mouthpiece and permitted her to live.

She must have come down just after I changed my last set of tanks, he thought.

When they had risen ten feet, an eerie and tearing sound filled the ocean depths. The loudness of it told Pres that something terrible was happening. Turning, he looked toward the underwater canyon, and at the two searchlights that still shone in the murky, swirling water.

He tried to see what was happening, but the angry ocean floor was swarming with every form of life and debris imaginable, and he could see very little.

Another loud, almost mournful wailing groan filled the depths, the sound hauntingly magnified by the very sea itself. Before it faded, Pres knew that the galleon was being pulled from the shelf.

An instant later the searchlights tilted. Pres, with Megan held close against him, saw the lights shift and begin to fall and slowly drop from sight. He knew the currents had torn the lights loose, just as he knew that the ship was no longer on the ledge.

Sadness at the loss of history as well as wealth tugged at his mind, while he tightened his arms even more securely around Megan. He cast away the regret of losing the ship and concentrated on getting the woman he loved to safety.

It seemed to take forever. They could have gone up faster, but after two hours of intense pressure, Pres could not take the chance of being hurt himself. Just before they reached the surface, he saw Megan's air-pressure gauge was just about on the empty mark. Pres quickly turned on her reserve air.

When they broke the surface, Pres was unprepared for the ferocity of the waves. His arms and legs were screaming with pain, but he ignored that as he held on to the equipment line.

Working as quickly as he could, he unhooked Megan's tanks but left the mouthpiece between her lips. Carefully, Pres timed the rise and fall of the giant waves. When the *Cervantes*'s diving platform was within a foot and still descending, he pushed Megan's limp form onto it while blocking the opening with his own body to prevent her from being thrown out again.

The mouthpiece was torn from her teeth when the tanks were carried away from the boat. But she was on the deck. Fighting the sway of the *Cervantes*, Pres pushed Megan farther in. Rolling in after her, he hit the switch that lifted the wooden platform into place and closed the opening in the boat's side.

Pres ripped off his tanks and, steadying himself against the pitch and sway of the boat, lifted Megan and carried her into the cabin.

He didn't bother to undress her, but after taking off her mask, his fingers roamed over the wet mat of her hair. Finding a large bump near the crown, Pres surmised that this was the cause of her unconsciousness. Pres gently opened one eyelid with a thumb and forefinger. Her pupils were dilated, and he knew that she might have a concussion.

"Why, Megan?" he asked her. "Why are you here?"

She could not answer, and the boat heaved, tossed about by another giant wave. Megan's body lifted off the berth, and Pres was barely able to stop her from falling to the floor.

Moving quickly, Pres opened the upper cabinet and took out two long canvas straps. He tied Megan to the berth, making sure that he did not cut off her circulation. Slowly, he bent and kissed her forehead.

When he was satisfied that she would be all right, Pres worked his way back onto the deck, where all the primordial furies of the world conspired to destroy the *Cervantes*.

Before he weighed anchor, Pres went to the second winch and started its electric motor. If nothing else, there were the three bags of gold.

The electric whine was a thin whisper against the force of the howling wind. While the winch worked, Pres went to the life preserver compartment and took out one iridescent orange vest. He pulled it over his head and secured it around his waist and chest before returning to the task at hand.

Just as he reached the winch, the sea erupted in a foaming cascade that washed over the side of the *Cervantes* almost swamping the cabin cruiser.

Pres felt a great, straining pressure on the *Cervantes*. Its stern whipped around madly and was lifted high. But the bow stayed down, and the ocean rushed over it. Before Pres could move to another winch, a loud snap pierced the gale winds. The *Cervantes* lurched; its bow flew straight up. The boat spun around again, freely, and Pres knew that the anchor rope was broken and the *Cervantes* was now at the mercy of the sea.

Still, Pres had no choice but to hold on to the winch and keep himself upright. The boat was tossed high again, and suddenly the sound of the winch became strained as the weight of the gold and equipment attached to the line dragged back at it, while the ocean moved the cabin cruiser in whimsical directions.

"Come on!" Pres shouted, hammering his fist futilely against the metal winch. But the winch was in a battle too— a battle against the weight of the treasure and the currents that must have been plaguing the three sacks of gold.

As if in agreement with his thoughts, the winch groaned. Sparks flew from its casing at Pres's feet. Then the winch died.

"But Megan's alive," he whispered, knowing exactly what he had to do. He half walked, half stumbled to another compartment aft and withdrew a buoy. He inflated it with the pull of a string before he bound its steel wire to the rope on the winch.

Pres freed his knife and, gripping the equipment line, cut the line free from the winch. He tried, his muscles protesting painfully, to tie an extra knot where the buoy was attached. But the movement of the boat, and the weight of the line itself, tore it from his already numbed fingers.

Pres watched the buoy fly out of the boat. All he could do was hope that somehow the buoy would stay attached to the rope. If not, there would be no chance of finding what little of the treasure he had salvaged. Pres had no doubts that since the anchor had snapped, the *Cervantes* had been flung along madly and was far from its original position. Without the marker to lead him to the hoard of gold, it would never be found again.

Pres pushed that thought roughly aside and worked his way to the controls. He started the engines, thankful that they caught and had not been flooded by the ocean.

He looked at the compass, turned on the navigational equipment and shoved the throttles forward. Now, he told himself, the real fight was on.

Pres had no idea how long the storm had been raging while he was underwater, but he was sure it could not have been too long, or it would have torn the *Cervantes* apart. Also, he might be hours from the calm eye of the storm, or he might be minutes.

Whichever it was, Pres could not sit and wait for the eye; it was too dangerous. Nor could he be certain that the *Cervantes* could take much more of the storm's vicious pounding.

While he fought with the wheel and kept his eyes glued to the navigational equipment, he reached for the radio and sent out an SOS. He expected no reply and received none.

As he battled the hurricane named Ariel, his muscles knotting with the effort of keeping the *Cervantes* on course, time began to blur. Whenever he could remember, and whenever the ocean gave him a chance, he would repeat his distress signal.

No thoughts of the galleon that had been lost played any part in this journey. His mind and his body were set upon only one task—survival.

The storm-maddened sea tossed the *Cervantes* about, while Pres fought back with his muscles and his will. He refused to be beaten down, and stood strong against the giant swells that washed over the *Cervantes*'s bow and came spilling over the forward deck in an effort to wrench him into the sea.

But Pres had a purpose, and that purpose was to get Megan back. Nothing would stop him, he swore, nothing. Five hours later, when the mighty tropical sun should have been shining down in all its glory, Pres felt the first lessening of the storm.

Glancing around, he realized the heavy downpour of rain had become a light misting. Above him, the clouds still whirled angrily, but the winds that blasted at him were retreating.

The eye of the hurricane had finally arrived.

The ocean was still a boiling eruption of chaotic waves, but its ferocity had lost its edge. Carefully, Pres picked up the microphone with his left hand and pressed the button.

He couldn't take his right hand from the wheel, where it had been for five straight hours, his muscles and joints had locked tight. He spoke his call letters and gave his SOS. Just before he put the microphone down, several things happened: the rain stopped completely; the shrouding mist cleared to show him the first hint of St. Thomas on the far horizon; and, through the static on the radio, a voice blared out.

"*Cervantes*, this is Coast Guard Control. Do you read?"

Chapter Sixteen

Cervantes, this is Coast Guard Control. Do you read?" the hollow voice coming from the shortwave radio's speaker repeated.

Pres's breath whooshed out in a mighty swoop. He breathed in and tried to smile, but the saltwater that had caked and hardened on his face had turned it stiff. "Coast Guard, this is *Cervantes*. I'm about three miles off the coast."

"Well done, *Cervantes*. We thought you were lost. We hadn't heard your signal for almost an hour."

"Too busy," Pres said. Glancing at his instruments, he noted his location. "I should be off Mandal Point. I've got an injured passenger and will require an ambulance. I'll dock at my place within fifteen minutes."

"We'll have the ambulance dispatched," said the Coast Guard radio operator.

Before Pres could sign off, another voice came over the airwaves. It was Lieutenant Peter Malcome's hard-edged island clip. "What the hell are you doing out there, Wyman?"

Pres smiled, relieved that his long ordeal was almost over. "Easy, Lieutenant, you said the storm was fifteen hours away—if it came in our direction."

"Damn it, Pres!" Peter snapped.

"Relax, Pete," Pres replied, his voice suddenly sounding as tired as he felt, "I'll tell you the whole thing when I see you."

"Just be glad you *can* see me again. Coast Guard Control out."

"*Cervantes* out," Pres said, and he dropped the microphone and grasped the wheel. Twelve minutes later Pres, again using his left hand, cut the *Cervantes*'s throttle and glided into his dock, which surprisingly was still there. The ambulance attendants were already waiting, and with them was the large shape of his old friend Simon.

When the *Cervantes* bumped into the rubber bracing, Simon hopped onto the boat and moored her to the dock. The two ambulance attendants rushed on board after him.

"In the cabin. Treat her gently. She may have a concussion," he cautioned.

The two men disappeared as Pres tried to take his hands off the wheel. The left one came away, but he could not move the numbed fingers of his right hand.

"You did it good this time, Pres-ton," Simon said when he stepped next to Pres and reached for his hand. Gently, the older diver pried Pres's fingers free from the wheel. As he worked, he smiled.

"I told you, you be a crazy man. Only crazy men to after treasure. Was it worth it?"

Pres watched Simon work as if his friend were working on someone else's hand. "We'll never know. I found her, but she's gone."

When Simon freed the last of Pres's fingers, he stood. "At least you found her. That be better than most. Better than me."

With Simon's last words, the ambulance attendants emerged onto the deck, carrying Megan in the litter between them. Pres followed them onto the dock, where they transformed Megan to a wheeled gurney.

Bending over her, Pres stared at her face. "Megan," he whispered.

Megan's eyelids flickered and opened. Her eyes darted around until they found him, but Pres, seeing their glassy stare, was not sure she even saw him. Her next words changed his mind.

"Oh, Pres. Thank God you got out in time." On her last word, her eyes closed.

The attendant nearest Pres asked him to stand aside while they moved Megan to the ambulance. Pres stayed with Megan until the attendants secured her inside the ambulance and closed the doors, cutting him off from her.

When the ambulance pulled away, Pres kept thinking about Megan's words. But while his only concern was that she recover, he also made himself face the truth. He could not accept what she'd said meant she had been there to help him—his knowledge that she had not believed in him was too strong to ignore.

Yet his love for her tore into his heart and lent deep meaning to the words that came forth. "Let her be all right," he whispered. "Please let her be all right."

Megan, strapped into the ambulance's gurney, was sure that she was moving across land and not sea. She tried to open her eyes but could not, although she was aware of everything. She heard the ambulance's siren and felt the attendant's hand on her wrist, monitoring her pulse. What all those things did was to assure her that seeing Pres's face had not been a dream, and that he was safe. With that thought, and with a special warmth rising in her, Megan gave in to the calling darkness.

When she awoke again, it was to a blurring vision of white. People in white gowns surrounded her. White walls were behind them, almost making the people fade into them.

Her head was spinning; her lips were parched. "Miss Teal," came a voice rich in its island accent, "I'm Forman. You've had a rather nasty blow to your head. Are you feeling any nausea? Is there anything else hurting you? Are you in pain?"

"No," Megan whispered. Darkness started to draw her away, but she fought it. "Where am I?"

"The St. Thomas Hospital in Charlotte Amalie."

Megan sighed, once again realizing that her ethereal dreams had been reality. Closing her eyes, she let the darkness wash over her.

When she succumbed to the combination of exhaustion and pain, she drifted off into sleep. The barest hint of a smile curved along her mouth, making the doctor and three nurses look at one another in surprise.

After securing the *Cervantes* for the next and last assault of the hurricane, Pres called the hospital to check on Megan's condition. He was informed that she was sleeping and was expected to stay that way for several hours. They assured him that they were monitoring her carefully. The doctor Pres spoke with said it was likely some of Miss Teal's symptoms were signs of extreme exhaustion.

After hanging up, Pres stared at the torn net pouch that he had forgotten about when he found Megan floating on the equipment line.

A bitter, sardonic smile twisted his lips at what had been the final loss of the dive. Shaking his head, he tossed the bag on the desk and, seven hours after he had first put it on, he removed his wet suit.

His right hand was almost back to normal now; the tightened muscles and locked joints had eased with the return of circulation. The hard, caked mask of salt covering his face brought little twitches of pain with every change of expression.

Simon had been the last to leave, after helping him secure the *Cervantes* and explaining that Peter Malcome had called him when they got the first radio message for help.

Simon had waited for the eye to come, and when it had he'd gone to the Coast Guard control base to wait with Peter to find out Pres's fate. He had just arrived when Pres radioed in.

After helping Pres get everything in order with the *Cervantes*, Simon had offered to stick out the storm with him; but Pres had wanted to be alone and sent his friend back to his family, not a half hour before the storm picked up again.

Wearily, Pres finished undressing and went into the small apartment in the rear of the salvage shop. He spent twenty minutes under the shower, and when he emerged he felt much better.

After brewing a pot of coffee, which fortunately finished perking just before for the storm knocked out the electricity again, he sat at his desk and contemplated the future.

The only two things Pres knew with any certainty, were that he would have to accept Bud Shaeffer's job offer, and that he would have to forget Megan Teal.

Now that the danger was over and Megan was safe, he could not help but remember her distrust of him. The puzzle of how she had gotten to the bottom of the ocean was easy to solve now, with a cup of coffee in one hand and no outside forces battering at his mind.

She had not gone to the villa as he'd thought; rather, she'd stayed on the boat to make sure he wouldn't go back to the dive sight without her.

"How could I be so blinded by her beauty?" he asked aloud. A tree cracked somewhere nearby. The hurricane winds howled in fury as they threw themselves against the concrete block walls of the shop.

"Because I wanted to be," he answered himself as honestly as he could. Pres would not lie to himself about his feelings for Megan. He knew it was pointless. He loved her, and he had lost her. All he wanted to know was what had made her do this to him. And, he decided, he would find out.

The next time Megan awoke, it was to the increased sounds of the hurricane. Forcing her reluctant eyes open, she looked around the dimly lit hospital room. The overhead light was off. A small emergency light glowed yellowishly over the door. The windows were covered with wide bands of tape, in case the glass could not bear up against nature's forces.

Near her head was the electrical pulsing of a machine. Carefully, Megan raised her hand to her head. Her fingers touched something metallic and, as she traced the attached wires, she turned her head to see a machine with green phosphorous lines rippling smoothly along.

"Easy now," came a gentle female voice. A moment later a white-capped nurse leaned over her.

"What...?"

"You're fine."

"Pres? Where's Pres?"

"Hush," the nurse crooned. "Don't worry yourself about anything right now. Just go back to sleep and get stronger."

Megan wanted an answer but her strength was gone, and she had no choice but to obey the nurse's command.

"Pres," she whispered once more before letting sleep claim her.

Megan didn't know how long she slept this time, but when she finally managed to rise through the foggy layers and open her eyes, her window was open and the evening sky was ablaze with color.

There were no crashing sounds of wind and rain, only calm and peace. As she stared out the window for several minutes, Megan wondered where Pres was and what he was doing.

She tried to remember what had happened on the *Cervantes* but could not. All she remembered was putting on the Aqualung. After that memory, everything was blank except for the fleeting glimpse of Pres's face.

What will happen to us now? she wondered, knowing that Pres must not only be puzzled by her appearance on the *Cervantes*, but raging mad as well.

Suddenly, she sensed eyes watching her. She started to turn but ended up wincing because she had moved her head too quickly. She brought her head around slower. Her breath caught, trapped in her throat by her surprise.

Pres was sitting in a chair across from her, but he hadn't seen that she was awake. He was staring down at his hands, rolling something between his palms.

She didn't call out; rather, she took this moment to study him. Unexpectedly, the memory of her last few conscious minutes aboard the *Cervantes* returned. She remembered the boat pitching, lifted high by an ocean swell, and then crashing down. She saw herself falling, twisting, and ultimately slamming her head into the deck. She even remembered how it felt when the water tugged at her as it drew her off the boat and into its huge and wet maw.

"Pres," she whispered.

Pres's head rose slowly, a reflection of his bone-deep tiredness etched upon his face. But as tired as he looked, his clean-shaven chin surmounted by his generous mouth sent a ripple of pleasure through her.

"It's gone, Megan," Pres said when he gazed into her eyes.

She started to speak, but her tongue felt like cotton. Shifting in the bed, she saw a glass on the tray near the table. She reached for the glass, brought it to her lips and sipped. "What's gone?" she said when she put the glass down.

"The ship," Pres said. "The storm currents tore it from the shelf. It's gone, Megan. It's somewhere on the bottom of that canyon."

Pres stood and walked to the window. His right hand was balled in a loose fist. He looked out at the calm island and saw all the evidence of the storm's violent path.

Trees littered the landscape. There was an overturned car near the hospital's entrance. Shaking his head, he turned back to Megan.

"I had three bags of gold bars, coins and art-work," he said, breaking the silence. "They were hooked to the equipment line, and now they're somewhere in the middle of the Atlantic. I tied a buoy to the line, but it couldn't possibly have survived the storm."

Megan felt all the heartache that she knew was Pres's. Unlike herself, Pres had needed to salvage the treasure to save his business. Now he had nothing. She wanted to comfort him, but she wasn't sure if he would allow her to.

"It doesn't matter, Pres," she whispered, wanting to tell him that she would help him with whatever he wanted to do, that she would stand by his side; but he didn't give her the chance to speak.

"No, it doesn't," he stated, fixing her with a suddenly hard stare. "You've already gotten what you came after. Or at least Bruce did. I know all about the funding for Bruce's foundation, and his wanting to cancel the dive. I found out about it before I went back after the galleon."

"Pres, I . . . I wanted to—"

"No!" Pres spat. "I trusted you because I loved you. But you've never done the same for me, have you? Why couldn't you trust me, Megan? Why couldn't you tell me?" Pres demanded.

Finding herself floundering helplessly in the path of his anger, Megan shook her head. A wave of dizziness washed across her, but she fought it down.

"It wasn't what you think," she said, as the need to explain what had been happening within her mind these past few days became overwhelming.

"What do I think? Or should I ask, what *else* can I think? You used me! You used me in a lot of ways. But it all keeps coming back to the same thing: for you, I'm someone to play with but not to trust or to love."

"No!" Megan cried, her heart splitting at his words.

"Yes! If you had really loved me, you never could have believed that I was after the treasure for myself."

"No!" Megan cried again. Tears sprang to her eyes with the bitter ferocity of his words.

Megan's tears had no effect on Pres. His anger and hurt would not let him weaken. "I made a mistake twelve years ago, but I was sixteen years old and I told myself that it was because of the way I looked. What excuse do I have now, Megan? I'm twenty-eight, and I made the same damn mistake all over again. I believed in you. I loved you!"

Suddenly, Megan could not take his unfair words. Ignoring the throbbing in her head, and the waves of dizziness that followed, Megan sat up.

"That's right!" she shouted. "Blame me for your own inability to understand anything other than what you think is right."

"My inability?" Pres replied, unbelieving. Stepping closer to the bed, he bent to stare down at Megan's upturned face and defiantly outthrust chin. They both held that taut, challenging pose for several seconds before Pres stepped back.

Shaking his head sadly, he said, "Perhaps you're right. Maybe it is my inability to see you as you are instead of seeing you the way I want you to be."

The air hissed forcefully from between Megan's clenched teeth. "I can't be something I'm not!" she retorted hotly. "And I won't be some figment of your fantasy."

Megan quelled the anger that had made her speak so strongly. "Pres, I'm not perfect, but I'm not the horrible creature you're making me out to be. Please let me explain what happened." As her words reached him, she could discern no softening of Pres's features, and her heart grew heavier.

The love she needed, the love she craved from him, was nowhere to be seen, and she was afraid that it was gone forever. Slowly, Megan lay back down and closed her eyes, unable to look at the man she loved but had lost.

Strangely, she heard Sandi's voice in her head, telling her not to deceive Pres. *I should have listened*.

"You don't owe me any explanations, Megan. You told me once that your career was the most important thing in your life. And I believed you. But you were wrong!"

His last words, so acrimoniously flung, were the catalyst that snapped Megan's eyes open, only to find Pres, his face drawn into angry lines, glaring down at her.

"The most important thing in the world, for you," he continued unrelentingly, "is anything *you* want! Not just a career, but anything! Anyone who stands in your way, who wants to share your life and be a part of it, is a fool!"

Instead of feeling the heat of Pres's anger, she felt something else. While his unfair charges should have sent her temper soaring into battle with him, she felt no need. Once again, Megan sat up in the hospital bed and drew her shoulders proud and straight. Her green eyes reflected no anger. Her low voice held no hostility. Her love for him would not let her retaliate and add to the pain she had already caused him.

"You may not believe me, but I understand how you feel. I even know why," she said, meeting his eyes without fear. "I'm sorry, Pres. Sorrier than you'll ever know. I handled things the wrong way. And yes, I did doubt you. Yes, I found my trust in you lacking these last days. But with good reason," she finished each of her last words accented by a painful pause.

When Megan paused after the last word, she wondered if Pres would let her go on, or continue with his own heated tirade. When he did nothing except stare at her, Megan took a shallow breath.

"You had become so...obsessed with finding the galleon that I thought it was the only reason you said you loved me. But whether you believe me or not, everything that happened between us was real—at least for me."

Pausing again, Megan studied Pres. His face was still an immobile and stern mask. The only reaction she could see was the ticking of his jaw muscle, which she had learned was a sign either of anger or of thoughtfulness. This time she couldn't tell which.

"And it wasn't just you I didn't trust. It was myself as well." She saw his eyes flicker briefly and then go blank. "But I didn't recognize that until last night, when I woke up in the middle of the storm and discovered that you were diving. All I could think about was you. Not that damned ship! Not my career! Only you. I was scared to death, and I was afraid I'd never see you again. It was then that I knew how much I loved you, no matter what else I might have thought."

"Just what in the hell were you doing on my boat?" he asked, using his question to stall for time. When Megan had spoken, Pres had heard the truth in her words and now needed time to comprehend and adjust his mind to their real meaning.

"I fell asleep on the berth while you were unloading the equipment," she said. "Pres, I hadn't slept in two days. I didn't even know you had taken the boat out."

A wry smile flickered across Pres's mouth. Megan's heart beat erratically.

"I never realized how much alike we are," he said in a soft voice. "Maybe because of that, I thought everything we wanted was so opposite." Pres took another step closer to her. "I was obsessed with finding the galleon, but I wasn't looking for it for myself. Megan, I was looking for it for you."

Megan's throat constricted. She tried to swallow but could not. She tried to speak but words failed her. She reached tentatively toward him. He took her hand, grasping it tightly.

"Because I realized that our love was more important than my business, I wanted you to have the freedom to go to school and have your career. I was afraid that if we didn't find the ship, I would somehow lose you. That's what my obsession was."

Megan squeezed Pres's hand, and as her eyes misted, she moistened her lips. "Wh...what about your business?"

"I just told you. My business isn't as important to me as you are."

"But what will you do now?"

"Today, when the storm ended, I called Miami and accepted a job I'd been offered by a salvage company based there."

"Oh, Pres," she whispered, feeling the loss of the business he had worked so hard to save. "I'm so sorry." Pulling her hand free, she levered herself higher in the bed. "Maybe we can still find the ship. Maybe it didn't go too deep into the canyon." Megan's green eyes, reflecting the optimism in her voice, turned her features into a brightly lit picture of hope.

"It doesn't matter, Megan," Pres said. "I've already found my treasure."

Megan's heart thudded. His words echoed endlessly in her ears. Her hands trembled. "What treasure?" she asked in the barest of whispers.

"You," Pres said. "If you want to try again."

"There's nothing to try," Megan said. When she saw Pres start to draw away, she hesitantly reached out to him. He stopped, but he drew no closer and didn't take her hand. "We've already tried. Now what we have to do is enjoy what we've found, and keep it. And Pres," she said with a smile, "I think I'll like living in Miami."

Pres stared at her, unable to follow this latest twist in their conversation. "What about school?"

"I understand the University of Miami has an excellent anthropology department."

"Does it?"

"That's what I've been assured of by a very knowledge-able person—my brother."

"I see," Pres replied, his face so deadpan that Megan's heart almost stopped.

"Pres," she asked quickly, "what's wrong?"

"Well, knowing how important your career is, I would imagine you'd want to wait until you finish school before getting married."

"Is that a question or a statement?" Megan asked.

"A question," Pres replied. "Do you want to wait until you've graduated school to marry me?"

Megan smiled. The smile was slow in coming, but it built steadily until she thought it would become a permanent part of her face. "Absolutely...not!"

"Megan," Pres said, still not going to her yet. He raised his right hand, which was formed into a light fist, and extended it toward her. "Not everything was lost last night. Which," he asked as he opened his hand, "would you like for your engagement ring?"

Megan's eyes widened, her breath rushed out and her teeth caught her lower lip between them as she stared at the two large, perfect gems centered in his palm.

The first stone was an oval emerald, as deeply green as the ocean. The second stone was a sapphire, as blue and as clear as Pres's eyes.

She looked up from his palm, her heart thudding in her chest, her hands still trembling. "Oh, Pres," she whispered, reaching out to him, catching him and drawing him down to her.

When their lips parted, she trailed her mouth across his cheek until her lips hovered above his ear. "All I want is you, forever you."

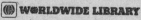

Silhouette Romance

Enchanting love stories that warm the hearts of women everywhere.

SIL-ROM-1RR

FOUR UNIQUE SERIES
FOR EVERY WOMAN YOU ARE . . .

Silhouette Romance

Heartwarming romances that will make you laugh and cry as they bring you all the wonder and magic of falling in love.

6 titles per month

Silhouette Special Edition

Expanded romances written with emotion and heightened romantic tension to ensure powerful stories. A rare blend of passion and dramatic realism.

6 titles per month

Silhouette Desire

Believable, sensuous, compelling—and above all, romantic—these stories deliver the promise of love, the guarantee of satisfaction.

6 titles per month

Silhouette Intimate Moments

Love stories that entice; longer, more sensuous romances filled with adventure, suspense, glamour and melodrama.

4 titles per month

SIL-GEN-1RR